HIDING IN THE SMOKE

OFELIA MARTINEZ

READING CACTUS
PRESS

READING CACTUS
PRESS

First Edition

ISBN 978-1-954906-06-8 (hardcover)

ISBN 978-1-954906-04-4 (eBook)

Library of Congress Control Number: 2021912616

HIDING
IN THE
SMOKE

To all chingonas. You are my inspiration.

1

SOFIA

On most days, it's feast or famine at *La Oficina*—my bar. But tonight is surprisingly steady and mellow, so I can't hide a face-splitting grin when my two best friends show up with one of their coworkers from the hospital, and I actually get to hang out with them.

I don't even go over to greet them before heading to the kitchen to put in their order that I know by heart. My best cook, Martín, glances at the order and his own grin grows wide. "Carolina is here?" he asks.

I nod. "So is Sara," I say.

"*¿La comelona?*"

I laugh, but nod again. "You know what that means."

"You need the salsa," he says all businesslike.

The *Salsa* is Carolina's mom's recipe and a fan favorite on the menu, which means we run out on most days. Martín always hides a secret stash for when Sara comes by because she sulks if we're out and don't save her any.

I head to the table where I can already tell from Carolina's furrowed brows—and from Sara looking everywhere but at her friends—that they are arguing about something with their coworker Mandy.

"How about you, Sofia? Are you free tomorrow night?" Mandy asks with hope in her eyes. She presses her palms together in front of her chest like a prayer and juts her lower lip into a pout.

"Oh, no. I don't know what you three are fighting about, but I know I don't want to be dragged into it. I just came to see what you want to drink."

Carolina and Sara call out their drinks, and I repeat them to make a mental note of the order. "A beer and a Horsefeather. Coming right up. You, Mandy?"

Mandy relaxes her shoulders and shakes her head. "No, I'm fine. Thank you."

Joe, my bartender and manager, is busy, so I go behind the bar to pour the drinks myself. When I get back to the table holding a tray of food and drinks, they eye me with conspiratorial smiles spreading across their faces.

Oh, no. This can't be good. Carolina, Sara, and I have been best friends for a while now. Ever since Carolina, a doctor, helped me without charging me when I needed stitches. We became instant friends. Sara was a bonus—a sort of package deal—since she's practically attached at the hip to Carolina. She is a nurse at the same hospital, Heartland Metro.

My bar sits conveniently in front of their emergency room entrance, so I see them quite often. And when those two women get together and look at me like they are looking at me now, I know they have something up their sleeves. Something I'm not going to like.

I set the platter, filled with zucchini blossom quesadillas fanned out into the shape of a flower, in the middle of the table. My cooks, Rubén and Martín, are artists, and they didn't forget the salsa. Sara nearly starts drooling and is the first to dive in, followed shortly by Mandy and Carolina.

"What?" I ask and take a seat next to them.

"We think you should go with Mandy," Carolina says, chewing on a bite of quesadilla, her thick, black brows shooting up along with her smile.

"You should totally go," Sara adds in her signature bubbly voice that has grown on me over the years.

"Go where? I have no idea what you three are talking about."

"Mandy has tickets to the *Industrial November* concert tomorrow night," Carolina says, turning her attention to Mandy, who is flashing me a toothy grin.

"I do! I called the radio station and got front row tickets and backstage passes. Can you believe it? I never win anything. I'm still on a high from it. But I have no one to go with me, and I really don't want to go alone."

I blink at Mandy. I barely know her through Carolina. Mandy is her research assistant at the hospital and a kick-ass artist, but we've never really socialized on our own. I'm not sure we have much in common. To be perfectly honest, I've avoided her. Mandy is super-hot, but she is also Carolina's favorite research assistant, so I never dared spend time with her alone. Carolina would never forgive me if I did a number on Mandy.

"What about your cousins?" I ask. I know she is close friends with her two cousins.

"Tlali and Izel both have to work tomorrow. They get out way too late to make it to the concert."

"I'm sorry, Mandy. Wish I could. But Friday nights are the busiest around here. It will be hard to get away."

"Come on," Carolina says. "You're too much of a workaholic. When was the last time you took a night off?"

"Are you calling the kettle black there, Dr. Ramirez?" I ask Carolina. Her brows furrow because she hates it when I call her by her professional title.

Carolina crosses her arms, annoyed. The truth is, I haven't seen much of either of them. Carolina's career has taken a bit of a stumble, and she is nursing a broken heart—caused by the same guy who messed with her career. Sara, too, had a tumultuous relationship with a scumbag who beat her to a pulp only a few months ago. Both women threw themselves into their work at an alarming pace.

I know people deal with heartbreak differently—I probably would do the same—but I'd be lying if I said I don't begrudge them for hardly being around anymore. It takes a miracle for me to see them these days. I'm sure it is their guilt of not being around as much that has them pushing Mandy and this concert on me. As if I have no other friends. I mean, I don't, but that's beside the point.

"Look," Carolina says. "I know you like *Industrial November*. I also know Sara and I have been a bit absent—"

"A bit?" I scoff, but I smile because I can't be too mad at them.

Carolina raises an eyebrow at me. "Fine. A lot absent. We just want to make sure you don't fall into your tendency to *only* work."

"Tell me," I say to both Carolina and Sara, "why, exactly, aren't either of you going with Mandy?" I raise my eyebrow right back at Carolina, even if my brows aren't as spectacularly thick and sculpted as hers.

Sara hangs her head, her blond tresses falling over her face like a curtain she hides behind to avoid any and all conflict, and Carolina has to answer for the both of them. "We're working."

I bite my lip, trying to suppress laughter. They can't get out of work, but expect me to?

"Look, I know we're total hypocrites, but we are slaves to our schedules. We can't take off on such short notice. You, on the other hand, are your own boss. You can do anything you want, even close if you have to," Carolina says.

I shake my head. "I can't close."

"Can't Joe handle it on his own?" Sara asks, looking up at me once again.

I glance over at Joe. He's been my bar manager for a year, and I have yet to leave him alone on a weekend night. I don't doubt he'd be able to handle it, but I'm not sure I'd have any fun worried about the million things that could go wrong. I've built my business from the ground up. It's successful because of all the hard work I put into it.

Mandy, for her part, is looking at me like I'm holding her new puppy. Talk about peer pressure. I roll my eyes.

"You're the *Industrial November* super fan, Carolina. I know their music from it popping up on some of my playlists, and I like them well enough, but I couldn't name a song if you had a gun to my head."

"I know. Trust me," Carolina huffs. "It's killing me that I won't get to meet them."

Rolling my eyes again, I look over at Mandy. "Let me talk to Joe. If he's okay with it, and we can get at least one backup waitress to come in, then yeah. I'll go with you."

I take my place back behind the bar—my favorite spot to be. I worked hard to give this place—my baby—an edge that felt like *me* without being kitschy. *La Oficina* is a modern bar with a moody feel, including exposed brick walls, tall, black-framed windows, dim lighting, and black and white photographs of my favorite Spanish rock bands. The likes of *Café Tacvba, Maldita Vecindad, Molotov,* and *Panteón Rococó* adorn my walls. *Industrial November* isn't amongst their ranks in my heart, even though they are the world's most listened-to band.

I don't admit to my friends that if the tickets were to *Café Tacvba*, I'd jump at the opportunity and close the bar faster than Mandy could say *Hot Potato*.

"What was that all about?" Joe asks, breaking my thoughts.

"Mandy wants me to go to the *Industrial November* concert with her tomorrow."

"No way! You get to go? I'm so jealous. I'm not too ashamed to admit that I actually wept when I couldn't get tickets. They sold out within an hour."

"I'm not sure I'm going. It's our busiest night," I say to him because he clearly hasn't considered the ramifications for him if I were to take off.

"Hey, if you don't go, please say I can have your ticket."

"What part of 'it's our busiest night' are you not getting?"

"Sorry, boss," he says. "But you really should go. I don't think I can work for a woman who, when given a chance to see the best band on the planet, declines. I'd have to question your judgment."

If Joe weren't married, or Mandy weren't quite as forward as she is, it wouldn't be inappropriate for them to go together. But given the realities, it's me or no one.

"Are you sure you can handle it, Joe? Like, really handle it?"

"You haven't given me a chance to prove myself yet. This might be the perfect opportunity."

"Okay. If you can get Tracy to come in tomorrow night, and you swear you'll text me the minute you need me for anything at all, I'll go."

I don't much care for our backup waitress Tracy, but she's gotten us out of some trouble in the past.

"You won't regret it, boss," he says. "Oh, and before I forget, David Price called again today. He really wants to buy the place?" Joe asks, with a slight look of concern straining his face.

"Joe, I'd never sell the bar."

"Next time he calls, want me to tell him to go to hell?"

I laugh. "No. He's still a colleague. Be professional. He'll get the hint one day."

When I get back to the table with the girls, I only smile at Mandy before she jumps up and hugs me. She doesn't even give me the chance to tell her I'm going.

"It'll be amazing, you'll see," Mandy squeals. "Drinks are on me. All night tomorrow night."

"Nope. Not drinking," I say. "I'll be driving." I grin at her.

"You don't mean . . ." Mandy trails off and covers her mouth from the gasp she let out. Seriously, what a drama queen.

When I nod, Mandy jumps again and hugs me tight one last time. "I get to ride Bonnie? No freaking way. It's going to be the best night ever."

When I sit with them, Mandy announces she has to go home and get ready for the next day. I watch her leave the bar with a pep in her step, her calves accentuated by the red pumps she's wearing.

When I look back at her, Carolina tilts her head to the side and crosses her arms. When her right eyebrow floats up, and her perfect lips form into a scowl, I know I'm in for it. "What did I do now?" I ask, annoyed. This is what she wanted. Isn't it? For me to take her assistant to the damned concert?

"Mandy's straight," Carolina deadpans.

"I know."

Sara interjects before any further questioning. "It looks like you two are going to be arguing for a while. I'm going to hit the hay. Caro, I'll get you next time?" Sara says and leaves me alone with Carolina.

"Please don't put the moves on her," Carolina says when we're alone.

"I wasn't going to—"

"It's your MO. Whenever you have the mood for a woman, you wow her with Bonnie, then take her to bed, and it always ends with the poor woman's heart broken."

I do my best to look offended. "My god, you're paranoid. I don't only take *lovers* for a ride. I thought it would be fun for Mandy. That's all."

"You promise?" Carolina asks.

"What's it to you, anyway?"

"I care about Mandy. You're both important to me. I'd hate to have to pick sides here."

The thing is, Amanda "Mandy" Gomez is very attractive. She is short, barely five-foot-three, and her frame is slender in a muscular sort of way that's always been catnip to me on a woman. She always makes me smile because she basically lives in high heels, trying to be just a little bit taller, and it's adorable. Her cool-toned, light-brown skin brightens with her broad toothy smiles that can cheer anyone up. But I'd never go there. She's a big part of Carolina's life, and I respect those bonds.

"Look, Mandy's hot and all," I finally admit. "I'm not blind, and I'm only human, but you know I don't date. I wouldn't jeopardize any friendship for a fuck. It's not that important." I don't say out loud what Carolina already knows. I don't do relationships. Period.

"I'm going to trust you here—"

"Have I ever given you a reason not to?" I ask my friend.

Carolina eyes me warily and takes too long to respond.

"And if you remember, it was you and Sara who pushed me to take her to the stupid concert," I add.

"Okay, I'm going to let go of the fact that you just called my favorite band 'stupid.' But you're right. You can't win tonight, can you? I'm sorry. I've been in a mood."

My eyes soften when I take a moment to study Carolina's tired features. Her eyes are sunken, and she looks a little worse for wear. "I know. Hey, how are you doing—*really* doing?" I ask her, worried about my stubborn friend trying to pick up all the pieces of her life by herself when she doesn't need to do it alone. She has friends, damn it.

But I also get her. I'm just as fiercely independent as she is, if not more.

"Not ready to talk about it," she says. "Besides, I have to get going. Early morning tomorrow. Close out our tab?"

"You got it."

Joe walks over to me at the register. "Tracy said she'd come in."

"Good, cuz I already told Mandy yes."

"You won't regret it, boss. Nothing will go wrong tomorrow night."

Famous last words, I think.

When it's nearly closing time, I walk over to the last straggler, who's been checking me out all night but has been too afraid to talk to me. He is tall, handsome, and well-built—a little burly—just how I like my men.

"Can I get you another drink?" I ask him.

"Nah, but maybe close out my tab?"

Once I hand him his credit card, I place my elbows on the bar counter, letting my cleavage swell over my tank top. "So, Nick. You gonna ask me out or what?"

Nick blinks quickly. "How'd you know my name?"

I point to his hand. "Your credit card."

"Oh."

"You've been checking me out all night." I lick my lips slowly as I stare him dead in the eye—my favorite flirting move. My luscious lips are my favorite part of my body, and whenever I lick them, it makes men crumble, if I do say so myself. "We're closing now, so you could say you've missed your chance."

"Oh. Have I really?" Nick chuckles nervously, scratching his jaw.

"Yeah, sorry. But if you'd like to fuck, my place is close by."

Nick does a doubletake. "What?" His mouth falls open.

"Hey, I'm sorry if I misunderstood. I just thought you—"

"No. You didn't misunderstand . . ." he hastens to add.

"So," I say. "You're interested in going to bed with me tonight?"

Nick nods. "Very."

I lean in closer until I can feel the heat of his breath. "Okay. I have rules."

"Okay," he says, looking at me—a mischievous smile curving his mouth. "What are they?"

"One night and one night only. No repeats and absolutely no sleeping over. Are those acceptable terms?"

"Fuck yeah," Nick says and slams down the rest of his drink.

"Oh, and you have to be sober," I add.

Nick smiles. "I only had two drinks. I'm completely sober."

Joe smirks at me and shakes his head as he leaves the bar. Undoubtedly, he heard the exchange, but he's used to me taking customers to my place and doesn't bat an eye—anymore.

I lock up *La Oficina*, and Nick trails me home.

2

SOFIA

There couldn't be a worse place to be than at the front row of an *Industrial November* concert. Hell would be cooler. I made the mistake of not looking into the band's live shows before showing up at the concert.

The arena is packed to the brim with screaming fans, and apparently, the lead singer, Brenner Reindhart, has a thing for pyrotechnics. Much like the *Pink Floyd* laser show, *Industrial November* also attacks their audience with a light show, only they use real fire. I will be surprised if those of us at the front leave with our eyebrows and eyelashes intact.

Fire erupts from below, from the sides, and even outward over the audience's heads—at a safe distance, but still close enough for the scorching heatwave to graze our skin. Midway through the concert, their microphone stands light on fire. At one point in the show, when they play "Metal Red Day"—their most popular single and the song I am most familiar with—the singer places a thick helmet over his head that sprouts a massive mohawk made of fire. I have to admit it now—I'm impressed.

This is the concert that turns me into a fan. Experiencing their music live is an entirely different experience than hearing it over my headset. Though the same is true for probably any rock band, there is a spectacular visual element to *Industrial November* that elevates their show to a form of performance art.

They don't rely on the visuals, though. The music is just as powerful as their studio albums produced with sound engineers. I can see how it would be easy to slack on the musicality when fans are clearly here for the spectacle, but they do both, and they do it well.

I do feel a bit out of place. Everyone all around me knows the lyrics to every single song. If only they sang in their native language—German—I'd probably be in better company. But as is my luck tonight, every single song is performed in English.

All four members of the band are exceedingly handsome— tall, muscular specimens. Brenner is the tallest, though perhaps the least attractive of the four men on stage. His face isn't classically handsome, but more a type of beastly sort of ugly-handsome with a strong jaw and slightly wide nose. His straight, black hair falls to his forehead with every head-bang, and he pulls it back with one hand, slicking it into place with his sweat. He is drenched with sweat after the first three songs and exudes the type of virile sexiness that I've always been attracted to in men. He moves on stage like a brute, with powerful thighs, firm steps, and one of the broadest sets of shoulders I've ever seen.

Midway through the concert, when Brenner takes off his shirt, revealing chiseled abs below a barrel chest, I am done for. To put it plainly, the heat emanating from the concert isn't only coming from the fire.

As the audience's energy winds down after an impressive four-hours, and the band turns to their slower songs, Mandy rests her head on my shoulder. She's tired from all the jumping, screaming, and singing of the night. As she leans on me, Mandy sways to a rock ballad she informs me is called "Bed of Eyelashes."

That's the moment when Brenner sweeps me away. His deep

voice carries a power in the hard metal songs, but I never expected he would be able to carry that over and actually sing. His voice in the rock ballad borders on operatic. It flows like authentic Mexican hot chocolate, silky smooth and hot with a hint of spicy. I know then that I'll go home and listen to all their albums, hoping I'll find more ballads there.

Then it happens. I can't believe it when he does, but midway through the ballad, Brenner Reindhart, the one and only, lead singer of *Industrial November*, locks eyes with me. I'm not singing along like everyone around me, and he shakes his head lightly as he smirks between lines of the chorus. He locks his gaze on me for the entirety of the ballad after that, effectively serenading me.

I look around and behind me, wondering if I'm imagining it, and he's actually looking at someone near me, but when my gaze lands back on him, he shakes his head and points, nodding, almost as if to say, *Yes, you, stupid.*

"Holly, hell," Mandy says when the song is over. "Did you see the way he was looking at you?"

"I didn't just imagine that?" I ask her.

Mandy grins, turning me by the shoulders to face her. "No. You didn't."

I've been to my fair share of rock concerts, and not once have I seen anything close to what *Industrial November* does when the show is over. They exit the stage, and the crowd stomps their feet until they return for the encore. All four men come back out, line up in a straight line, grab hands, and take a bow. The concert is heavy metal, performance art, and theater all rolled into one. It's pure art.

"Ready to go backstage?" Mandy asks.

When we get backstage, Mandy and I are escorted to a room packed with other fans and groupies. I find a spot on a couch and take a seat to check my phone, which I now realize I haven't done all night. I frown. I got so lost in the music, in the magic of the singer. Brenner Reindhart actually made me forget about *La Oficina* for four hours.

Three missed text messages from Joe await me.

Joe: *Tracy was a no-show. We are short-staffed.*

Joe: *Never mind. Don't worry. I was able to get Ileana to come in. Enjoy the concert.*

Joe: *Did you not get change for the register?*

I rub my temples. Joe's never had any issues like this before. He is probably nervous and, I'm sure, figuring things out on his own. Not that it eases my nerves any.

The door opens, and all the women in the room, including Mandy, jump to their feet, if they aren't already standing, as the bass player walks in, followed by the guitarist. Two security guards flank them.

"Hello, ladies," the guitarist says with a wide smile. He has the look of a golden, blond god as he opens his arms wide for two women to fall under his wings and fawn over him.

"That's Karl," Mandy says. "And that one over there, the brooding, muscular one with the beard, the bass player, his name is Fritz. We should go over and say hi."

"Why don't you go ahead? Get their autographs or take a selfie or whatever you want. I have to deal with Joe."

"Everything okay?" Mandy asks.

"Yeah. Go on. Enjoy what time you can with them. When I'm done with Joe, I'll join you."

Mandy shrugs, and I can almost see her skipping toward the two band members—surely her high heels are the only thing stopping her. I still can't believe she wore those shoes on Bonnie. I had to hand it to her, the woman was committed to her high heels.

It is a little tempting to go meet the band now that I have a better understanding of what they do, but they are so outnumbered by fans, I imagine any real conversation likely won't take place.

Instead, I decide to take my seat once again and text Joe about how to access the safe and get the change he needs. Joe and I are in the middle of that text conversation when someone sits next to me, but assuming it's Mandy again, I don't pay much attention.

"Why aren't you tripping over yourself to meet Karl?" a husky voice says.

"One second, please," I say without looking up.

Me: *Were you able to get into the safe?*

Joe: *Yeah. Got it. Sorry to have bothered you. I got it from here.*

Me: *Are you sure?*

Joe: *Yeah. You're distracting me now.*

Me: *I have every faith in you.*

Whoever sat next to me clears his throat, grabbing my attention for real this time. "Um, sorry about that. Work." I shrug apologetically as I tuck my phone in my back pocket and turn my attention to the man speaking. I have to do a doubletake to realize who is sitting next to me.

Brenner Reindhart.

I look around the room, and the groupies are all still huddled around Karl, plus a few around Fritz, along with Mandy. Had no one noticed Brenner walk into the room? I sure hadn't. But he would be hard to miss, being the tallest person in the room. Or did they just not care?

"So?" Brenner asks.

"Um—so what?" My heart starts to race, and I can't believe I'm having a hard time forming words.

I always imagined that if I ever met someone famous, I wouldn't be a fumbling moron like everyone else seems to be. I also am not the super-fan of *Industrial November* that Mandy is, so it catches me by total surprise when my brain stops working in front of Brenner Reindhart. His chocolaty-brown eyes bore into me, and I melt under his gaze. Brenner exudes a virility that overtakes my senses, and I decide it is that—and not his rock-god status—that attracts me to him.

He asks again, "Why aren't you over there with the other groupies dying to meet Karl or Fritz?" His voice carries the slightest hint of a German accent that sounds so sexy from his lips, I almost liquefy into the couch.

Words come out chopped, and time slows around me. "Oh, I'm not really a fan . . ." Crap. That's not what I meant to say. My eyes widen with panic, and I clasp my hand over my mouth.

Brenner throws his head back with laughter. "Well, this is a first." He rubs his fuller bottom lip with his thumb, keeping his eyes locked on mine. "So, if you're not a fan, what are you doing backstage?"

"That came out wrong," I offer. "I guess I'm a new fan of the band, but tonight's the first time I've been to one of your concerts."

"Oh?"

I point to Mandy. "That girl over there, Mandy, she won tickets from a radio station and invited me."

"So she's the fan?"

"I really didn't mean to say I wasn't a fan. I, um—I like your music."

My phone dings again. I close my eyes and count to ten. I am going to kill Joe. "I'm so sorry. Really, it's work."

I barely have my phone in my hand when Brenner speaks again. "You Americans are so rude. Always glued to your phones or work—or both."

My jaw drops, and I can only stare at him. What the hell? "Excuse me?" I say, my voice clearly laced with disdain.

"Get back to your *work*." Brenner stands and walks over to where Fritz and Karl are standing as Mandy runs over to my side. What an arrogant ass. To think I found him handsome and talented. Though, from what stereotypes I hear about musicians, especially front men, they are all arrogant. I shouldn't have expected anything less, not even after he basically sere-naded me in front of thousands of people.

His rude comment and prompt dismissal cure me of any celebrity-induced blindness I may have had.

"Ohmygawd, ohmygawd, ohmygawd," Mandy whisper-screams at me and squeezes my forearm like a boa constrictor. "You aren't going to believe this!"

"What?" I ask, prying her hand from my arm before she bruises it.

"They want to come over to *La Oficina*! Karl said he wants to party, but the band didn't want to go out because they don't feel like dealing with fans all night."

"You think they won't have fans at *La Oficina*? I'm pretty sure they'll get recognized anywhere they go."

"Yeah, but you have that private party room. I told them I know a bar with a private room and discreet staff, and they could go there. Karl is all for it. Fritz agreed. Please tell me it's not booked tonight."

"No, it's not, but—" Mandy stops listening to me then as she turns to give Karl a thumbs up.

"Mandy, focus," I say. "I think Brenner and I got off on the wrong foot. I doubt he'll want to go to my bar—"

"Oh, they said he probably won't go. He rarely goes out drinking with the band."

Leave it to Mandy to know all the inner workings of a band she met only minutes ago.

"I don't know," I say. Rock bands are notorious for property damage and rowdy behavior. *La Oficina* isn't that kind of bar, and I don't want it getting the wrong reputation.

My typical customers are hospital staff or the families of patients. They come to celebrate new babies or near-death recoveries. Sometimes they come to mourn. But all of it is a mellow sort of vibe—the local watering hole. I always knew what kind of ambiance I wanted my place to be, and high-profile expensive clients don't quite fit the bill.

"Come on!" Mandy whines. "Think about it. You'll make a killing from them alone."

Mandy makes an excellent point, and I'm not renting out the private room tonight, so I am fresh out of excuses for her.

"Let me text Joe so he can get things ready—"

"Really? This is amazing! I'm going to party with *Industrial November!*" Mandy all but squeals.

I shake my head at this strong, beautiful woman reduced to teenage antics as she fangirls over the German band. "Tell them to use the back entrance. I'll leave empty boxes they can lift to cover their faces and carry them into the private room so no one will see them go in. They'll pass for staff."

"You're brilliant!" Mandy gives me a peck on the cheek and is about to run off when I stop her.

"Hey, we should get going. I need to be there to help get ready for them."

Mandy shoots me a wicked grin. "No worries. I'm going with the band."

───

As I speed-walk to Bonnie, I text Joe about the private party, leaving out the details about who exactly our VIP guests are. I don't need another fumbling idiot beside me. If I wait on the private room, no one else in the bar needs to know who is there. I'll let Joe know at the end of the night before they leave so he can meet them.

───

When they arrive, Mandy beams at me as she goes into the private room, followed by the band members, who all carry in boxes and successfully enter the bar under the radar. So successfully is my brilliant plan that I don't catch that one of the men carrying a box is Brenner Reindhart—the ass. I don't notice him until I go into the room to take drink orders.

The private room has six tables, and they are packed with the band, their security detail, and various groupies, including Mandy. The only band member not present is the drummer—Adrian, I think.

"What can I get you all to drink?" I ask, ready to start jotting down orders.

"Just get us a bottle of vodka and a bottle of tequila for every table. Waters for everyone too," Brenner says, not looking at me.

"I'll have a beer," Mandy adds.

"And a beer for the lady," Brenner says, smiling at Mandy, letting his eyes linger on her. "All on my tab," he adds, still looking at her. He never turns to look at me during the exchange. When he lifts his credit card in the air and waits for me to grab it without so much as a 'thank you,' I decide I'll be over-charging him out the ass for his arrogant entitlement. I can't believe he had the gall to call me rude when he behaves like this to waitstaff.

When I return, clutching a tray of water glasses and shot glasses, the mention of my name stops me in my tracks outside the entrance to the private room.

"So, what's the deal with that girl who came to the concert with you?" the voice I recognize as Fritz asks. "The hot one with the short black hair. The one who took our order."

"Sofia," Mandy says. "She's a friend. I kind of dragged her out tonight."

"But what's her deal? She single?" Fritz asks with interest, making me smile. Maybe the night isn't a total dud. Fritz is hot in his own way, even if he doesn't have Bren's dangerous voice.

"Aww, man, you claiming dibs on the hottie? Didn't even

give a guy a chance," says another man, who I'm pretty sure is the guitarist.

Then Brenner's thunderous voice rises over everyone else's. "You all sound like idiots. You can't claim dibs on women."

Someone laughs, and I think it might have been Fritz. "Looks like dad already claimed dibs," he says, and I can picture the grin on Fritz's face even without looking at him.

"I hate it when you call me that. And I'm not calling dibs. I wouldn't call dibs on an insignificant waitress," Brenner answers.

"That's not cool, man," Fritz says. "Who cares if she's a waitress?"

"Yeah," Karl chastises. "Nothing wrong with being a waitress."

That does it. I walk into the room, my hands shaking so much the glasses tilt and water sloshes, nearly spilling over the rims. Mandy must see murder in my eyes—and I can't deny I'm seriously considering turning the tray upside down on Brenner Reindhart's head—because she calls out to me to grab my attention.

"Sofia! Hey. Thanks for the drinks."

Her loudness draws everyone else's attention in the room, and Brenner looks at me for the first time. In his defense, he grimaces and slides a bit down in his chair.

Good. I hope he is embarrassed.

Mandy begins offering an explanation, "Actually, Sofia isn't—"

"Done getting all the drinks. I'll be right back with more. Mandy, can you come help me, please?"

"Um, okay."

Joe has the vodka and tequila bottles ready to go with buckets of ice by the time I get back to the counter, Mandy trailing behind.

"What was that about?" Mandy asks.

"Don't tell them I own the bar."

"Why not?" she asks.

"If that pretentious ass thinks I'm a waitress and that he gets to look down at me because of it, I don't want him to change his tune. I will never see him again after tonight. Let's just get through the night and leave me out of it."

"You promise you won't pour a drink over his head?" Mandy asks sweetly.

"I promise I'll do my very best."

3

BREN

I insulted Sofia, our waitress, not once but twice. The first time at the meet-and-greet backstage, when I flat out called her rude to her face, and the second when I put down her profession just now, and I'm almost sure she heard me.

I'm almost certain of it because her icy glares send shivers down my spine the rest of the night, and when I sign for the bill, I pay about twice what I usually do. Given we are in Kansas City, I expect the bill to be less than at a major American City, not more. I can't fault her for padding the bill, though. I've been a total ass.

I've tracked her all night, hoping to find a moment to explain myself and apologize, but she's a slippery one. In my defense, after the concert, I was exhausted. At thirty-four, I am the eldest member of the band and the front man. I need to keep up with the younger guys, but I also need to deliver our overly ambitious performances. When I saw her sitting there alone, I couldn't believe there was a woman as hot as her not kissing Karl's or Fritz's feet. An excitement I hadn't felt in a long time bubbled in my chest, and I had to talk to her.

It doesn't help matters that she is perfect. Her raven-black, short hair falls in straight tresses around her perfect, heart-shaped face. She is wearing black jeans and a black t-shirt. Despite her simple outfit, her body is fucking killer. The instant I saw her sitting by herself, my cock twitched. Then I got close, and she bit that perfect full bottom lip of hers as she typed on her phone.

I wanted that perfect mouth on me—anywhere.

Then she kept her attention on her stupid little phone and texted away. And I'm Brenner fucking Reindhart. I'm not used to women dismissing me. Sure, I'm not the first one the women go to, but once Karl, Fritz, and even our drummer, Adrian, pick, I get the same kind of attention from their castoffs.

Usually, it doesn't bother me to be last pick. Karl, Fritz, and Adrian are still looking for the next hottest groupie for the night. But I want something real. Something more. And I think women realize that when they get to know me.

But after Sofia's cold shoulder the rest of the night, and the effects of the vodka taking over, I grow increasingly more pissed at her indifference. Does she not care who I am?

Now we're waiting for the bar to empty out so we can leave unnoticed. Once Karl keeps ignoring a gorgeous redhead, she saunters over to my table.

"Hey, you're the lead singer, right?" she purrs. Then she tosses her red hair over her shoulder.

"Yeah. Please, call me Bren. Nice to meet you."

"Bren." She giggles as she says my name.

This is always the most infuriating part. Waiting for people to adjust to who I am. It takes some longer than others to see that despite it all, I am just a guy. Same as any other.

"I'm Amber," the redhead says. She bites her lip, and that gesture forces my thoughts to Sofia as she had bitten her own lip earlier in the night. What the fuck? Why am I still thinking about her?

"So, it's getting late," Amber says. "You thinking about heading out soon?"

"Yeah. The bar is already closed. We're just waiting for it to empty out so we can go."

"Want some company tonight?"

For some unfathomable reason, my instinct is to say no. I want no one if I can't have Sofia, but as I scan the room, she's nowhere to be seen. Besides, I've been such an ass to her, I'd probably have a better shot at her throwing a drink in my face than wanting to spend the night together.

"You know what, Amber? Yeah. I'd love some company."

ALMOST THE SECOND I CLOSE THE DOOR TO MY HOTEL ROOM, Amber's miniature dress comes off, and she stands there in her underwear. She drags me by the hand until I sit on the bed, and she straddles me to grind on me.

"Brenner Reindhart. I can't believe I'm in Brenner Reindhart's bed." She keeps giggling, and the sound is like the screech of audio feedback.

She also keeps saying my full name, and I have to resist the urge to roll my eyes. When she kisses me, I feel nothing. She is beautiful and hot and exactly my type, and there is absolutely no reaction from my body.

Amber keeps grinding over my groin, waiting for a reaction that never comes—pun intended. "Everything okay?" she asks after her ministrations end up fruitless.

"Sorry. Bit tired. And distracted."

She stops moving for a moment. "What are you thinking about?"

I don't lie to women, so I became apt at workarounds a long time ago. "Don't worry about it," I say and press my lips to hers. I close my eyes and think about Sofia and Sofia's lips only. My pulse quickens and redirects blood to my dick, stirring it alive. I dart my tongue into her mouth, and she purrs in response.

As I harden, she picks up the pace of her grinding over my jeans. Then she cups the shaft through the fabric and pulls away from my lips. "Oh, there you are, Brenner Reindhart."

The sound of my full name in a voice that isn't Sofia's pulls me out of the fantasy, conquering my brain. The voice is too high and chirpy to be Sofia's. Sofia's voice is seductive and honey-thick. My eyes fly open, and it's Amber, the redheaded groupie, grinding against me—not Sofia. I stand, nearly tossing Amber off my lap, but I steady her to her feet.

"Sorry," I say. I scan the room until my eyes land on her dress. I pick it up and hand it to her. "I guess I'm more tired than I thought. Do you need money for a cab?"

Amber's nostrils flare, and she huffs. "No. I don't need money for a cab."

She hastily gets dressed again and storms out of my room, slamming the door behind her.

What the fuck was that? Why can't I get an insignificant woman out of my head? We barely met, hardly talked, and it took thinking about her to get a hard-on. I've never, not once in my life, had a difficult time with that.

Kicking Amber out was a mistake. My erection presses against the zipper of my jeans almost painfully. I had already taken a shower before going to the bar, but I know if I want a shot at sleep, I'll have to shower again before bed.

After shedding my clothes, I jump into an almost-scalding shower, letting the water ripple down my body. I hang my head, letting the strong water pressure beat at the back of my neck, and I shut my eyes, thinking of her.

Sofia's thick lips wrapped around the head of my dick. Her tongue licking the length of me. I wrap my hand around my hard-as-steel shaft and squeeze with thoughts of Sofia on my mind. I stroke myself, picturing her mouth in the place of my hand.

Seconds pass before my load erupts from me, and my body tenses. I open my eyes, disoriented to time and place. I need to stop thinking about this woman.

Dreams of Sofia lull me into the best sleep I've had in a long time.

WE HAVE A DAY OF REST IN KANSAS CITY BEFORE WE MOVE ON TO our next tour destination, and I'm determined to apologize to her, so I show up at the bar from last night. I don't expect her to be there, but I can ask someone for her phone number.

It is two in the afternoon when I arrive, and per the hours on the door, they won't open for another hour, but I see movement inside, so I try the door. I turn to my security guard, Andreas, before going in. "Wait out here."

Andreas nods.

I enter the bar and freeze when I see her. Even from her backside, I can tell it is her. My eyes glue to her slender frame as she stays busy taking chairs off the tops of tables and placing them on the floor. She has the body of a super-model. Why the fuck is she waitressing?

"I'm sorry, we won't open for another hour," she says.

"Lola, you forgot to lock up when you got in this morning!" Sofia calls out, though I can't see anyone else.

"Sorry!" A voice drifts into the room from elsewhere. Then the same woman yells something in another language —Spanish, I think—and Sofia yells back, also in Spanish. Sofia is smart, I think to myself, and I smile. That is such a turn-on.

"Um, actually, I was hoping to speak to you," I say.

Sofia spins around, and her breath hitches as her posture stiffens.

She has a uniquely rare beauty that almost leaves me speechless. I can't tell if her heritage is American, American Indian, Hispanic, Asian, or a combination of those things. But the sound of her voice in Spanish carries a sensuality to it that I shouldn't be thinking about, especially after I jerked off to thoughts of her last night.

"You," she says, her eyes narrowed. "I don't see what we need to talk about."

I clear my throat. "I owe you an apology. Last night—I acted like an ass. I'm sorry."

Sofia uncrosses her arms. "I appreciate that. Apology accepted. Anything else?"

"See, you accept my apology, then you're short with me."

"So?"

"So, it makes me think you don't really accept my apology."

"Look, I appreciate you making the trip. You apologized. I accepted. I'm not sure what else you want from me—"

"Dinner," I say, surprising us both. That was not my plan.

"What?" she asks, stunned.

What the fuck did I just do? I swore I'd apologize and get on with my life, my next tour destination, forget all about the waitress named Sofia. "Yeah. Dinner. I'd like to make it up to you and explain why I—"

"It's really not necessary, Brenner—"

"Please. Call me Bren. All my friends do."

Sofia cocks her head to the side with interest. "We're not friends." She keeps her hands busy pulling more chairs off tables as we continue our conversation. It doesn't escape me I'm trailing her like a puppy. *Pathetic.*

"I'd like to be. Please. Just one dinner."

"Even if I wanted to, I can't." She spreads her arms as if she were showcasing the room. "I work tonight."

"All right. How about a nightcap after?"

The woman who matched the voice in Spanish from earlier materializes, interrupting our conversation.

"Oh, sorry," she says. "Am I interrupting?"

The woman, if she can be called that because she looks like a teenager, is short and wears her blond curls in a mess of a bun like a bird's nest on top of her head.

"No, Lola. It's fine. This is Bren. Bren, meet Lola. She helps out a bit around here."

Lola can't bring her eyes to meet mine, but I don't think she recognizes me, so I step forward and offer my hand, but she only shakes her head and apologetically shows me the cleaning gloves covering her hands.

"I'll get out of your hair," says Lola. "Just, are we out of this?" she lifts a spray bottle of cleaning fluid for Sofia to see.

Sofia shakes her head. "We should have some. Try the cabinet in the office."

"Okay. It was nice to meet you," Lola says and keeps on working, not interrupting the few times she walks by us again.

"So, where were we?" Sofia asks.

"Nightcap."

"Bar closes at two in the morning. Bit late, don't you think?"

"You're really making me work hard here, aren't you?"

"I'm not trying to—"

"Night cap, morning-cap, call it whatever you want. Just have one drink with me."

She looks past me out the window, a question in her eyes as she takes in my security guard.

"That's Andreas. My security."

Her eyebrow quirks up.

"Purely a precaution."

Sofia's posture relaxes, and I can see the minute her resolve wavers. "Fine," she says. "One quick drink. Here."

"Perfect. I'll be back at closing."

ONCE THE LAST OF THE STAFF LEAVES, SHE POURS US TWO SHOTS OF tequila and places the bottle between us. She takes a seat next to me and leans on the bar, cupping her cheek in her palm as she waits for me to talk. She looks tired.

"Look," I say. "I was a fucking asshole last night. Not that it's any excuse, but I was exhausted—"

"You're right," she says. "It's not an excuse."

"No. It's not, but please, hear me out. I was tired, and the texting thing . . . well, it's a pet peeve of mine. I shouldn't have bitten your head off about it, though."

"Don't forget that you also insulted me for being a waitress—"

"You heard that, huh?" I ask.

Sofia nods, but there is a teasing glimmer in her eyes. She picks up a lime wedge between her fingers and brings it to her mouth to lick it once.

When I recover my senses after watching her tongue dart out and slide over the flesh of the fruit, I speak again. I smile because I'm fairly certain her licking that lime wedge was her intentional flirting. "I didn't really mean to insult you. If

I'm sincere, I thought you were really hot—still do. When Fritz and Karl expressed interest, I admit I put you down, but I did it to try to get them to stop sniffing around you like hounds."

"So you don't know me, and you're displaying possessive behavior?"

"Again, I was an ass, and I'm sorry."

"Possessiveness is really unattractive, Brenner."

My full name on her lips grates at my ears. "Please, call me Bren."

"You said that's what your friends call you."

"It is," I say.

"We're not friends."

"I'm hoping we could be."

Sofia fills our shot glasses a second time and sips on the tequila, not once making a face, which I'll admit impresses the hell out of me. She leans forward, and I have difficulty keeping my gaze on her eyes and not on her cleavage. Then she licks and bites her lower lip, and my dick stirs alive. This woman is going to be the end of me.

"Is that what you want from me, Bren? To be friends?" Her voice is low and sultry when she delivers the question.

"No, actually. If I'm honest, that's the last thing I want to be." I rub my bottom lip with my thumb. I can almost anticipate the feel of her lips on mine.

"What do you want, then?" Her eyes are hooded when they freeze on my lips.

"More," I say.

For a moment, Sofia considers my one word and all the implications we both know I placed in that one syllable. We let the silence stretch for a long moment, but it isn't uncomfortable. I could stare at her rare beauty for hours without exchanging a word and die a happy man.

For some reason I can't explain, I feel light around Sofia.

Women have used me in the past. For press, or to make a quick buck on my name. Normally it takes me a long time to trust a woman. But Sofia is different. I don't know for sure that I can trust her, but my gut is telling me I can, and I need to find a way to spend more time with her. I'll take crumbs from her if that's all she offers me.

Finally, she breaks the silence. "I can't give you more."

"Why not? I know you don't know me, but I'd like for us to get to know each other."

"Even if we got to know each other, and you were the perfect man, I don't do more."

"Okay . . ." Shit. This isn't going my way at all.

"I'll admit I'm surprised. The last person I'd expect to be looking for something serious would be the lead singer of a famous rock band, but—"

"Who said I'm looking for something serious?" I try to backpedal.

Sofia leans back and crosses her arms in front of her, deepening the distance between us so she can study my face. "It was implied, Bren."

"All I'm proposing is that we spend some time together."

She bites her lip while she considers her next words. "You mean it?"

I nod.

"Fine. Here's the deal—if you want it," she says. "One night. No strings. No repeats. No sleeping over."

I blink. What the fuck did she just say? I'd hoped for lunch the next day, and she has turned it into something much more indecent.

"One night?" I croak out, incredulous.

"One fuck. That's it. That's all I can offer. Take it or leave it."

"I'll take it," I say, because really, who in their right mind says 'no' to this woman? I'll woo her later, and she'll take back her conditions. I just know it.

She grins devilishly at me. "All right. Let's go."

"What, right now?"

"Want to risk me changing my mind?"

"Definitely not."

4

BREN

When we get to her apartment, I smirk, taking in the pristine, if small, living space. She's as much of a neat freak as I am, if not more. But I don't get to explore her home further before Sofia basically jumps on me when we close the door behind us.

She is a fine master in the arts of seduction. She undresses me swiftly but always holding my eyes and drawing my attention to her mouth—which makes me think she likes her mouth, and she has every right to. It's perfect.

She bites her lower lip and lets the tip of her tongue rest gently between her perfect teeth, followed by a swift lick of her upper lip.

I am fully naked before she lets me taste her mouth.

"A big boy, aren't you?" she asks when she looks down at my rock-hard erection. I can only stare at her through eyelids at half-mast. She takes my length in her hand, slim fingers wrapping around the shaft and squeezing tight. My eyes close with pleasure at her intimate touch.

"This is a bit unfair, isn't it? You being fully dressed."

"Would you like to see me naked, Bren?"

My preferred name on her lips does something to my heart that I don't quite comprehend, and I rub my thumb over her upper lip, tracing its shape and admiring the dent of the deep cupid's bow. I nod because words escape me at her proposition. I've never been shy with women, and I had two full years of fun when the band first started getting serious attention. I'm a tried-and-true lover, but something about Sofia's extreme beauty, unlike anything I've ever seen, has me feeling sensations anew.

She is different . . . somehow, and I get the feeling it's not just her physical beauty. She isn't waiting for me to act—to make a move. She makes all the moves for herself, and she sure as hell isn't afraid to speak her mind. She doesn't care about my celebrity status, and for the first time, I feel like just a normal person. The pressure of my status washes away every time she treats me as she would anyone else, even if it simultaneously annoys me a bit. It shouldn't bother me—it's what I want— but I also have an inexplicable desire to impress her.

I know she claimed to only want one night; I'll have her tonight, and I'll let her have her way with me. In the morning, I'll beg, if I have to, for a second and then a third night, because I doubt I'll be satisfied with having her only the one time.

She ditches her jeans by the doorway, and I help her peel off her top until she's in nothing but a black bra and thong, leaving me breathless.

I want—no, need—to touch her smooth skin, but more than anything, I need to unclasp that bra free.

But Sofia beats me to it. She takes two steps away from me so that I can admire the length of her body and then unclasps the bra, letting it fall by her feet.

She grabs my hand and leads me to her bedroom. As I walk behind her, my eyes are glued to her thong-clad ass—

that strip of fabric disappearing between perfectly plump ass-cheeks—and for the life of me, I can't piece together why this woman is waitressing at a fucking bar when she could be a top model. But even top models would pale next to Sofia's beauty.

My cock throbs like it needs to explode, and I have only looked at her so far. I lead her to her bed, and it is me who claims her lips the second time. As I devour her mouth and taste her tongue and every corner of her mouth, only one word runs through my mind. *Mine.*

I have one hand tangled in her short hair as I let my free hand sneak lower toward her center. I hook two fingers into the thin cloth of her thong and tuck it to the side, letting my thumb hover over her clit. I pull away from her mouth and search her eyes. "Do you want me to touch you, Sofia?" I ask.

"Fuck yes!" she nearly screams, and I reward her by pressing my thumb to the bundle of nerves I know will drive her wild.

Sofia's eyes draw closed, and her head leans back, exposing her smooth, thin neck to me. I bring my mouth down to that delicate flesh and draw my teeth gently across the span of her neck, feeling her shudder under the sensation.

She moans while I circle my thumb over her clit, and almost as if the moan instructs her body, an even deeper wetness gushes out of her, soaking the cloth of the thong. I lean back so I can help her out of it; as much as it pains me to not see her in a thong, I need to see her bare even more.

Once completely naked, I return to my work on Sofia's body. I let my index finger dip inside a second time, and she clenches around it with a firm and slippery wetness. "Fuuck," I gurgle out as I picture burying my cock inside her balls-deep. I can't take it any longer.

"Condom?" I ask.

"Yeah," she says and crawls over the bed to the bedside table where there's a decorative bowl full to the brim with condoms. My jaw tightens at the thought of why she has that bowl there, but I also recognize I'm being a hypocrite with the number of women I've been with, so I shake the thought and take the condom she offers. I peel it open and sheath myself.

I help Sofia onto her back and position my tip right at her entrance all frantic, when she takes me by surprise and wrestles me to my back, placing herself on top.

She hovers over my body, the lips of her pussy barely tasting the head of my cock, torturing me. My instincts are to wrestle her back into the conquered position, but I'm enthralled by the view above me. Sofia sitting tall over my cock, her hips rolling gently in circles, driving me insane.

I freeze, and all I can do is stare. She brings me back to action when she takes my hands in hers and leads them to each of her breasts. The hardness of her nipples making contact with the palms of my hands brings me back to earth.

"Sofia." I say her name because it is the only word that my brain is capable of right now.

Holding on to my forearms for support, she slides lower and lower on my shaft until she takes me all in. Once I fill her to the hilt, my hands float to her waist, and my hips buck, making her cry out.

"You okay?" I ask, worried the cry could be from pain. But Sofia smiles down at me sweetly and nods.

"I'm perfect," she says and starts rolling her hips, first slowly, then incrementally picking up the pace.

She bends over me so our lips can connect again. I thrust my tongue deep into her mouth, and the sensation of invading her mouth with my tongue and having my dick deep inside her—those two critical points of contact are everything I never knew I was missing.

I'm afraid her lips are bruising from our rough making out while she rides me, and my entire body is a live wire. I can't lay here any longer. I have to regain control before I'm too far gone. I sit up and handle her until I'm on top, dipping my head to take her tan nipple between my teeth. Her back bows off the mattress, pushing her breast deeper into my mouth, forcing me to growl against her flesh.

Her hand grips my hair, pulling it tightly, and she brings me up to her face so she can nip my lip again. Then she smiles up at me and bites that lip of hers. I slam into her with deeper, rougher strokes, forcing her eyes to roll to the back of her head. Her body convulses under me, and I sit up so I can watch her writhing in ecstasy, oblivious to anything but the climax taking over her body.

When the spasms ebb, I pull out from her and make quick work of flipping her on her stomach, and, probably with too much force, pull her back by the hips until she's kneeling at the edge of the bed.

Her ass is fucking perfect. I massage each cheek, taking a moment for a deep breath, because fuck, I want this to last forever.

But then Sofia reaches down with one hand to play with herself, and it's the fucking hottest thing I've ever seen. She scoots back, searching for me, moaning as she rubs her own clit.

"Yes. Keep touching yourself, Sofia," I growl, and thrust in —deep, long, and hard.

Each hard thrust pushes her further up the bed, and she claws at a pillow with one hand when her legs begin to shake, moaning into the pillow. My grip on her waist is slipping with the slickness of her perspiration, and the slapping sounds of my hard thrusts fill the room.

She shudders, and her walls clamp around my cock in a pulsating rhythm that pulls my climax out of me. She keeps coming as I unload in her, milking me as she convulses with each wave of her pleasure.

I stay inside her far too long while we catch our breaths. I'm in awe of her, of us, of what our bodies can be together.

We could ignite fires, Sofia and I.

MOMENTS LATER, I DROP MY FOREHEAD TO HER BACK, BOTH OF US gulping for air. I stroke her back gently, but at the sensation, Sofia pulls away from me, releasing my half-limp dick from her.

I've done worse things, dirtier things, more erotic things, with countless groupies, and yet, Sofia was the best sex of my life. The comparison is not even close. The chemistry is unlike any I've experienced. I can't put my finger on it, but suddenly I am reduced to the primal needs I remember from my teenage years, and all that energy is directed at this one waitress.

I lay next to her for a long, quiet moment, until our breathing becomes less erratic.

"That was fantastic," I say.

Sofia turns and smiles sexily at me. "Sure was."

I'm getting ready to roll on my side and wrap my arm around her when the bed shifts and she sits up, then stands. She walks over to a dresser and changes into black sweats and a gray tank top.

"That was great," she says. "Thanks for that, Bren. Really."

What the fuck? "Okay, yeah. You're welcome?" I prop myself up on my elbows so I can look at her, but instead of coming back to bed with me, she hovers by the door.

"So, thanks for stopping by. The apology and all. We're good. Really," she says, staying by the door.

"You're serious?" I ask.

"What do you mean?"

"You're kicking me out?"

"No, I—um, I thought I was clear earlier. No sleepovers."

"The rules . . . you were serious?"

Sofia blinks at me. "Yeah . . ."

I blink at her, flabbergasted. "You're really kicking me out?"

She brings a hand up and rubs her temple. "Okay, I'm not sure how we got our wires crossed, but—"

"Oh, no. You were perfectly clear," I hiss, my jaw so tight, I'm afraid I'll break a molar.

"Then I don't see the problem."

"Clearly."

"So I guess your request to be friends is retracted?"

"Fuck yeah, it is! What the fuck was this, Sofia? I told you I want to spend time with you, and you what? Want to be able to tell your friends you fucked a rock star? You're just some fucking groupie who wants to brag she nailed Brenner Reindhart?"

Her eyes narrow, and her calmness is maddening. "You can't help but be an asshole, can you?"

"I'm the asshole?" I yell.

"You came looking for me, Brenner. It wasn't the other way around, so you better watch your accusations. Trust me, I'll never tell anyone I took an asshole like you to bed."

"Unbelievable," I say. I'm fuming as I gather my clothes from all corners of her apartment, a task that only takes longer in my fury.

"I'm unbelievable?" she says, her voice rising now as she follows. "I told you what this was, exactly what it was, and now you want to act all butt-hurt because I meant it—"

This woman is infuriating. Finally, I'm almost done dressing and pull my shirt over my head. "I can't believe this—"

"What?" she challenges. "What can't you believe?"

"I'm Brenner fucking Reindhart. I can't believe a fucking groupie used me and is kicking me out without so much as a—"

"Ugh! I'm not a groupie. And before you fall off your mighty high horse, consider you don't even know my last name. You don't know anything about me. So how hurt can you really be?"

"I wanted to spend time with you to learn those things—"

"No, you wanted to use me for sex and didn't expect that that's all I wanted too. You're just pissed I beat you to it."

I blink at her. No. That's not what I'm mad about. I study her rigid features. Is this what she's used to? Men using her for sex? Empathy wants to take over, but then my eyes track her hand still holding the door, pointing out, and the anger takes over again.

"It's not a competition!" I yell.

"Agreed. Then why are we yelling?" she shouts.

I shake my head as I make my way to the door and mumble under my breath, "Fucking Americans."

Sofia must have heard me because I hear her cry out after me, "You don't even know where I'm from!" Then she slams the door.

5

SOFIA

"You look tired," Ileana, my part-time waitress, says.

"Thanks. Love you too."

"You're just not your normal self this morning. What's wrong?"

"I had quite the night," I say.

After the fight with Bren and kicking him out of my apartment, I promised myself I would take the memories of that night to my grave. Still, I'm unsettled by how everything went down. I am not sure why, but I regret how things ended.

I reason it is because I always, and I do mean always, remain on friendly terms with my lovers. The fight with Bren threw me off, and I have thought of little else since he left.

Ileana and I aren't particularly close, but I know I can trust her with anything. She's a motherly, supportive presence at the bar and takes care of all of us in any small way she can. She brings us meals when she cooks something yummy and helps Joe iron his shirt when he shows up to work looking a mess. I know if I tell her about Bren, she will take it to her deathbed if I ask her to. And I really need to vent, to process why I'm feeling so unsettled about the whole situation.

"Ileana, if I confide in you about something, will you promise to keep it to yourself?"

She smiles brightly at me. Ileana is the girl-next-door type of beauty, and when she smiles, I feel like a cat basking in the sun filtering through a window. "Of course. I won't tell anyone anything you don't want me to."

The docking door opens before I can tell her about Bren. Ileana showed up late-morning to help me put away my weekly delivery. While each of us could lift the heavy beverage crates alone, it is sometimes easier to double-team it. Not to mention faster.

While my delivery guy dollies crates upon crates into the bar, Ileana and I busy ourselves with organizing everything. I table the conversation, not wanting strangers to be privy to such personal details.

"Hey, are you busy after this? I'm going to the distillery for some tequila tastings. Would love the company and to talk to someone."

"Sure," Ileana says. "Lola's babysitting. Let me just make sure she can stay a couple of extra hours, and I'm all yours."

"Great!" I say.

I know Lola moved in with Ileana after Lola's parents died last year. Ileana claims she needs help babysitting her son while she works, and Lola can stay at her place rent-free if she helps out with that, but everyone at the bar knows that Ileana wants to help. Before her eighteenth birthday, Lola lost her parents and really has no one else. They aren't the first two people I'd put together as roommates, but they make it work. I'm slowly starting to consider them friends and find myself confiding in them both more and more.

When we finish working, we both make our way to my apartment next door to freshen up before heading out.

I am in the process of putting on a little makeup when the call from Mom comes through.

"¡Mami!" I all but squeal into the phone.

"*Mija*, how are you?"

I love when Mom calls. She is the only person I know who speaks proper impeccable Spanish. Ileana and Lola both speak Spanish, but theirs is even more butchered than mine. So Mom and I always keep our conversations in Spanish.

"I'm great, Mom. Getting ready to go out with Ileana."

"She's the waitress, the single mom you really like?" Mom asks.

I tell Mom everything—well, almost everything. Nothing about my lovers because she likes to pretend I'm still chaste and saving myself for marriage. "That's the one," I say.

"Well, you're busy. I'll call tomorrow."

"No, it's fine. We can chat while I get ready. How's Nana?" I ask. She and Mom are the reasons I work so hard. I want them to have everything they need.

Mom sighs long and deep into the phone. "She's fine, but she won't stop complaining about her arthritis. The doctors have done everything, prescribed everything—I hate to say it, but I think she just likes the attention and plays it up."

"Just let her, Mom. At her age, Nana deserves to be pampered a little."

"I know. You're right. Anyway, the last prescription they prescribed for her is a bit on the expensive side. I hate to ask for extra this month, but—"

"¡Mami! We've been over this. Please, I'm begging you, tell me when you need anything. It's no trouble."

"I just hate thinking of you there, in the U.S. all alone. I know it's expensive—"

"¡Mami! Please stop. I'm really not lying to you when I tell you the bar is doing great. Trust me, if it ever gets tight, I'll let you know, and we can all start pinching pennies, but until then, things are good. I even have a little left over every month for savings."

Mom is quiet for a long moment. "You wouldn't lie to your mother, would you?"

I laugh because she says it so seriously. "No. I'd never lie to you about that. How much is the medicine?"

Once she gives me a list of new expenses for the month, I adjust the monthly amount and make the bank transfer early so she can get the prescription filled.

"Gracias, *Mija*. You're an angel. I don't know what we'd do without you."

"I promised you when you moved back to Mexico, I'd take care of you. I meant it. I'll always take care of you. But . . . I do wish you'd move back. I miss you and Nana so much."

"*Ay, Mija*. I know. We miss you terribly too. But this is our land. Our people. At your grandma's age, she should feel at home."

"I know," I say. "You're right." My heart aches a little whenever we have this conversation, reminding me that I have no family here.

"Maybe you can visit us next summer?" Mom asks, hopeful.

"Yeah. Maybe. Joe, my manager, did great on his first weekend night alone. I think I could leave him in charge for a month."

"Wow. A whole month?" Mom asks, disbelieving.

"Yeah, I have a friend moving there next year. It might be nice to help her settle in too."

"She's moving here? To Chihuahua?"

I laugh. "No. She's moving to Acapulco. But maybe we can all go there for a week?"

"You have a deal," Mom says.

"Listen, Mom. Ileana is waiting for me. I have to go. Give Nana a kiss for me. Love you both."

"We love you too."

ILEANA AND I STARE AT THE TEQUILA FLIGHTS IN FRONT OF US. I'M glad she came with me so she could drive because while Ileana has made good use of her spit-bucket, I haven't. Half my testers are gone, and we stupidly planned to have lunch after and not before, so I'm nice and loose before our conversation.

"Who were you on the phone with earlier?" she asks.

"Oh, my mom."

"They're in Chihuahua, right? How is she? And your grandma?"

I blink at Ileana, surprised she has paid such close attention to my life. "Yeah. They live in Juarez. They're good. My grandma needed some medication, so I transferred some money over to them."

"That's right. You take care of them."

"Least I can do," I say truthfully.

"You're a good daughter," Ileana says.

"Ha! I try to be, but I'm not always a good daughter."

"What do you mean?"

"I'm a grown-ass woman. I'm twenty-eight, have an MBA, and own a successful business I built from the ground up—and yet, Mom doesn't think I'm a success."

"Mexican parents are tough." Ileana offers a sweet smile as we both take a small break from the tasting.

"Tell me about it," I say. "Mom thinks success means being married and going to med school or law school. She doesn't think what I've accomplished is enough." I smile sadly. Owning a bar isn't quite the proper, respectable path Mom had in mind for me.

"But it is enough." Ileana tries to reason with me. "Maybe not to her but having a profitable business before you're even thirty is amazing, Sofia. I have such admiration for you and everything you are."

I cock my head to the side, studying her, trying to determine if she's sincere. "Really?"

"Why does that surprise you?" she asks with a teasing smile.

"I don't know. I guess you're so proper; I always assumed you judged me for sleeping around."

Ileana throws her head back with laughter. "No! Not at all. I envy you. I wish I could be like that. To be so self-assured that I could pick people like you do and have sex without intimacy. But I'm just not wired like that. I'm a serial monogamist. Not because I'm a traditionalist like our moms, but because I need an emotional connection to be able to enjoy a physical one."

I purse my lips. "I've never had an emotional connection with a man—at least not in an intimate way."

"What?" Ileana's eyes are wide with surprise. "You're so stunning—I guess I always assumed you've had boyfriends by the dozens."

I shake my head. "No. Even through school, I worked to support my family and to save up for the bar. Between school and bartending, I worked eighty—sometimes ninety—hour weeks. Doesn't really leave time for dating."

Ileana's hand drifts to my shoulder, and she looks deep into my eyes. "Are you sure that's the only reason?"

After another sip of the next shot of tequila and some thought, I answer her. "Why do you have to be so damned smart? No. It's not the only reason. There are others . . ."

"Like?"

I shake my head. "I'll sound conceited if I tell you."

"I know you aren't conceited. Out with it."

"I know the way I look, okay? Everyone always says I'm beautiful or hot. And I definitely don't cringe when I look in the mirror. But looking like this, it does attract the type of people I'm not really interested in."

"What do you mean?" Ileana takes another sip of the tequila.

"The few times I did try dating before giving up on the entire thing, I realized I attracted two types of men only. The really clingy ones who were ready to propose, and honestly, they creeped me out a little."

"And the second type?"

"The users. The ones more than happy to take me to bed, but just not to meet their mom. You know?"

"I see," Ileana says thoughtfully. "So, you'd rather use people before they use you or kick them to the curb before they become squatters."

We both burst out laughing. This is the first time I've experienced sarcasm from Ileana.

"We should do this more often," I say. I'm thoughtful for a long moment, and Ileana doesn't seem uncomfortable in the quiet. Then there's the cold hard truth. "But really, Ileana, I've never, not once had someone in my life who gave me an example of a healthy relationship. I'm not sure I believe it's possible."

"It is possible," Ileana reassures me with a sad smile, and I know she's thinking about her late husband. "But back to you. I don't think you've really told me what was bugging you earlier. What's got you thinking about all of this?"

I take the remaining shots on the flight in quick procession and tell Ileana everything about my night with Bren. She takes a long moment to answer as she considers my predicament.

"I see. And you say he is really famous?"

"I can't believe you don't listen to *Industrial November*," I say as if I, too, had listened to them much before meeting Bren.

"I don't like rock," she says simply.

My jaw drops at Ileana's admission. "You realize you work at a Spanish rock bar?"

Ileana laughs. "Yeah. Tell me about it. But I tolerate it for the people."

"Gee, thanks," I say with a chuckle.

"Well, for what it's worth, I think you like Bren."

"Of course I like him. He's superhot, and while our night

together was pretty standard, at least sexually speaking, he kinda blew my mind. Our chemistry was incredible . . ." I smile. "Even when we were fighting."

"You haven't experienced this before."

"What's that?"

"Someone picking you. Think about it. You take all your lovers from the bar. You always open up the conversation and flirting. Sure, it's after you've noticed they can't stop staring at you, but it's always your pick. With Bren, it was different. He approached you. Then you both took a dislike to each other. Then he came back to apologize. I think you like having someone bend to you, for once."

"That's crazy," I say.

"Is it?" she asks.

"You should have your head examined."

"Just give it some thought, okay? You don't know what it's like to like someone, *really* like them, beyond a physical attraction. This is new to you, but I think that's what it is."

My nose scrunches up at her, and she laughs.

"Can I see a picture of him?"

I type Bren's name into a search engine on my phone and show her.

It's Ileana's nose that scrunches up now. "He's ugly," she says.

"He is not! Give me back my phone."

She laughs as she hands it back. "He is the ugliest in the band. All the other guys are really cute, though. Maybe you should trade up. Like the drummer. Now, he is hot!"

I shake my head. "No! The drummer is too . . . pretty. I think Bren is the hottest. Sure, he isn't pretty, but I like that beastly handsomeness of his."

"That's new too," Ileana says.

"What is?"

"You always take the hottest people to bed. This is the first time you're physically attracted to someone for another reason."

"I think it's his voice."

"Oh?"

"It's deep and beastly too." I grin, and Ileana smirks know-ingly at me.

"What?" I ask.

"Beauty and the Beast."

I laugh. None of this matters anyway. I'll never see him again.

6

BREN

We're supposed to be on our way to our next tour stop the day after our Chicago concert. Instead, Roger, our band manager, calls a band meeting in my hotel suite, but it's Karl who shows up first.

"Do you know what this is about?" Karl, the youngest member of the band, asks. It's early morning, and his blond hair is a mess while he looks half dead.

"Not a clue," I say, ignoring his ghastly appearance and choosing not to comment.

Fritz shows up, followed shortly by Roger.

Roger tries to start the meeting, but I have to stop him. "Wait a minute. Shouldn't we wait for Adrian?"

We are all used to our drummer showing up late and causing trouble in general, but we always wait for him.

Roger shakes his head. "He's not coming."

My jaw tightens. Whatever this meeting is about, it has everything to do with Adrian. We've budged a lot for Adrian because no one wants to replace a second original band member. Our original guitarist fell into addiction, along with Adrian, during our first year touring. The guitarist declined rehab, so we had to find a replacement—which is how we ended up with Karl.

But Adrian agreed to get help, so we work with him.

As many headaches as the band gets from Adrian, we all know he is trying, and for that, we protect his place in the band.

I finally ask what's on everyone's mind. "Did he relapse?"

Roger nods. "It was minor, and he called me right away."

"So at least he's doing what he's supposed to," I say.

Fritz's beard shifts with the tensing of his jaw. He has little patience for anyone who he feels isn't taking the band or its success seriously. But Fritz fails to see what I see: Adrian has a disease—one he has been working really hard to overcome. He deserves our support. To his credit, Fritz doesn't say anything. He knows how both Roger and I feel, and he won't go up against both of us. One, maybe, but not both. *Industrial November* is a democracy.

If there is a bright side to this shitshow, it's that all the fucking drama with Adrian scares the daylights out of Karl. He knows why our old guitarist got sacked from the band. Being the youngest, Karl still has something to prove to the rest of us. He drinks when the band parties together, but it never gets excessive. Somehow, his predecessor in the band and Adrian both serve as the best cautionary tales. Karl sits through the band meeting unusually quiet and avoiding all eyes as Roger and I set a plan in motion.

"What's next?" I ask Roger.

"He wants to do a week in rehab."

"For one night of relapse? Isn't that excessive?" I ask.

"It's not about that night. It's that he wants to keep drinking and doesn't think he'll be able to stop himself."

"Okay." I agree that this is the best plan of action.

"We'll postpone our next two concerts and loop back

around when the tour ends. Can you make the changes?" I ask Roger.

"Already done," Roger says.

"I'm heading back to Kansas City," I say, surprising even myself.

That gets the attention of both Fritz and Karl.

"Why do you want to go back to KC?" Fritz asks, an eyebrow raised.

"I liked it there. Less paparazzi to deal with than here in Chicago. I found it easier to get around without being recognized. Plus, a week's stay there will be cheaper."

"Worried about money, Dad?" Fritz asks, and I want to smack the back of his head but don't.

"Don't call me that," I hiss. Ever since Karl joined the band, he and Fritz have taken to calling me *Dad*, and I fucking hate it—which only encourages them further.

"Wait a minute. This is about that girl, isn't it? What was her name? That waitress from the bar?" Fritz asks.

"What girl?" Roger asks, his interest piqued.

"This major babe who showed up at the concert in Kansas City," says Fritz, "then we found out she was waitressing at the bar where we ended up. Cool place too. We were able to get into a VIP room under the radar."

"So you're going back to Kansas City to chase tail?" Roger asks.

The darts I shoot Roger with my glare propel him to take a step backward. "Whoa, sorry. Man, you really must have it bad." Roger laughs, and both Fritz and Karl join him with guffaws.

"You all better shut up now," I say. What are we, in kindergarten?

"You know what?" Fritz says. "I think I'd like to go to Kansas City too. I agree; it's easier to get around. Plus, I've been writing some music. Bren, I was hoping you'd whip up some lyrics to go with it?"

I send Fritz a knowing glare. It's time for payback, fucker. "You're not heading off to Mexico for the week?"

Fritz's jaw ticks, and I know he would like nothing more than to punch me right now. We worked it out a while back that it's Mexico he disappears to whenever we lose track of him. To our annoyance, we have yet to figure out why he takes those mysterious trips. Though I suspect our curiosity only makes him want to keep that secret closer to his chest.

I let him off the hook and change the subject. Whatever's in Mexico isn't pleasant for Fritz. "It would be good to stay on track and not treat this completely like a vacation. That's a good idea. Karl? What do you say? Keep the band together for the week before we start making our way to the west coast?"

Karl considers it for a moment. Chicago has more allure to him than Kansas City—especially this being his first touring experience. But if he wants a larger role within the band, he'll have to contribute to new music. This is a chance for him to show us what he could do creatively other than play the music written before his time.

"Sure. I'll head back with you guys," Karl says finally, though I know he's a bit annoyed.

"Roger? Can you make the arrangements?"

"Way ahead of you. I'll also look into getting a rehab center there so we can visit Adrian," Roger says.

"Anyone want to work out in the morning before we fly out?" I ask.

Roger and Karl look away from me, saying nothing. "I'll go," Fritz says, rubbing his belly. "Don't wanna get a beer gut."

WHEN I TURN THE GYM TELEVISION ON, FRITZ AND I KEEP THE news channel on. We barely start a light warm-up jog when the band name on a news report draws our attention.

A female reporter in a red blazer speaks, "Adrian Köhler, drummer to the world-famous German heavy metal band, *Industrial November*, is set to return to rehab this week. This will be Köhler's third stint in rehab since the band's formation nearly eight years ago.

"An anonymous source claims Köhler allegedly passed out outside a Chicago nightclub. The embarrassing incident comes not two years after they replaced their original guitarist with the youngster Karl Sommer due to the former guitarist's alcohol and drug addiction.

"We have confirmed Köhler is heading to a Kansas City rehabilitation center. The shows in Denver and Phoenix will be postponed until later in the tour. The band is expected to resume the rest of their planned American tour in Los Angeles after one week of treatment for Köhler.

"In a supporting move from the rest of the band, lead singer Brenner Reindhart, Friedrick "Fritz" Hartmann, bass, and Karl Sommer, guitar, will be staying in Kansas City until Köhler completes treatment.

"A statement from band manager Roger Kemp was released this morning as the news broke. 'We are a family,' Mr. Kemp said. 'We will support Adrian in getting any treatment he needs for this disease, and we will stick together to see him through this tough time. We want Adrian to know we love and support him. His fans have been extremely supportive, and we ask that you continue to keep him in your thoughts and prayers. We will return to Denver and Phoenix as soon as we can. And Los Angeles, we will see you next week.'"

"Shut that shit off," Fritz groans.

"Wow," I say. "Roger works fast."

"Yeah. I appreciate he got ahead of it by being up front, but goddammit. Now every reporter in the world knows we will be in Kansas City. Kinda wish he hadn't released the location," Fritz says.

"If he hadn't, it would only have created more intrigue, and we would have even more media attention. He did the right thing," I say in approval of Roger's management.

"Yeah. You're probably right," Fritz huffs.

I'm going to have a hell of a time keeping the band, and especially Karl, focused on work while technically having a week off. Luckily, Fritz has a good head on his shoulders, for the most part, and I can count on him to keep working during our downtime if he doesn't sneak off on his secret Mexico trips as he tends to do. The same can't be said for Karl.

We move on to weightlifting after our jog and are better able to talk through that part of the workout.

"So," Fritz says nonchalantly, "are we really supposed to believe this little band relocation has nothing to do with our gorgeous waitress?"

I glance at him sideways and continue with my bicep curl reps. "Stop it, Fritz. I already gave my reasons."

I'm annoyed that he hit the nail on the head. When I stormed out of her apartment after being kicked out, I swore to myself I'd never contact her again. But then I cooled off and realized that that was the first time anyone had kicked me out of their bed. I didn't think I had many more firsts with anyone, and annoying as it was, it was also refreshing. I don't remember the last time I had to work to woo a woman.

And fuck if the chase wasn't exciting.

"So, if I were to look her up when we got back, you would be okay with that?" Fritz teases.

"Only if you don't enjoy breathing," I hiss.

Fritz laughs, and I want to slap that stupid grin off his

face. "I knew it," he says.

My only priority should be keeping my band together. *Industrial November* is susceptible to loss of momentum after the lineup change with Karl. The kid hasn't recorded with us yet, and this is his first tour—one interrupted by Adrian's rehab.

The only thing I need to focus on is keeping it all together and getting us through this challenging year. Few bands last as long as we have, and I am not about to fold at the height of our popularity. I still have songs in me—albums—ideas I want to see realized before the band retires.

But I can't focus because a waitress named Sofia in Kansas City occupies my every thought. Her beauty is the magnet that lands all of us in KC once again.

I wait until almost closing time to show up at the bar, hoping she'll be working tonight. I'm fully prepared to return the next night, but she is behind the bar when I get there.

I'm puzzled—so far, she hasn't had a day off on any of the days I've surprised her with my presence.

Then I notice the man sitting at the bar. Sofia leans on the counter, letting her cleavage bulge—a move I recognize as her heavy flirting.

My chest tightens with a scorching fire I can't tame. Does she flirt with anything that moves?

I put the hood of my sweater over my head, hoping to avoid recognition by the man, and storm up to the bar. I practically yell my order. "A beer, please," I hiss. "When you get a moment," I add.

Sofia flinches at my bark and blinks rapidly when she realizes who I am. "One second," she says to the man and walks over to my spot. "What are you doing here?" she asks and crosses her arms. She clearly has no intention of getting me the requested beer.

"I wanted to talk to you. I don't like how we left things."

"I don't either—"

"But then I get here, and you're offering yourself up on platter for—"

Sofia chuckles bitterly. "Oh, this is rich. I never thought I'd see the day I'd be slut-shamed by a rock star who has undoubtedly fucked thousands."

My nostrils flare as I try to think of a response. I have no comeback because . . . she's right. Not only am I slut-shaming her, I'm being a complete hypocrite.

Our attention momentarily lapses when a woman joins the man at the bar and sits next to him. It's then that I notice his wedding band in a gold that matches the band on the woman's ring finger.

My gaze returns to Sofia's face only to find her staring, her gaze darting between the couple and me. I open my mouth to speak, to apologize, but she holds up one finger. "Hold on. Let me get rid of them. I don't want round two of our fight to be witnessed by customers."

I listen as Sofia offers to buy their last round in apology, then closes out their tab. The couple leaves the bar looking a bit stiff, and I don't know what turned their moods sour.

"I'm sorry. Here I am being an ass again," I say when we're alone at last. Sofia locks the door before shutting off the 'Open' sign.

"Yeah. You're being an ass."

"I was jealous," I admit.

"Jealous?"

"Yeah. I didn't realize he was here with someone, and I thought you were flirting, I—I'm sorry, I assumed—"

"You assumed right, Bren. I was flirting," Sofia says.

7

SOFIA

H e rears back, and his eyes narrow. "With a married man? Have you no shame?"

"Who the hell do you think you are? I owe you no explanations," I say to Bren. I can't believe him. My blood is boiling with fury because I hate possessive assholes. In large part, I know deep down that a big part of me avoiding serious relationships like the plague is a severe aversion to feeling like property . . . like I'm being owned.

I've known men like that in my life. From what I hear, my father was that way with my mother, and that didn't end well. My friend Sara's boyfriend was a possessive asshole, which led to his laying his hands on her.

The list goes on and on. If that's what it means to be in a serious relationship, to be the property of another to claim whenever they chose, then I want no part in it.

"Are you telling me you've never not once fucked a married woman?" I challenge Bren, who is looking like he wants to break something.

He averts his eyes. "I, um—" he starts to say, but I can't take it anymore.

"And not that it's any of your business, but I wouldn't take a married person to bed without their spouse's consent. I do have a moral code, not that you would know anything about that."

He seems flabbergasted. "What—"

"I was flirting with *both* of them. Not just him," I say, crossing my arms.

"What . . ."

It's actually kind of funny to see Brenner Reindhart the Great reduced to that one little word. I enjoy leaving him a stuttering mess more than I'd like to admit to myself.

"I was taking them *both* to bed, Bren. Not just him. Thanks for the cunt-block," I say and roll my eyes.

He spins around to take a look out the glass door, but the couple is long gone, so he turns once again to me. He blinks, then looks at the spot where the couple had been sitting. "Both of them?" he asks.

Bren stands there, rooted to the ground, unsure what to say next. My anger doesn't soften my features, and eventually, he lets his shoulders droop.

"Look," he says. "For some reason, I always say the wrong thing to you. The truth is, I can't stop thinking about you. I was serious before—I'd like to spend time with you. Get to know you—that's all. No expectations. I promise. And I've been feeling really guilty about how things ended last time. I overreacted. You're right. You were perfectly clear about what it was to you."

I unfurl my arms and offer a light smile at his admission. "Thank you. I appreciate that."

"That said, is there any way I can change your mind? Persuade you just to get to know me? That's all. I'm going to be spending the week here before our next concert. I'd like to spend it with you. If it doesn't work out, or you don't enjoy my company, I'll go on with my tour, and you'll never see me again."

"I don't know . . ." I say, unsure I want the chaos that I'm sure will come if I were to be spotted with the rock god.

"What's stopping you?"

"You are, *Tonto*."

"What does that mean?"

I smile but say nothing.

Bren shakes his head and chuckles, and I realize too late I am offering him hope.

"Bren, that's three times now you've been demanding or possessive of my time. Backstage, you threw a fit because I dared take an important text from work. Our night together—well, I don't have to repeat our hurtful words, but then tonight, you come in here ready to pummel a guy because I was flirting—"

"I wasn't going to hit him!"

"It looked like you were."

"I didn't say I didn't *want* to hit him, but I wouldn't have acted on it."

"See? You're making my point for me. I'm not property. I don't like to be owned or possessed. And I have a strong feeling that's what you want to do."

"If I promise to be on my very best behavior this week, and I don't show up at the bar unannounced, would you please agree to spend some time with me?" He smiles, and it looks so out of place on his beastly physique.

I shift my weight from one leg to the other. Ileana's words echo through my mind. *You like him. You aren't used to being picked.* Damn her. Is she right? Do I like him more than any other person I've ever gone to bed with? The very fact that I am asking these questions is the answer.

The thing is, I can't stop thinking about our night together, and not just because his body was built for mine. It's his voice, and the way it sent goosebumps down my arms when he growled in my ear. Bren didn't fuck me. He claimed me. And

I'm disgusted with myself for inwardly loving his ownership of my body. One night. That's all it took, and I gave myself over to him.

"Fine," I say finally and watch as Bren lets out a long breath. "But if this doesn't work out, you go on your tour, and you never contact me again. Got it?"

"I promise," Bren says.

"What're you doing tonight?" I ask.

"Other than grovel at your feet? Nothing."

I smirk at him. "I went to a tasting this week and got a few bottles of a tequila not yet sold outside of Mexico. Would you like to try them?"

"I would love that," he says, smiling.

As I make my way around the bar and grab the chilled bottles from the fridge, Bren settles on a seat. I place glasses by him, along with the bottles, and hop on the bar, swinging my legs around to go over it and sit next to him. I pour us each a shot of the blanco variety of the tequila first.

Bren picks up one of the bottles and reads the label. "The bar thinking about carrying this variety of tequila?"

"Well, the distillery is toying with the idea of distributing in the U.S. They already export their main line, but this is an exclusive reserve batch. They drummed up some press to local businesses to gauge interest, but it's far from settled. But this is some of the best tequila I've ever tasted, so I will definitely consider carrying it if they do open up their market for the Yoali line of reserve tequila."

"You?"

"Me what?"

"You're considering carrying it? I guess I didn't realize you were like a manager or anything like that. I'm surprised you can decide that kind of thing."

I throw my head back with laughter. Somehow, over the multiple arguments Bren and I have gotten into, I'd forgotten he thinks I'm a waitress. There would be nothing wrong with being a waitress, but the fact that it bothers him bothers me.

"Try the tequila, Bren," I say to shut him up. I sniff my glass, enjoying the aroma before taking half the shot. I close my eyes, feeling that familiar heat radiate from my stomach through my bloodstream. When I open my eyes, Bren is setting his glass down and twisting his face. I laugh again.

"You're not a tequila man?" I ask.

"I am."

"You didn't seem to enjoy that."

"What's there to enjoy? I mean, I enjoy the effects of it, but the flavor is awful—"

"What? It's not! You're missing it. You didn't taste the crisp agave flavor with a hint of citrus?"

Bren shakes his head. "I tasted Drano."

"You're breaking my heart, Brenner Reindhart."

I pour us each half a shot from the second bottle of reposado. "This one is aged just a little bit. The flavor profile is a bit more complex."

Because it is a reposado, I sip that second shot and savor it. Bren takes his shot like a bullet and slams the glass on the bar, twisting his face again.

"I'm guessing you didn't taste the flavor profile of that one either?"

Bren shakes his head.

"You're missing out. It was lovely. A little bit of grapefruit and silky caramel finish."

"All I got was Drano," he teases.

"A stab to the heart, Bren."

"Sorry," he says.

"Okay, this next one I genuinely believe is the best tequila in the world. If you can't enjoy this one, you're a lost cause, my friend."

"No pressure, Sofia." Bren's lips spread into a crooked

smile that heats my core more than the tequila. I've never wanted a man a second time. I've never wanted to get to know a man beyond his physical body. But sitting across from Bren while he listens to me geek out about my passion is comfortable in a way I'm not used to. A way I like. A way I want more of.

Before I pour the tequila from the last bottle, I think better of it.

"This one is an añejo, aged several years in whiskey barrels. You should get hints of cocoa, spice, and oak with a smooth vanilla finish."

"I'll do my very best to pay attention," Bren says.

"Lean your head back," I order.

"What?"

Instead of pouring into the glasses, I bring the bottle to my lips and take a healthy sip into my mouth, holding it there. I stand and hop onto Bren's lap, then kneel over his powerful thighs. He doesn't so much as grunt from my weight.

I take him by surprise, and his eyes are wide when he looks up at me, so I grab him by his short hair and pull his head back.

When I bring my lips down to his, and his mouth opens for me, I let the tequila slowly flow into it. His eyes widen further with the surprise of the nectar dripping from my tongue. Once the last drop of agave leaves my lips, I follow its trail with my tongue deep into his mouth, and Bren's eyes draw closed.

I press my palm to his throat so I can feel him swallow the tequila, the muscles of his thick throat contract, and my skin reverberates with his groan as his tongue seeks mine.

When I break our contact and lick my lips for any stray liquid, Bren is smiling ear-to-ear.

"You were right," he says. "That was the best tequila in the world."

"So glad you liked it," I say with a massive grin of my own.

"I'm a convert, Sofia."

He pulls my legs apart, so I'm no longer kneeling on his thighs but instead straddling him.

"Hold on tight," Bren says, and he stands while holding me up. I wrap my legs around him and lick his neck while he walks around to the other side of the bar with me in his arms, then sets me down on the counter behind the bar.

"Now, I think I need another taste of that añejo," he says and lowers his mouth to mine. That Spanish word comes out of his mouth so smoothly and so sexily, my thighs tighten around him in response.

The day-old stubble framing his mouth and jaw scrape my skin with the most pleasurable pain, and I moan into his mouth.

I pull away from him to peel off my top and shed my bra, tossing it to the dirty bar floor. Bren's hands drift to cup a breast in each palm. "Sofia," he gurgles my name out in a hoarse voice.

He bends down to trail his tongue and lips down my neck and chest until he reaches my breast and can take a nipple into his mouth. My back arches in response, pushing my breast deeper into his mouth.

"Fuck me, Bren," I plead. "Right here. Right now."

Bren frees my breast from his mouth and leans back to undo my buckle and help me out of my jeans and underwear. I return the favor in kind, and his jeans drop to his ankles, but not before he pulls a condom from his back pocket. I smile at his preparedness.

As he rolls the condom on, I grab the last bottle of tequila we drank from.

"Would you like another taste?" I ask and smile up at my German rock god.

His eyes are hooded as his gaze roams my breasts, abdomen, and then moves lower between my legs. He nods, and I hand him the bottle. He takes a swig from the bottle and tangles his hand in my hair, pulling my head back like I did to him earlier.

As his lips hover over mine, the tip of him parts my flesh with a maddening lack of urgency. I gasp at the sensation, and Bren lets the tequila flow from his mouth into mine. I drink the rest of the liquid he offers as he slides the length of his shaft in until there is no more tequila and no more of him to devour.

My back arches with the pleasure of all the sensations, and I have to force my gaze to stay on his body. While I had already shut off the lights, the dim backlight behind the bar still illuminates Bren's torso. The deep blue light casts shadows below each of his abdominal muscles. I draw my hand down those rippling muscles, admiring a body that seems to be that of an athlete.

Each thrust deeper into me forces his muscles taut, and I bask in the view of his perfect body.

Then Bren chuckles. "Like what you see?" he asks.

"Very much," I say.

And as if my voice were a whip, Bren drives into me faster and faster until he brings me to the edge, pushing me over it and making me fall for the longest orgasm of my life. My cream slickens between us where we join, and Bren's forehead pearls with sweat as I look up at him while I come down from my high.

I grab his neck and pull him down so I can taste his tongue again—the tequila flavor still lingering there deliciously. I break my mouth away from him so I can see his face. "I like the way you taste," I say.

With one last harsh thrust into me, Bren's head jerks back. The veins in his neck bulge, and he stills inside me as he lets out a groan followed by a long string of curses.

When he collects himself, he pushes aside some of the hair matted to my face with sweat. Then, his hand falls to my mouth, and he traces the shape of my lips with his thumb. "You're so beautiful, Sofia."

"And you're very hot, Bren."

He smiles wickedly at me. "I think I'll have a great night's sleep tonight."

"Who said anything about sleep?" I ask, biting my lip seductively.

"What do you mean?"

"You said you want to spend time together. To get to know each other. We only have one week, so why not start now?"

Bren leans down to kiss my forehead. "You mean it?" he asks.

I nod. "That bottle of tequila isn't going to drink itself."

8

BREN

The tequila doesn't taste quite as sweet, not coming from Sofia's lips, but it isn't as terrible as my past tequila experiences. It also isn't quite as sweet now that we're both fully dressed. Sofia tips her head back with the next shot and uses her thumb to wipe an escaping drop from the corner of her mouth. I'll never be able to look at tequila the same way again.

"So, you said the point of this exercise was to get to know each other better. What do you want to know?" she asks.

"Let's start easy. What's your last name?"

Sofia smiles. "Ocampo. But that's not what you want to ask."

"What do you mean?"

"You want to know about my ancestry, but you're too polite to ask."

I avert my gaze from hers. "You don't have to tell me—"

"I'm Mexican-American."

"I wondered if there was some Latina in there." I smile, remembering her seductive voice rolling those r's when she spoke Spanish.

She smiles like my words bring her pride. "Mom is Mexican. She lives there now. Her ancestry, like the majority of Mexicans, is mixed Indigenous and European. Don't ask me what specifically, though. The family was too embarrassed by their indigenous roots, so they hid them for the longest time. It kills me not to know what tribe I come from. And the European side—well, they were mighty proud of that. There are rumors of Spain and France, but I couldn't say for sure."

"And your dad?"

When I mention him, Sofia's smile evaporates.

"I'm told he was Chinese."

"Chinese?" That takes me aback.

"That's what I hear. He split when Mom got pregnant. She came to the U.S.A. to give me a better future, and the rest, as they say, is history."

The mystery of her rare beauty is solved. Wherever the roots of her mixed-race originated, they culminated in all the most beautiful features in one single specimen. Sofia Ocampo is the perfect woman, physically speaking, and I have a sneaking suspicion that her inner beauty more than matches.

"Your turn," she says.

"My turn?"

"Background, parents, whatever you want to share. Don't want to pry."

"Well, I had the typical suburban upbringing. Mom and Dad married young. Been together over fifty years. Still very much in love. I'm an only child, so they are mad as hell not to have grandchildren."

"Do they?"

"Do they what?"

"Have grandchildren?"

I blink at her. "No. I don't have any children, Sofia—"

"That you know of," she deadpans and busts out laughing.

I join in with laughter. "That's not funny. But really, I've always been cautious with that sort of thing. You could say I'm career-minded."

"I'm surprised the band has survived, thrived even, for so long."

I beam at her. She understands what this is. *Industrial November* is my passion. My baby. She gets it. So many people don't. It's not about fame or money for me. It's about making something that, at the end of the day, I am proud of. It's about art. And I'm one lucky bastard when I get to relive my art-making on the stage at every concert.

"Hey," I say. "Will I get you in trouble with your boss for staying after hours here?"

Sofia laughs. "Bren, I am my boss."

"What?"

"I'm the owner of this fine establishment." Her grin grows wide with pride.

I have to do a doubletake. Then I feel like an imbecile. "Oh. I'm sorry," I say and hang my head. "Why did you let me assume you were only a waitress—"

"Because of that right there." Sofia points at me, jabbing her index finger to my chest, with accusation in her eyes. "What would be wrong with being a waitress?"

"I—uh . . ."

"Nothing, Bren. It's honorable work. I love many of my waitresses. It's a pitstop for some of them, a career for others. And every one of them deserves your respect." Her tone changes during that little speech and my mouth dries up because . . . she's right.

"I'm sorry, I didn't mean to—"

"I don't like snobs, Bren. And you were one. That's why I

never corrected you. I didn't care if you thought that's what I was because I wouldn't be ashamed to be a waitress. There is nothing shameful about it."

"I'm sorry, I—"

"You're forgiven," she says, like the matter is settled. "Can I ask you a personal question?" she asks with apprehension, clearly trying to change the subject.

I shift in my chair. Have I become an arrogant asshole with the growth of my fame? Sofia brings my feet to the ground, and I can't believe how far I've strayed all this time. I might just need her around all the time to keep myself firmly planted on earth.

"That's the idea of tonight. You can ask anything. Nothing's off-limits."

"I'll admit, before the concert, I only knew topically about your music, but since then, I've listened more carefully—"

"Oh?"

"Well, don't let it go to your head." She rolls her eyes.

I chuckle. "Go on."

"That song. 'Late Night Legs.' You wrote it, right? Who's it about?"

That's a change in topic I'm not expecting. "I regret saying nothing's off-limits now—"

"Forget I asked—"

"No. It's okay. Um, just—I think I'll need another drink if I'm going down that rabbit hole with you."

Sofia smiles and grabs the bottle between us so she can fill our glasses. I lift the small shot glass in front of me, watching her carefully through the clear, amber liquid. She clinks her glass to mine.

"*¡Salud!*" she says.

"*Prost!*" I respond.

Our glasses thud on the counter when we slam them down. I ask her for a beer as well, only so I can hold something. I need to grip something in my hands in order to relive what "Late Night Legs" is about. Sofia doesn't skip a beat before retrieving a glass and filling it with beer from the tap.

I have trust issues. Many women have tried making a buck on my name after spending a night with me. I should be wary of revealing too much to Sofia, but somehow, I'm not. I am ready to trust someone, and if I am burned in the process, well, I'll cross that bridge when I get to it. This is a risk I need to take. She seems like she's worth taking that kind of risk.

"I'll tell you, but first, can I ask why you want to know about that song specifically?"

Sofia considers that for a moment. "I guess it stood out. All the other songs on that album are powerful and either angry or about having fun and fucking around. They all fit together, except for 'Late Night Legs.'"

"You would make a good music critic," I say, and she rolls her eyes.

"Then there's that one line . . ."

"Which one?" I ask.

"I think it's something like, 'Late night legs, wrapped not around me.' Your voice changes when you sing it. It's a bit . . . broken. Like maybe you're sad? I'm thinking someone hurt you, and that's what the song is about?"

I smile at her but can't hide the hurt inside.

"I'm sorry," she says. "You really don't have to tell me if it's too personal."

"It's about my ex, Emma."

"Oh."

I nod. "I came back early from a tour date to surprise her and found her in our bed with someone I thought was my best friend."

"Oh, Bren," she says. "I'm so sorry."

"Me too." I take a sip of my beer.

"Did you love her?"

I consider that for a moment and decide to be honest with Sofia. "I thought I did. I thought she was the one. But looking back, she clearly wasn't."

"I'm sorry it ended like that. Must suck to also lose your best friend in one fell swoop."

She doesn't cease to amaze me. Not only did she pick up on a subtle shift in my voice in that song, but Sofia looks at my situation and doesn't focus simply on the relationship. She understands I lost two people that night, not just Emma.

When I'd come to beg Sofia for her time, the last thing on my mind had been Emma. I've never wanted to speak of it to anyone. Fritz and Roger don't even know the whole story, though I'm sure they suspected when my best friend was no longer a constant presence around us. They never asked.

"Hey, thanks for telling me," she says.

"I'm trusting you here to keep my secrets. I have trust issues, so treat them gently," I warn her.

"You're not alone," she says. "For different reasons, but I have trust issues too. Especially with men. I think that's what sometimes draws me to women—"

"So, are you bi?" My eyes widen at how stupid that just sounded.

Sofia only laughs. "I don't really like labels. I mostly enjoy men, but every now and then, for the right woman, I don't know." She shrugs. "I guess I feel . . . safe. Less on guard than I do when I'm with a man."

"I'm sorry. I shouldn't have asked that."

"It's okay, Bren. I'm not offended."

I relax a little. "So, tell me, where do these trust issues with men stem from?"

"That, my friend, will take you and an army of psychologists to figure out. Though I suspect my father's abandonment or witnessing the heartache of literally every one of my friends at the hands of men has something to do with it."

"I have an uphill battle here, don't I?"

"You sure do," she admits.

"Hopefully, we'll learn to trust each other, then?"

We cheer to that notion and remain silent for a long while as we both digest the information we have so willingly and recklessly shared with the other. We've both placed lethal weapons in the other's hands, and now only time will tell if they were earned.

After a long moment and another round of drinks, Sofia speaks again. "You know, I'm breaking all my rules with you."

"How's that?" I ask. "Sharing too much?"

"Well, that too, but I meant my more practical rules."

"What do you mean?"

"I never sleep with the same person twice. Not once. Not ever. You're a first."

The heat in my body raises as my blood starts to sizzle. What the fuck did she just say? My nostrils flare, and Sofia rears back when she takes in my face.

"What's wrong?" she asks.

"You have more of the rock star lifestyle than even I do. That's what's wrong," I say with disdain.

"Oh boy. Here we go again," she says, followed by a dramatic yawn as if she's bored.

"What?" I hiss.

"You're about to slut-shame me and turn into a possessive asshole you have no right being. Am I wrong? You're so predictable, Bren. It's boring."

I take deep breaths and count to ten. This woman is infuriating.

She stands and puts away the tequila bottles and grabs the shot glasses off the bar top. She is clearly ending the conversation.

"Unbelievable," I mutter under my breath and storm out of *La Oficina.*

9

SOFIA

The week Bren claimed he wanted to spend with me came and went, and not one peep from him. I'm not sure if I'm expecting him to at some point show up or if I even want him to. I hurt his ego, and apparently, he couldn't take it.

On the day I know Adrian is being discharged from rehab and they will be flying to LA, I receive an enormous bouquet of flowers. The vast majority are still buds in a velvety black. The few that have started to bloom reveal a deep crimson hue inside. I don't have to open the card to know an extravagance that screams 'heavy metal' like this is from Bren.

WHY CAN'T WE STOP FIGHTING?
    We should explore that together and give us a chance.
    Still thinking of you,
    Bren

. . .

HE IS LONG GONE, SO I FAIL TO SEE THE POINT OF STARTING anything with him. But then the very thought of not starting anything at all with Bren doesn't sit well in my stomach. I don't want to want him. But I do. Now I just have to find a way to stop all the want because Brenner Reindhart will try to own me and my heart if I let him.

"Whoa, those are, um . . ." Ileana's eyes bulge as she appraises the flowers. "Something," she says and chuckles nervously. Ileana is a sunny-side-up, sun-dress-wearing, girl-next-door type who wouldn't appreciate a dark beauty like this arrangement.

I, on the other hand, love them. And they do precisely what Bren intends them to. They make me think of him every time I glance over at the bouquet.

"Who are they from?" she asks.

"Just this guy."

"It wouldn't happen to be this guy named Brenner Reindhart, would it?"

I smack her playfully on the arm with the card in my hand. "Shhh. Someone will hear you," I warn her.

We don't have many customers through the door yet—it's still early—but I don't want anyone to get wind of the fact that Brenner Reindhart has been at the bar. I shiver at the thought of paparazzi casing the place.

"You going to see him again?"

I shake my head. "Don't think so. They're gone. Besides, even if he were still here, we can't go a day without one of us picking a fight. It wouldn't work out."

"That's too bad," Ileana says. "It seemed like you really liked him."

We set the flowers in one of the tables at the center of the lobby where anyone at the bar can appreciate them.

After the bar closes and I'm getting ready for bed, I receive a text from an unknown number.

Unknown: *Did you get my flowers?*

Me: *How did you get my number?*

I save Bren's number under my contacts and mask his name in the most delicious way. I chuckle when his next text comes through.

Tonto: *I have my ways.*

Me: *They're beautiful. I have a few suggestions on where you can shove them.*

Tonto: *I meant it, Sofia. We need to stop picking stupid fights. I want a chance. A real chance.*

Me: *What's the point? You're touring, and I'm bound to KC by my business.*

Tonto: *I'll find a way to work it out.*

Me: *You never showed this week.*

Tonto: *I was angry. I'm sorry. I was in a foul mood, and I think it's because I was there without you in your city.*

Me: *No point in talking about the past. I'm sorry. I've moved on. You should too.*

Tonto: *What?! Moved on? What do you mean?*

I need to stop engaging him in conversation and vow that was my last text to Bren.

Tonto: *Sofia?*

Tonto: *What do you mean you've moved on?*

Tonto: *Sofia! Answer me, please.*

THERE ARE NO MORE TEXTS FROM BREN AFTER THAT. THE following day is a busy one at the bar, and I hear not another word from Bren, so I start to relax and won't allow myself to admit I'm disappointed I will never see him again. Ileana is doing a great job of keeping the flowers alive, trimming their stems, and changing the water. I'm glad someone is because if they were in my apartment, I'd let those roses die a slow, painful death.

I'm exhausted by closing time, and I leave Joe to finish up closing procedures. Once I get home, I jump straight into the shower because—I realize after I catch a whiff of myself—I badly need one.

The shampoo is barely rinsed out of my hair when I jump at the sound of loud knocking on my door. I shut the water off, wrap myself in a towel, and hurry to the door, worried it's Ileana or Joe and something happened at the bar. But when I look through the peephole, I find a murderous-looking Bren instead.

Clinging to my towel so it will stay in place, I open the door. "Bren?"

"Moved on?" he says, his eyes dark with fury. Then he takes a step forward, but I don't budge. He isn't going to intimidate me.

"What do you want?"

"We need to talk."

I stick my head out the door to make sure the halls are clear and none of my neighbors have seen him. Down the hallway, a tall figure in a suit stands, crossing his arms. I recognize him as Andreas, Bren's security guard. His dirty-blond hair is combed back neatly, and he keeps his eyes on Bren. Andreas, I think, is rather handsome, and other than him, there is no one around. I don't want him to be recognized and associated with this apartment, so I let go of the door to let Bren through and close it behind me before anyone has a chance to see him.

"I don't know what there's left to talk about," I say, gripping my towel tightly in front of me.

"You've moved on? What the fuck does that mean, Sofia?"

"Which word is giving you trouble?" I ask and arch an eyebrow.

"Such a smartass," he says but he smirks this time. "I'll show you how much you've moved on," he says and charges for me until he has my back pressed against the wall.

His hand snakes to the back of my head until his fingers tangle in my wet hair. He pauses to look into my eyes, waiting to hear a word of protest from me, but I'm incapable of one.

My traitorous body wants him here, in front of me, naked, his bare skin flush against mine, even if my head doesn't. I stand on my tiptoes, ignoring the pain from him pulling on my hair so that I can close the distance between us and take his mouth in mine. I suck his bottom lip between my teeth and bite it. Hard. Until a single drop of a metallic taste laces over my tongue.

Bren's groan of pain fills the room, and he uses his free hand to rip the towel away from my body. My hands hurry to free him of his clothes until he is as naked as I am. His kisses rain down fiercely, making my lips ache. His stubble rubs my chin and the skin around my mouth raw as he nibbles on my lips and tongue like a starving man. We hardly come up for air, and I worry my mouth will be swollen tomorrow.

"You want me to move on?" he asks again, teasing me, then bites the gentle skin between my neck and shoulder. "Before you decide to really move on, let me show you what you are moving on from." Bren's voice is vicious, more vicious than on any of his angriest songs, and the sound sends electric shocks down my body.

Those massive arms of his pick me effortlessly off the ground, and I wrap my legs around him. He positions his tip at my entrance, getting ready to feed himself to me when I remind him of the condom, and he pauses to put one on frantically before he resumes his earlier position and bangs me against the wall.

Hard.

It is so different than the last two times we were together. All the passion from our tequila night is long gone, replaced with fury and a hunger I'd never experienced in bed with anyone. His eyes are pitch-black in the dark apartment; the danger of his large size, of his strength, of his rough movements only turns me on more.

My thighs squeeze around him tighter, not wanting to be dropped, and he responds with a firmer grip on my legs. I know, just know, my thighs will be bruised in the morning.

"How about now?" Bren asks with a hoarse voice between deep, punishing thrusts. "You moving on now, Sofia?" He drives deeper into me and faster, making me gasp for air. He is so large and deep in me, with gravity pulling my body down around his cock, I can almost imagine the length of him reaching my belly-button from inside.

"Tell me, Sofia!" he growls. "Are you moving on?"

That harsh, sexy voice combined with the deepness of him inside me forces an explosive orgasm that renders me speechless. I couldn't answer him, not even if I wanted to. All I can do is scream and shake my head.

"Tell me!" he demands and pumps harder into me. "Are you moving on?"

"No," I pant, finally, when the words come back to me.

He kisses me harshly again, devouring my mouth, and I wince at the pain still there from our earlier kiss. I bite his lip, more harshly than I intended, so that he will break away from my mouth, and he rears back before I have the chance to draw blood a second time.

I smile wickedly at him and lick my lips to soothe them. "That all you got?" I taunt him.

He grabs my ass with both hands to keep me off the ground, and his fingers dig into the flesh of my glutes. I imagine the matching bruises I'll find in the morning. Then he drives into me with a ferocity I didn't think possible, making me come a second time before he finds his own release and buries himself in me, stilling as he catches his breath.

He brings his head to my shoulder, gasping for air. "You are driving me crazy, Sofia." Then he pulls out of me and lets my legs come down to the floor.

"You drive me crazy too, Bren. But the rough sex is good."

He laughs.

10

BREN

The concert couldn't have gone better. The arena was packed, and our performance was better than it's ever been. Even Adrian brought his best to the stage tonight. And yet, the thrill of the stage, the roaring fans—they don't quite hold my interest like they once did.

Something is missing.

And I know that something is actually someone.

After the show, Fritz and Karl go out to party as per usual with their groupies. Adrian goes straight to his room to avoid temptation, and I also stay in, hoping Sofia is still awake after closing the bar.

When she texts back that she's up, I'm like a kid on Christmas morning. This woman has brought me down to my knees, and she doesn't even know it.

Or does she?

I smile when the video call icon appears on my phone, and I sit up on my bed. When the call connects, my jaw nearly drops at the sight of her.

Sofia is sitting up against her deep-blue velvet headboard. She wears a white ribbed tank, and grey satin sheets cover her legs. I don't want to be anywhere but with her between those sheets. I almost think I feel . . . homesick.

"Hi," she says and bites her lip, which drives me wild.

"Don't do that," I say.

"What?"

I smirk at the camera. "You know damn well what. Don't bite your lip."

She blinks for a moment, then bites it again—the insolent woman that she is. "Why not?" she asks demurely as if there is an ounce of demureness in her.

"It does things to me," I warn her.

"Oh?" She continues to play dumb.

"Yes. Now tell me. How was your day?"

She shrugs. "Same old, same old."

I sigh. "I don't know what that is, Sofia. You're going to have to give me a little more than that."

"Okay. Let's see. It wasn't too busy tonight, so I let my waitress Tracy go home early. Joe closed up. Nothing spectacular, really. How was your concert?"

"It was okay. I'm a little jaded at this point," I admit. "So, can I ask about why you opened up a bar?"

Her nose scrunches up. "I guess we're talking about me tonight."

"If you don't mind." I flash her a smile to hopefully make her comfortable. She laughs.

"Well, I knew I wanted a business of some sort once I got my MBA. I bartended through college and really loved it. When I got my business degree, I knew exactly what I wanted to do with it."

"I can tell you love what you do."

She grins wide. "I really do. It's a lot of hard work, but it's worth it. It's pretty successful, actually."

"That's great," I say.

"Yeah. I even have this restauranteur from Chicago interested in buying it, but I'd never do that."

The pride she takes in her work is refreshing, and I find myself feeling proud of her and her accomplishments too. I already knew she came from a single-parent family and that her mother lives in Mexico. For her to have such a successful business so young is pretty fucking spectacular and damned impressive.

Then she bites her lip again, and I doubt she realizes she does that when she is thinking. "Stop biting your lip, Sofia—"

"Sorry. Didn't mean to that time." After a half-smile, she asks, "How did you get into music? I want to hear about you."

"I didn't. I got into writing first."

"Writing?"

I nod.

"How boring," she says.

Great. I huff. The admiration is entirely one way. This woman doesn't care who the fuck I am or about my fame. It's so . . . different, but also refreshing in a way I'm not expecting.

"I wanted to be a poet, but then I learned poets make no money, and I wanted money more—"

Sofia laughs. "But you know you got lucky, right? Most bands don't make it. They don't see the kind of money you do."

I agree with her, but even back then, I'd had a gut feeling that *Industrial November* would be successful. We chat for about an hour, and I almost forget about how tired I am, so I tell her the band's origin story.

I met Fritz in college. He was studying economics at the time and playing bass as a hobby. After I showed him some of my poetry, we became friends, and he started writing music to it. Eventually, we decided to form a band to get laid—honest-to-god, that's how most bands start. It was successful, but Fritz is first and foremost a businessman, and he knew we had something. He wanted to shake that money tree. He had the vision, and I had the writing and the voice, so that was that.

"Wow," Sofia says when I tell her everything. "So to him, it's a business?"

"Yeah. It is to me too, to an extent, even if it didn't start that way for me. I don't know how much longer we'll keep the band going. Fritz and I are a little tired from all the touring but adding Karl's youthful energy to the mix has . . . rejuvenated something in the band."

Unable to fight it anymore, I yawn.

Sofia bites her lip, and I snap. "Stop it!"

"Sorry!" She looks annoyed now as she crosses her arms, and it's so damn adorable.

"Do I really need to fly out there only to turn around and fly back here a few hours later? Are you trying to kill me, woman?"

"Oh, that's what you meant."

"What—"

"When I bite my lip. It turns you on. Oh, Bren, you shouldn't give me ammo like that," she teases me. She's damn well aware of my obsession with her lips.

I watch as she shifts in the bed, props her phone up with a cushion, and leans forward toward the screen like a cat. She bites her lower lip, and my cock twitches despite my exhaustion. Fucking hell. Then she gets on her knees to show me her short shorts, and I smile at the screen.

Bringing a finger to her mouth, she sucks it and trails it down her front until it plunges inside her shorts. The fabric bulges with her knuckles as she pleasures herself.

"Fuck, Sofia—" I stammer out and close my eyes. I'm about to reach for my now-hard cock when she speaks again.

"Tsk, tsk," she says, biting her lip. She shakes her index

finger side to side, motioning a 'no,' then grabs for her phone. "It's bedtime for you," she says and ends the call.

My eyes widen with horror at what she just did. I've never been so powerless in my life.

I'm so fucked.

And she is in for it now.

11

SOFIA

Joe and our two cooks, Rubén and Martín, show up at the bar early on Thursday. We have a food delivery, and they want to do some prep work. I write out the specials for this coming weekend on the chalkboard we place on the sidewalk Thursday through Saturday night.

Bren has been gone a week and is supposed to have a weekend off soon, so I have a bit of a pep in my step today.

He wouldn't forgive me for how I teased him that first night he was away. My punishment was a nightly video chat, text, or phone sex over the last three days. I don't mind too much being punished by an international rock god.

Poor me.

"What's that smile for?"

Joe's voice snaps me out of my nocturnal flashbacks. "Huh? What?"

"You're grinning like you did something dirty," he says.

"Get back to work," I snap, but the smile is still tugging at my lips.

Joe chuckles. "Sure thing, boss."

Then the smile really does vanish when I realize I'm missing him. Bren is taking so many of my firsts, I'm starting to worry my feelings are growing too much for him. Now I'm frowning because I can't let myself fall for him. We are meant to be an adventure. Fun only. But that thought only deepens my frown, so I try to distract myself with work, as usual.

Though the bar is empty, those of us here early are all busy with many tasks required to ensure our weekend runs smoothly. I really do have the best staff in the world. I can't fathom how I got so lucky.

It catches me by complete surprise when Bren shows up before opening, and I hate how much I'm squealing on the inside like a pathetic teenage fangirl. This isn't me. I'm losing it. But I'm also damn happy to see him—and *that*, I can't deny.

"In my defense," he says, grinning, "I showed up before opening, so I'm technically not getting in the way of work."

I shake my head. "Just because we aren't open yet doesn't mean there isn't any work—"

"And here I thought you were going to be glad to see me—"

I'm about to lean over the bar for a welcome kiss when the sound of glass shattering on the floor grabs both our attention. Joe stands down the bar from me. He's carrying a tray of clean glasses from the kitchen that he must have dropped.

Joe freezes. He doesn't hurry to clean up the mess he made. Instead, he blinks, looking at Bren, then at me. Back and forth, behind the bar, and in front of the bar. "No way," he finally says in a breathy voice. "You—you—you are . . ."

I chuckle because Joe can't bring himself to use whole sentences, and it's the funniest thing I have ever seen him do.

Bren steps forward, grabs a stool, and sits in front of the bar. His movements are natural, like he's used to this kind of interaction. Of course, he is used to fumbling idiots blinded by his fame. Bren then stretches his hand out over the bar toward Joe but keeps his gaze on me.

"Now that's the welcome reaction I was looking for." Then he turns to Joe. "Hello. I'm Bren," he says while sporting a warm smile.

Joe looks at his outstretched hand and blinks. Then he blinks a second time. I bring my hand to my lips, pressing them firmly down to hold back my laughter. Joe will never forgive me if I embarrass him in front of his hero.

"Joe," I finally say to Bren. "This is Joe."

It's still Bren who speaks first. "Joe. Nice to meet you, man."

To his credit, Bren never drops his hand, waiting for Joe to eventually snap out of it—which he does.

"Um, sorry," he says, shaking his head. He shakes Bren's hand with exaggeration for several seconds. "Nice to meet you. Um, we aren't open yet—what am I saying? You're Brenner Reindhart. We open for you. What can I get you?" All of that, Joe says in a single breath.

"I'm good, man. Thanks," Bren says.

"Are you sure? I'm happy to make anything you like."

"A bit early. Thanks though. I actually wanted to talk to your boss here."

When Joe doesn't move, I speak up. "Joe. Can you give us a moment?"

"Yeah . . ."

Joe throws me a glance like I've kicked his puppy as he walks through the swinging door that leads to the kitchen. He is a big, burly man, but he slouches, and his shoulders slump forward as he leaves us. I chuckle when he's on the other side of the door.

"Oh my god," I say. "Do you get that a lot?" I ask Bren and realize I have yet to see him interact with fans outside of that first concert I went to.

"You have no idea," Bren says.

Once we know we are entirely alone, I lean over the bar, keeping all my weight on my elbows as I stretch up on tiptoe to reach Bren's lips. He leans in across the counter, his breath hot on my face. Phone sex and sexting are not good substitutes for Bren in the flesh.

He kisses me with an open mouth and runs his tongue across my teeth. He nibbles, sucks and kisses until my arms start to shake, and I have to let go and bring my feet back to the ground.

When we break contact, I am grinning, riding the high of a kiss I had no idea I'd missed so much while he was away.

Then I frown because this has disaster written all over it. I don't like this feeling. Me missing him is not part of the deal. When have I ever sat around waiting for someone? Not ever. Not once. Bren is the first, and he can't be.

He is passing through. I am one tour stop of many. How many women does he have sprawled all over the country at every major city where *Industrial November* stops? I don't want to think about it. And that right there is the worst of it all—I've never cared about that before.

Not once have I wondered about my lovers' past lovers. I'm not a jealous person because I have no right to be, given my past and my sexual preferences, but suddenly I care a lot about Bren and how many women he is currently seeing—because it isn't just me. He has to be seeing more women. He is a rock star, after all. I am not the only idiot currently enthralled by him, am I? No thought could be more unsettling.

"What's wrong?" he asks. "You aren't happy to see me?"

"No, I, uh, I'm very happy to see you."

"You were frowning—"

"I was?"

Bren nods. "Come on. Tell me what's wrong."

"Nothing. Really. Why didn't you tell me you were coming?"

He grins in that boyish way that looks so out of place on that angry-looking face of his that so rarely smiles for the camera. "I wanted to surprise you," he says.

"Well, I'm surprised . . . and sorry. I can't get away tonight."

"It's all right. Can I wait at your place until you get off work?"

"Then what?"

"I was hoping to persuade you to come to Napa Valley with me—"

My eyes bulge. "Napa Valley?"

He nods. "You ever been?"

"No! I'd love to go. The wine tastings alone! I could make great contacts for distributors—"

"Whoa, whoa." Bren cuts me off. "It's only for the weekend, and it's not a working weekend. I promise I'll take you back some other time for business if that's what you want, but this weekend, I don't plan on sharing you with work."

"This weekend?" I ask.

Bren nods. "We fly out tomorrow afternoon. We have the evening Friday and the rest of the weekend, then fly back Monday."

He is so damn pleased with himself, it only pisses me off more. "I can't go this weekend."

"Come on. You own the place. You can do whatever you want—"

"No, Bren. I can't."

Is this man serious? Many people assume that because I own my own business, I can take off whenever I want. Nothing could be further from the truth. I am harder on myself than any other boss could ever be. I am not a slave to my business, because I love doing what I do, and it's true what they say: when you do what you love, it's not work. But I am not about to drop the ball and let myself be whisked away by someone who is so out of touch—he clearly doesn't get it.

"Why can't you go this weekend?"

"You should have mentioned this last night on the phone. I could have told you it wasn't possible."

"You have yet to give me an explanation."

I glance at the partition between the bar and the kitchen. Through the small circular window on the door, Rubén's baseball cap comes into view along with the top of his head. When my gaze lands on him, his eyes widen, and he ducks out of sight. Martín follows, peeking through the window until he mimics Rubén with the same look of alarm on his face. Last to show his face is Joe. He just smiles wide, clearly happy that Brenner Reindhart is at our bar. I have the sudden sensation this must be what it's like to be in a fishbowl.

I pinch the bridge of my nose then turn back to Bren. "Look," I say. "We can go on a trip another weekend when I've had the time to make arrangements—"

"So you're telling me you can never be spontaneous?"

"Not when spontaneity gets in the way of my business," I fire back.

Bren frowns, and I see the clouds behind his eyes swirling into a full-blown storm. I'm fast becoming an expert at recognizing Bren's rising anger. Anger he can shove where the sun don't shine.

"Any woman," he says, "would jump at the opportunity to—"

"Do you not know yet, Bren?" I cut him off.

He raises a brow in question.

"I'm not like the women you know."

His forehead smooths out, and he smiles weakly. "I'm sorry," he says. "I really want to break this cycle of fighting just when things are starting to get good again. I was just trying to do something nice."

"And I appreciate it." I bite the inside of my lip, unsure I should ask him what's on my mind. But if I am trying new things, then communication should be a part of it too, because what do I have to lose? Nothing. Not my heart. That's for sure.

"Bren," I say with a voice like I'm approaching a wounded wild animal. "Besides models, have you ever dated a woman with her own career or business?"

Bren's jaw slackens. He blinks, then shakes his head. "I hadn't thought about it, but no. Not really."

I smile at him. I know he really did mean well with the trip and his attempt to whisk me away. "I know you meant well with the surprise trip, but I can't drop my business at a moment's notice any more than you could cancel a tour midway through."

His eyes avert from mine when I say that, like I'm actually making some sense.

The swinging door busts open. "She can go!" Joe all but yells as he comes into view, his voice an octave too high for him. I glare at him, and he doesn't so much as flinch. "I can handle it, Sofia. Really. You can go."

This idiot listened to our entire conversation? Bren looks at me with equal parts shock and a question in his eyes. I know what he wants to ask. Can he trust Joe to keep his trap shut about us? I tip my chin in affirmation, and Bren's shoulders drop as he relaxes them.

"Joe, I can't—"

"Yes, you can," he reassures me as he keeps looking at Bren. "Let me earn the raise you just gave me."

Joe's raise was well-deserved. I can't afford to lose him. He is my right hand, and I need him exactly where he is. Even if he oversteps when he shouldn't.

"Joe—"

"See?" Bren interjects. "He can handle it."

I shake my head. "We still need staff."

"I'll get Tracy or Ileana to come in. Don't worry about it."

I know what Joe is doing. He is kissing Bren's ass. Bren, for his part, grins at Joe and nods in approval. I don't like the bromance brewing here—not one little bit.

"Ileana has worked more days this month than she wants to. I don't want to push her too hard to where she no longer wants to come in anymore."

"Fine, I'll get Tracy or someone new. Don't worry about it."

Bren is nearly bouncing where he sits, and I can't keep finding excuses.

I sigh from deep within my chest. "Fine," I say. "Let's go to Napa Valley."

12

SOFIA

As we approach the villa, Andreas drives us through the tapestry of the vineyard. Pine trees flank the winding road leading to the secluded property. He enters a code into a keypad, opening the massive gate in front of us. He drives forward until we get to a circle of trees encasing a water fountain in front of the villa.

An impressive stone archway in front of the door greets us as we exit the car. I take in the massive villa, or rather, estate, and laugh. Bren takes off his glasses and looks at me.

"Do you like it?" he asks.

I nod, my eyes still roaming the face of this mansion. "Bren, it's just the two of us. This is ridiculous. We don't need so much space."

He turns me to him, breaking away my concentration from our surroundings. My hand is in his; I didn't even notice him taking it when we got out of the car. Bren lifts my chin so he can look at me, amusement dancing in his irises. "Schatz, first, you deserve the world. Second, we won't be able to explore much if we want to avoid paparazzi. And lastly, I wanted a place big enough to have a pool house so that Andreas can be both comfortable and out of our way."

"Or out of earshot," I mumble under my breath, and Bren laughs.

"Yeah. Out of earshot is a bonus. Now answer me. Do you like it?"

I glance at the expansive villa again, something straight out of a French country fairy tale encased in foliage and flowers. I take a deep satisfactory breath of the air that smells almost green—if green had a smell. "It's unlike anything I've ever seen, Bren. It's . . . it's breathtaking."

When Bren nods and lets go of my face, the double doors open, and out walks a short man in a suit. We walk toward the door, and he greets us with a broad smile halfway to the entrance.

"Mr. Reindhart, it is such an honor. Welcome to Maison Madrone."

Bren tips his chin and shakes the man's hand, introducing me as well.

"It is a pleasure to meet you both," the man says. "Calvin Brown. I'm the estate manager—at your service."

I move to reach out my hand for a shake, but Calvin takes a bow, and I wonder if I have stepped into some bizarre alternate reality. Is this how the other half lives? With people *bowing* to them?

"Would you like a tour of the estate?" Calvin asks.

"No, thank you. I'm sure Miss Ocampo here would rather explore on her own."

"I would," I say, reassuring Calvin with a smile. "But thank you."

"Of course," he says and bows again. I scratch my head. This is weird.

"Why don't you show my security, Andreas, to the master

bedroom so he can take our luggage. You can hand him keys and arrange any particulars with him."

"Of course." Calvin smiles, and Andreas trails him toward the side of the villa. I have to force a snort to die inside me at the realization that they're using a separate entrance. Like, for the help.

"You're not planning on carrying me in, are you?" I ask Bren, causing him to laugh.

"And be endlessly mocked by you?" he asks. "No, Sofia. I'm not carrying you in."

Feeling giddy with a child-like excitement I'd long forgotten, I smack him playfully in the middle, catching him off-guard, and yell, "Race you in," before dashing toward the door.

I'm barely across the threshold before Bren's brawny arms catch my waist and pull me in, my back pressed against his chest. I wiggle, trying to break loose, and his grip grows tight around me. He lets go with one hand so he can tuck my hair behind my ear, and his lips touch the shell of my ear as he speaks slowly. "You didn't play fair, Miss Ocampo. And you know what happens to someone who doesn't play fair?" he teases.

I shake my head but don't speak as I collect myself, brushing away the goosebumps that have sprouted down my arms.

"They get taught a lesson," he says and chuckles sexily into my ear. Holy hell, Brenner Reindhart has game.

I spin around so I can face him, and he keeps his arms around me. "I think I'll enjoy any punishment from you."

Bren chuckles again, and I love how lighthearted and stress-free our trip has been so far. He's been attentive and playful, not to mention hell-bent on making sure I have a good experience.

"Come on. Let's explore together," he says and slaps my ass gently, forcing me into action.

The dramatic foyer with an open-beamed ceiling and check-ered stone flooring greets us first, taking my breath away.

Massive French doors lead to a terrace revealing an expansive vista of the valley below.

Bren holds my hand as we go from room to room, my jaw nearly at the floor over the opulence. The extravagance is a bit irresponsible, but I won't lie and say it isn't also spectacular.

Luxury doesn't begin to describe our private villa in Napa Valley.

"Do you really like it?" he asks again.

My insides are screaming *Yes! Of course, I do. Who wouldn't, you idiot*, but I only shrug a single shoulder. "It's all right," I say, averting my eyes.

Bren chuckles, seeing straight through me. "It takes a lot to impress you, doesn't it, Sofia?"

"No," I say. "Not really."

Someone clears their throat, and Bren looks past me. I turn around to find a woman who looks to be in her mid-forties wearing a maid's uniform. I smile at her. "Hello," I say.

"Hi," she says, keeping her eyes glued to the floor. "My name is Carmen. I clean for you. I cook—anything you want. You tell me. Okay?"

I approach her, ducking my head a little, hoping to meet the short woman's eyes, but she won't look up at me. Her English carries a heavy accent, but she isn't hard to understand. And I'm surprised. Carmen reminds me a little of my mom, making me feel homesick for her. "Carmen," I say and switch to Spanish. "Do you speak Spanish?"

Her face snaps up to meet mine with surprise, and her eyes sparkle. "Yes!" she nearly yells, and I laugh, glad she's looking me in the eye now.

"You speak Spanish?" she asks, this time in Spanish.

I nod. "I'm Mexican," I tell her, and she looks at me with skepticism, pulling another laugh out of me.

I lean in, taking her upper arms in my hands, and give her a customary kiss of greeting on the cheek. "It's nice to meet you, Carmen. I'm Sofia," I say as I pull away.

Carmen looks stunned, and she brings her hand to her cheek where I kissed her, her eyes a bit glassy. "You too, *Chinita*," she says and smiles at me. I laugh at the nickname my nana uses for me too.

I turn back to introduce Bren, who is watching our interaction quizzically. I purse my lips. Then I remember what a snob he was to me when he assumed I was a waitress and throw him a look that says, *Well? What are you waiting for, you idiot?* He is so high and mighty on that horse of his, he can't even stoop to the level of greeting his staff.

Realizing his blunder, he steps forward and shakes Carmen's hand. "I'm Bren. Nice to meet you," he says. Carmen smiles at him and switches back to English for Bren. "You too, Bren. I leave you. I be in the kitchen if you need anything. Okay?"

"Thanks, Carmen," I say.

I want to stay in my happy bubble, so I don't call out Bren now about how rude he was to Carmen when he didn't acknowledge her presence until he was prompted. But we both know there will be a reckoning for that. Brenner Reindhart has a lot of introspective work to do if he wants to be in my life. That behavior just won't do.

Instead of working myself up into anger, I refocus my attention on our self-led tour of the villa.

The living room is all drama with high ceilings, an impressive, distressed chandelier, and a view of the sweeping valley beyond the glass French doors that looks like a painting. I'd love to come back in the winter and sit by the marble fireplace, all cozy with Bren wrapped around me like a blanket—preferably naked.

Though grand in scale, every room is light and airy. The main floor is complete with an informal breakfast nook, a formal dining room, an expansive kitchen, a library that makes me drool, and all of it has a cozy charm to it. We take a peek at the wine cellar, but Bren doesn't let me in. "Later," he says. "I know you'll get lost for hours in there." I giggle because I know he's right. Maybe I can strike a deal with the vineyard to supply *La Oficina* if the wine is good. But I force myself to stop thinking about work, at least for today.

We ascend a white stone staircase with a black wrought-iron railing to the second floor.

When we get to the main bedroom, I stare wide-eyed at the four-poster plush bed with silk linens and a down comforter. My legs twitch, eager to jump on it and giggle like a little girl.

Instead, I run my hand over the exquisite fabric. I doubt my hands have ever touched something so expensive, and I pull them back with that thought.

"I'm sorry I couldn't take you to a luxury spa. There are some amazing ones, but I thought at least for this first trip, we would want some privacy."

"This is perfect," I say, looking up at him. "But how much privacy can we really have with Andreas around?" It's not a complaint, even if it sounds like it, but I find myself wondering more and more about Bren's everyday life.

"My lifestyle isn't for everyone, Sofia. I understand if it's too much for you to handle." He takes my hand in his and rubs the back of it with his thumb. "But I'd like for you to try."

I lie down on the bed, running my arms over the comforter's buttery fabric. This bed is as unreal as I imagined it would be when I first saw it. My pleasure doesn't last because now I am frowning. We have been lucky so far. News media hasn't yet picked up on the story that Bren is seeing someone. So far, we only see each other in private, and apart from this trip, we haven't gone anywhere together.

We flew on a private jet to get here, and when we arrived in California, Andreas drove us in a private car. Bren isn't letting anyone see us for a reason. I wonder how things will change when it gets out about us. I know Bren is shielding me from it, but I want to know how bad it can get before deciding to take this any further. The press has yet to take a whiff of me, and I'm sure I haven't seen anything yet, but that's a worry for another day. I'm determined to enjoy this weekend.

Almost as if Bren can read my mind, he kneels on the bed above me and leans in to suck on my earlobe. Then he whispers, "I know I'm asking a lot of you, Sofia. But I also know I can make any trouble worth your while." His erection presses against my hip bone, and I writhe under the hard feel of it.

"You're not playing fair." I pant, throwing his words back at him.

"Never have," he says and sits back to unbuckle his belt.

13

SOFIA

Our first night in Napa Valley, Bren and I stay up all night fucking. We take breaks between rounds to talk about anything and everything. The next day, I sleep in, missing most of it. I'm a little bummed I didn't wake up early enough to enjoy the majestic place, but I was utterly exhausted.

When I realize how late it is, I reach over for Bren, but the cold emptiness of his side of the bed greets me instead. I sit up, looking around the room for him until my eyes land on a note on his pillow.

WENT FOR A SWIM. YOU MAY WANT TO GET DRESSED.
   You will have visitors when you get up.
   — *Bren*

VISITORS? WHO THE HELL IS HE HAVING OVER WHEN IT IS supposed to be just us? I frown, but he is right. We have to stop picking stupid fights, so I won't voice my protest. My rebellion, however, knows no bounds. Instead of listening to him and getting dressed, I walk over to the French doors that lead to the upper terrace outside our room and open them. It's almost sunset, and the view of Mt. Elena and the sprawling hills of Napa Valley is spectacularly sun-kissed by the golden hour. I take a deep gulp of air. This must be what heaven is like— complete serenity surrounded by grapes and wine.

The sound of water turns my attention away from the spectacular view and downward. Bren's massive back and muscular arms glide and slice through the water of the infinity-edge lap pool. I bite my lip at the sight of all those muscles glistening under the water. The lap pool looks inviting, and I think about having my own swim when he is done. A naked swim, maybe, to enjoy those spectacular vistas. That sounds amazing.

I am watching Bren swim, unbeknownst to him, when the sound of Andreas yelling pulls my attention away. "Whoa, whoa! What are you doing?"

I was so busy watching Bren, I didn't notice when Andreas walked out of the pool house. He has a stack of towels in his arms and is now pulling the top one in front of his face to cover it. Confused, I look down and realize I'm naked. And he can see all of it through the iron railing. Shit. I cover my breasts with my hands.

Bren must have heard Andreas's booming voice at the sight of me, and he shoots straight up out of the water, startled. He wipes water from his face and looks around. "What's going on?" he snaps.

Andreas can only blindly point in my direction from behind the towel.

Bren's gaze follows the direction Andreas indicates, and I try to take a step back, but I am too late. He sees me. Shit. I dash back into the room and close the terrace doors behind me. Shit. Shit. Shit. I grab my underwear from the floor and have started dressing when the thunderous steps of an angry Bren roar over the stairs, getting closer and closer.

"What do you think you're doing?" he barks as he enters the bedroom. He holds a towel around his waist, and his rippling muscles are all taut from his anger. His jaw is set, his eyes black and murderous. "Sofia!" he snaps when I don't answer, but his mouth is turning upward into a half-smirk. I know he is trying to hold back a smile because I am checking him out. An Angry Bren is sexy as all hell.

"I was just watching you swim," I say and approach him slowly until I can press my palms to his chest. I draw my hands down his abs, and when I reach for the towel, he grabs my wrist and shakes his head.

"What am I going to do with you? Andreas saw you naked."

"I'm sorry," I say to appease him.

Bren's eyes narrow. Water is still dripping from his hair down his face. "Are you?" he asks.

I bite my lip, unsure if he wants my honesty or not. But what do I want from him if not honesty? I can't expect one thing and offer another, so I answer as truthfully as possible and shake my head. "No. Not really."

"*Scheisse!* Sofia!"

"I'm sorry, Bren. I'm trying to be honest here. I don't care if Andreas saw me naked. I don't care if anyone sees me naked."

His gaze turns murderous, and the smirk disappears into his setting jaw. "Sofia, no one knows about us yet, but as soon as it gets out, the paparazzi will go crazy over you. Do you want your naked body plastered on every tabloid in the world?"

In the world? I shift where I stand, uncomfortable, imagining a Mexican tabloid in the local store where my mother shops regularly. I shake my head. "No. I wouldn't want public photos of me naked." I don't point out the estate is secluded, and there isn't anyone around for miles because he is right. If there's a chance of photos in the future, I need to start being more careful.

"Will you please be more careful?"

"I will. I promise."

"Good. I'd hate to have to fire Andreas. He's been with me a long time."

I laugh, thinking he is joking, but stop when I see the wrinkle forming between his brows. "Sorry. Please don't fire Andreas."

"You just can't do what you're told, can you?"

I smile wickedly at him. "You'd have a better chance asking me to do the opposite of what you actually want."

He runs his hand over his face, exasperated, and I try to take his towel off again, and again, he stops me. "I'm serious. You have to get dressed. You have visitors downstairs waiting for you to wake up." I frown, still wondering who these 'visitors' are. Sensing my trepidation, Bren brings his hand to the side of my face and caresses my cheekbone with his thumb. "It's a surprise. From me," he says. "Oh, and I want to run something by you."

"Okay."

"You can say no if you want to."

"Out with it, Bren."

"An old friend of mine is in San Francisco with the band. He wanted to see me but didn't realize I'd be gone. Would you hate it if I invited him here tomorrow? Just for lunch, then I promise we will continue our romantic getaway alone."

"An old friend?"

"Yes. A good one. I'd love for him to meet you."

I shift my weight from one leg to the other. "It's not too soon to be meeting friends?"

"I met yours. Mandy was her name? And I've met Joe."

"Okay, Mandy is not really a friend-friend. And Joe, he's a colleague."

"Forget I asked—" he starts to say.

"He's important to you?" I ask.

Bren nods. "He's my best friend, and I haven't seen him in a while. We're both so busy, we don't get much of a chance."

He clearly wants to spend time with his buddy, and I would be a total dick if I got in the way of that. I wouldn't do that to him. "It's fine, Bren. Have him over."

"Are you sure?" His eyes search mine, and I nod. He plants a kiss on my forehead. "Thank you," he says. "It was not planned. I'm sorry we'll have an interruption, but I promise it'll be brief," he says.

Bren grabs some clothes from the closet, announces he is going to the guest bedroom to shower, and I hear him as he calls down the stairs for someone to come up.

Fully dressed now, I watch as a slender man in a pinstripe suit and rose-colored glassed walks into our room. Two people trail him, carrying a clothes rail between them. One is a young woman, and the other person helping is none other than Andreas, looking a bit rosy around the cheeks.

"Hello, Andreas, I'm sorry about earlier—"

"Nothing to be sorry about, ma'am," Andreas says, but his cheeks flush beet-red, and his gaze is glued to the cream carpet. I stifle a chuckle. "Excuse me," he says and leaves me alone with the other man and woman.

"Hello," I say, stretching out my hand. "I'm Sofia."

The woman takes my hand and smiles. "I'm Kikki," she says with a bright smile.

The man doesn't say anything for a while. He stands back and rubs his chin studiously, then his eyes grow wide. "You're so beautiful. We hardly get to work on anyone this stunning, do we, Kikki?"

"This is Marco," Kikki finally says, solving my mystery. "He

is your personal stylist, and I'm here to do hair and makeup."
Kikki smiles wide.

"So these are for me?" I ask as I approach the clothes rail and
run my hand through the expensive fabrics.

Kikki nods.

"Wow."

"Mr. Reindhart has special plans for you two this evening,
and he wants you to look spectacular," Marco says.

I don't know if I should be insulted and hide my eye roll. Of
course he does. Like I can't look spectacular without help. Sure,
so far, he's only seen me in concert or bar clothes. He's planning
a proper first date, but I can bring it. And I don't need any help
to do it, damn it. Still, I don't want to be rude to Marco, who
surely has been paid already.

Marco walks around me in a circle, eying me up and down.
He brings both hands to my body and wraps his hands around
my waist. "Great proportions," he says. "Boobs are a bit small,
darling, but I have this amazing pushup bra; we can fake some
extra cleavage."

"Uh," I say. The words themselves sound rude, but he says
them in such a friendly tone with a wide smile. I don't think he
actually meant for any of it to be rude.

"Why don't you look at what we've brought and tell me what
catches your eye. We can go from there," Marco says.

"Sure . . ." I scan the pieces slowly and frown. None of it
looks like me. These evening dresses are exquisite, feminine,
and eye-catching, but none fit my personality. I don't know how
to say that nicely.

"What's wrong, darling?" Marco asks.

"I'm not sure anything here screams 'me.'"

"Nonsense," he says. "You will bring him to his knees in any
of these dresses."

Kikki giggles. "I think she has already brought him to his
knees," she says.

I join in with her laughter. I think she understands what I mean.

"How about this one," she says, pulling out a metallic gold mini dress. It is stunning and has a revealing plunging back.

"Um . . ." I stammer.

Kikki keeps talking. "I could slick your bob back into a wet-hair look. We can get you a gentle spray tan and give your skin a glowy look—"

"A golden goddess," Marco says and clasps his hands in front of his chest in delight.

"Absolutely not," I say. Nothing could sound more unlike me than what they have in mind. Marco frowns. "I feel my sexiest with my bob straight," I clarify.

"Okay, that's good," Kikki says. "You know what you feel stunning in—"

"I do. And I'm sorry. I know you're just doing your jobs, but none of these things would help me feel comfortable, let alone sexy."

Marco's mouth drops slightly, and I feel a bit sorry at the distress plain on his face.

"Look. Why don't I show you what I brought, and you can see if there's any potential there?" I offer.

"All right," he says, but he is clearly annoyed.

I pull out the contents of my suitcase and splay them over the bed. My body-hugging little black dress is my favorite thing I've brought and what I had planned on wearing if we went out on a date. I also have a black leather, high-waisted mini skirt that is another one of my favorite pieces.

"I was thinking the dress," I say.

"That's a lot of black," Marco says. "It's not a funeral."

I chuckle. "I own other colors, but I went monochromatic for packing purposes."

"The dress is too . . . blah," he says.

"Blah?"

"Yes. Blah." He picks up the leather mini and holds it up to examine it. "This has potential. *If* we style it right." He walks over to the clothes rack, my skirt still in his hands, and he produces a black, button-up, long-sleeve blouse that is entirely sheer. "I'm not a big fan of black on black, but if you can wear a deep red or burgundy lace bra underneath it, it would break up the boring palette with a pop of color."

I rush to my suitcase again and pull out a crimson lace bra I thankfully packed. "Will this work?" I ask him, holding the garment like a surrender flag above me.

"Perfect!" he says. Try it on. "Kikki, you run to the car and get the black, strappy, heels. The Tom Ford sky-high ones, you know, with the gold heels."

"I think I need to take a quick shower before trying it on," I say, as I excuse myself for the restroom.

When I come out of my shower, Marco takes a seat on a chair in the room while Kikki sets up her makeup kit, and I start changing. I spin around when I am done.

"So?" I ask. "What do you think?"

"Hmmm," he says, studying me. "I think, let's tuck it in." But before I can start, he is tucking the shirt in for me. Then he takes a step back. "Yes! Much better. We can see your perfect little waist and heavenly wide hips so much better now. You look fantastic," he says. "For the least cooperative customer I've ever had, you look incredible," he says, arching an eyebrow at me. I chuckle and squeeze his forearm.

"Thank you," I say.

"You had no idea about this, did you?" he asks, and I shake my head. He is about to say something else when Kikki hands him a velvet bag and Marco produces the heels from it.

"Oh," Kikki says. "You look amazing. Brenner better have a healthy heart."

"It's not too sheer?" I ask, thinking of the gasket Bren blew when he realized Andreas saw me naked.

"Just sheer enough," she says and winks at me.

Marco hands me the shoes from the bag, and I put them on. They make me spin one last time for final approval.

"Makeup and hair time!" Kikki sing-songs.

"We're using my foundation. I'm very particular about that," I say.

Kikki smiles. "Of course."

Luckily, Kikki is more cooperative than Marco. She straightens and styles my asymmetrical bob perfectly and agrees to the smokey eye and dark red lip I request. Even if she took ten minutes too long trying to match the shade of the lipstick to my bra, I have to admit, I look great.

Once they pack up, Marco and Kikki give me a kiss on each cheek before leaving. "Your hunk is waiting downstairs," Kikki says and winks at me again before she exits the room for the last time.

"Thank you," I say to both of them.

I glance in the mirror for one last check. I look great, but the fact that Bren took the liberty of hiring stylists for me doesn't sit well with me. He is already pampering me too much with this trip, and now he wants to dress me like some sort of paper doll.

I wouldn't have looked quite this amazing left to my own devices, but I· wouldn't have been anything to scoff at either, damn it. I only let the stylists do their thing to preserve their dignity. I couldn't think of anything worse than being hired for a job only to have someone else sabotage my efforts. But if people and their feelings weren't involved, I'd have shoved this gift up Brenner Reindhart's ass.

Brenner Reindhart needs to be taught a lesson.

14

BREN

Andreas finds me at the foot of the stairs. "You ready to go?" he asks me.

"As soon as Sofia comes down. Should be any minute now."

"You're going to flip. Seriously," the girl stylist says, then proceeds to eat Andreas with her eyes. He clears his throat and follows her and the male stylist out as they leave.

When Andreas comes back inside, he apologizes for earlier.

"It wasn't your fault," I reassure him.

"I know, but you couldn't have liked for me to see her naked like that."

I grit my teeth. "Stop bringing it up," I bark.

Andreas chuckles. "Sure thing," he says but won't wipe that stupid grin off his stupid pretty-boy face.

Andreas was hired midway through the first year of the first *Industrial November* tour when crowds started to get a little bit too scary for our liking. After eight years, Andreas has more than proven his loyalty, and all the guys in the band consider him a friend.

And only because of that friendship is he entirely ignorant of how close to being fired he came today. Then his jaw drops as he gazes above me. I turn around, following the direction of his gaze, and Sofia looks down at us from the top of the stairs like the goddess she is.

I haven't seen her in heels before and am surprised at how graceful she is in those sexy strappy high heels. She descends the stairs slowly, allowing my anticipation of her to grow. I need to touch her. And god damn it, I am going to kill that stylist for the sheer blouse. I also need to seriously consider firing Andreas and getting a female bodyguard.

My eyes are glued to her figure until she reaches the bottom step, and I rake her body until my eyes lock with hers. "You look beautiful," I whisper into her ear, taking in the intoxicating aroma of a new perfume I haven't smelled on her before—a mix of floral and spice that sends goosebumps down my arms.

"You certainly clean up well," she says and smiles.

I offer my arm and let her lace hers through it. When I turn, Andreas's eyes are still dancing over Sofia's figure. "The car, Andreas!" I bark until he snaps out of it and fumbles with the door.

THE PRIVATE ROOM I ARRANGED AT THE TAPAS RESTAURANT IS ready by the time we arrive. Andreas waits just outside the door where he can still see us but not be in the room with us. I threaten his job if he keeps staring at what is mine, and he doesn't so much as glance Sofia's way the rest of the night.

The private room is dim, with dark walls and only candles, providing a romantic ambiance. I fidget with the napkin and place it on my lap. Dear god, am I . . . nervous? What is this woman doing to me?

When I order us champagne, Sofia's brow arches.

"Are we celebrating something?" she asks.

"A fresh start," I say with a smile.

When our glasses are filled, we clink them together. "¡Salud!" she says. "Prost!" I answer. A shiver shudders through my body, remembering our tequila night, and I wonder if we could replicate the process with champagne this time. She must have the same thought because she smirks sexily at me.

Watching Sofia eat is almost as erotic as watching her pleasuring herself. In fact, that's exactly what she seems to be doing as she places the aguachiles in her mouth and closes her eyes with a moan. "These are amazing," she says, licking her bottom lip.

Fuck. I can't even watch this woman eat before I'm hardening under the table. I clear my throat. "Yes. They're great."

We order plate after plate of tapas: stuffed mushrooms, mussels, and bacon-wrapped dates. We wash it all down with champagne, and Sofia moans with every last fucking bite. She is killing me here. And that look in her eye, the dark stare, with that playful smirk hinting at the corner of her lips, tells me she knows exactly what she's doing.

"We're in Napa Valley, after all. Can we switch to red wine?" she asks.

"Anything you want tonight, *Schatzi*."

We switch to wine after finishing our meal, skipping the dessert. Our dessert will come later.

I narrow my eyes at her. "I want to ask you something, but I don't want you to be upset."

"All right," she says, eying me carefully.

"That night we fought, when you were flirting with that couple . . . were you really going to bed with both of them?"

She smiles a sexy half-grin. "Would that bother you?" she asks.

I shrug. "I was just . . . surprised."

"I was thinking about it, yeah. That's part of why I was so pissed at you for ruining it. I thought I finally had a chance at a threesome."

"You've never had one before?" I ask, trying to come across as uninterested as possible while taking a sip of my wine.

Sofia throws her head back with laughter. "No, Bren. I have yet to be so lucky. Have you?"

I avert my eyes from her. It is difficult telling her of my sexcapades those first few years when the band started to pick up momentum. I've done far worse than threesomes, but I'm not that man anymore, and I want her to know the man that is here, sitting before her now.

"I know you're a rock god, Bren. I know you have."

"Then why did you ask if you thought you knew?"

She shrugs one shoulder. "For confirmation, and perhaps—equality. If you can ask those sorts of questions, then so can I."

"Fair enough. Then yes, Sofia. I've had threesomes."

"Always with two women?"

"Mostly with two women, but I've shared a woman with another man a time or two."

"I find that surprising, Bren."

"For her pleasure," I clarify, "not mine or the other bloke's."

She nods, and she bites the inside of her lip—the unmistakable sign she's thinking.

"Do you want a threesome, Sofia?"

She drops her glance to the table. "I'm afraid to answer honestly with how jealous you act—"

I sigh, remembering what an asshat I've been. "I'm sorry about that, Sofia. But I do see a distinction between an agreed-upon and shared sexual fantasy with other people and betraying someone behind their back. I'd never share a serious partner on an on-going basis, but I am open to exploring sexual fantasies on a one-off basis."

"Oh . . ." is all she can say.

"So tell me, Sofia, would that bring you pleasure? A threesome?" I look her dead in the eye when I ask her, then watch her lips part slightly. Her shoulders tighten, and I want to reach over and touch her. Instead, I grip the wine glass tightly in my hand.

She nods, then recovers her composure—and the upper hand. "But," she says. "I want both a threesome with another woman, and one with two men."

I nod. "I'd be open to both." I smile at her despite the heat in my belly at the thought of sharing her. But if that is what she needs, I want to be the one to gift it to her.

Sofia smirks and brings her wineglass to her lips again. Those lips I can't hold off on tasting any longer. Then she lifts her chin and glances past me out the door. "How about Andreas?" she asks. "He is very handsome." Her smirk is playful, and she seems oblivious to the anger building in me. I clench the glass in my hand so firmly, I'm afraid I'll break it, so I let it go and set it down.

"Absolutely not," I snap.

Sofia brings her glass to the table and raises her hands in surrender. "Okay, okay. Sorry."

"I'm sorry. Andreas is out of the question. Unless you want him fired. I couldn't do that and then have him around us all the time. Around you."

"Understood," she says. "Not with your bodyguard."

I relax in my seat. She can disarm me so easily. "Thank you. Besides, I think he and the stylist hit it off."

"Kikki? Really?" Sofia asks. "Well, if we're just staying in tomorrow night, why don't you give him the night off so he can take her out? We don't need him guarding us from the pool house, do we?"

"No, I guess not."

"Besides," she licks her lower lip seductively, "I'd love to swim naked."

I arch an eyebrow. "Would you now?"

She nods. "As for the threesome, it doesn't have to be this weekend. I think we'll both know when the time is right."

"Now, Señorita Ocampo. I believe it's time for bed."

BACK AT THE VILLA, WE DON'T MAKE IT PAST THE LIVING ROOM before we attack each other with our mouths and hands. I'm ecstatic Sofia had the forethought to give Carmen the night off, so we have the entire Villa to ourselves. The slight buzz from the wine—and the conversation about sexual fantasies over dinner—has worked us both into a frenzy of lust.

Sofia pushes me onto the sofa, hikes her skirt up a bit, and straddles me as she devours my mouth. She rolls her hips, grinding against my erection through our clothing.

I rip the flimsy shirt open, sending buttons flying and scattering with clinks on the hardwood floors. "I liked that top!" she protests, looking down at the wreck and the now-ruined top.

"I hated it," I hiss.

"Fucking liar. You loved it," she teases.

"Okay, I liked it, but so did everyone else who saw you in it—and that, I didn't like."

She smirks and resumes her grinding on me as her hand caresses my neck, stroking it to the rhythm of her hips over my hard length. I need to take these pants off and get inside her, but the feel of her movement is too good to pull her off me just yet.

"I'm going to come, Bren," she pants.

"No. Wait. I want to feel you when you come—"

She shakes her head. "No. It's too late," she says in a breathy voice as her pace quickens. Her body shudders and tightens over me, and I clench my jaw with anger at missing the feel of her clenching around my dick.

"You are in so much trouble," I say.

"No," she counters. "You are in so much trouble."

I blink up at her. "What? What did I do?"

She smirks down at me as she works my belt buckle. She slides down my body until her knees reach the floor. She unzips my pants and frees my cock from my slacks and underwear. Her eyes widen, and the sight of her face so close to my dick earns her a twitch.

She kisses the shaft gently, and I drop my head to the sofa's backrest, drawing my eyes closed. "You're in so much trouble," she purrs and licks my shaft from root to tip while she massages my balls with one hand.

"Fuck," I growl and snap my head back so I can look at her while she works. Her lips latch onto the head, and she sucks. Hard. Once. Then she lets me fall out of her mouth. "No!" I snap. She smiles innocently up at me and wraps her hand around my shaft, pumping, but the loss of her mouth is almost painful. As she pumps with her hand, she licks the head once. This woman is torturing me. She is fucking torturing me.

"Sofia," I snap. "Stop teasing me."

"What do you want, Bren?"

"You need to suck my cock, and you need to do it now."

"What are you willing to do for it?" she asks, still in that fake little innocent voice that is so out of place coming from her filthy mouth.

"Anything you want. Just please." I buck my hips upward, hoping she'll take me back in her mouth, but she doesn't.

"Let's see," she says and gives the tip of my dick one quick little suck before looking up at me again. She is driving me insane. "I want you to stop overstepping," she says finally, while she has me literally by the balls.

"What?" I can't think straight. What is she talking about?

"You need to stop assuming I can drop everything at the drop of a hat for you. And you don't get to buy things I have no part in selecting."

"What are you talking about?" I hiss, desperate and wild now.

"The stylists?" She arches an eyebrow.

Fuck. This woman is mad. She is fucking furious, and I'm in for it now. She has me where she wants me—balls in hand. This is coercion! How dare she? But I am her slave, and she knows it.

"I'll never overstep again. I swear! Now, for fuck's sake, will you just suck my dick?"

The innocence wipes away from her face and is replaced by a dark smirk. She has me where she wants—how she wants. She brings me into her mouth once again, but this time she sucks harder and brings me in deeper and deeper until I can feel the back of her throat relaxing and opening up for me.

She massages my balls again, and I almost lose it. "Sofia, if you don't want me to come in your mouth, you have to stop now," I say, but it comes out weak.

Her response is to suck harder, and my every muscle tightens. I look down at her disheveled state, the torn sheer blouse, the red lipstick smeared across her face—and my cock. It is such a sensual yet dirty look on her, it feels like I have defiled her, and she loves it. Just one look at her like that, and I explode in her mouth.

She gulps down every last drop of me as I come the hardest I've ever come in my life. When she lets me out of her mouth, I dust her bottom lip with my thumb, in awe of her mouth, of her beauty, and her dominating sexiness.

"That was really mean," I whisper as she looks up at me through her thick lashes from her spot on the floor.

"Was it?" she asks in a honeyed voice.

"It was."

"But did you learn anything?"

I chuckle. "Yeah. You sure taught me."

15

SOFIA

Bren is not in bed with me when I wake up in the morning—proudly at a respectable hour. I put on some sweats and a tank and wander out of our room and down to the kitchen in search of both Bren and coffee.

I'm surprised it's Carmen's voice I hear speaking with Bren as I get close to the kitchen, and I linger just outside, listening despite the heavenly smell of coffee luring me in.

"How about 'You look beautiful'?" Bren asks.

"*Estas hermosa,*" Carmen says, enunciating every syllable slowly for Bren.

He repeats after her. "*Estas hermosa.*"

"Yes!" Carmen says triumphantly. "Your pronounce is good," she praises him.

I smile, imagining Bren's grin of satisfaction at Carmen's approval. Maybe there's hope for Brenner Reindhart yet.

"You be good to her. Yes?" Carmen says, and it's not clear if she's asking him if he's good to me or telling him to be good to me.

Regardless, Bren answers. "Always."

"*Siempre*," Carmen says with a dreamy sigh.

"*Siempre?*" Bren parrots with good pronunciation again.

"*Siempre.* Means always," Carmen says.

I barge into the kitchen like I haven't been listening to them. "Morning. Any of that coffee left?" I ask.

Bren is sitting at the breakfast nook, and Carmen orders me to sit with him while she gets my coffee.

"Get yourself one too and join us," I tell her.

"Oh, no," she says. "I get in trouble with Mr. Brown."

I laugh. "We won't tell him. I promise."

Carmen shifts uncomfortably and glances between Bren and me.

"Yes, please," Bren says. "Mr. Brown won't know a thing."

"No, please. I need my job. Thank you." She smiles at me, appreciative of the invitation, but shrugs.

I let it go, not wanting to make her more uncomfortable, and she leaves us to dust the living room that needs no dusting.

When we're alone, I ask Bren, "So what were you two chatting about?"

"Oh, this and that," Bren says. He squeezes my thigh under the table. "Are you hungry?" he asks.

"Yeah, actually. Famished."

Bren takes off the tea towel from a small basket in front of us, revealing golden-crispy pastry, and my eyes widen. I gasp. "Are those . . ."

"Empanadas?" Bren asks with a wide grin. "Yep." He grabs one and devours nearly half of it one bite. "This is my fourth one."

"I haven't had good empanadas in forever!" I squeal with delight.

Bren laughs. "If I had known this was all it would take . . ."

I drop my head back with laughter because, really, that's all it does take to make me this happy.

"You looked happier at seeing the empanadas than at seeing the villa," he says with mock scorn.

I shrug, still gawking at the plate, my mouth nearly drooling. "What kind of filling are they?" I ask.

"These here are pumpkin, and these are pineapple. Though you'll break my heart if you want the pumpkin ones."

I laugh again. "I take it you have a preference?"

He nods, and I take one of each just to annoy him, though I've always been partial to pineapple ones.

I look up at his handsome, smiling face. "Thank you," I say.

"For what?" he asks.

"For being nice to her."

Bren lets out a long breath and hangs his head. "You shouldn't have to thank me for that, Sofia. Can you accept that I'm trying to be better for you?"

I lean my head on his arm, taking a bite of my empanada with a wide grin. I swallow, then answer him. "Yeah, Bren. I can accept you trying to be a better man."

After we finish breakfast, Bren announces we have to get ready.

"For what?"

"Finn is coming over this afternoon," he says.

"Finn?"

"Yes, my friend Finn. We talked about it last night."

That's right. We won't have the entire day to ourselves, and as much as that thought bothers me, I'm also looking forward to meeting one of Bren's friends. I haven't really gotten to know the guys from the band—and I haven't pushed the matter, not knowing where this is going. But now that I'm entertaining the idea of more, whatever the fuck that means, it seems like a good idea to start meeting some of his friends.

WHEN FINN JOINS US AT THE VILLA AND SEES BREN, THE TWO MEN embrace in a dude hug—the kind where they slap the other's back. Finn says something in German I don't understand, and Bren answers in English. "You too. It's been too long."

Finn wears a relaxed chambray shirt rolled at the sleeves to his elbows, revealing muscular and veiny forearms. Nearly as tall as Bren, he surpasses six feet tall. His wavy, light brown hair swoops upwardly from a side part in a purposeful bed-head style. He is clean-shaven, allowing a spectacular view of a perfectly carved jawline. Calling him handsome would be the understatement of the century, and I have to wonder if he models professionally. Or perhaps plays soccer? He certainly has the thick thighs for it.

When they break away, Finn takes his aviator glasses off his face, revealing hazel eyes, and hooks the glasses to his shirt. "Who is this?" he asks, pushing past Bren.

"This is Sofia. Sofia, this is my good friend Finn."

"It's nice to meet you," I say and take Finn's hand to shake it. He holds it tightly in his grip.

"You're stunning," he says and flashes an expert toothy grin. Oh, this man is smooth.

"And not for you," Bren says, clasping Finn on the back, forcing him to let go of my hand.

"Though what you're doing with this bastard here, I don't know. When you come to your senses, please give me a call." Finn winks at me, and I throw my head back with laughter. I know a player when I see one—I recognize my own breed.

"If you want to die," Bren says with a glare at Finn, but his mouth upturns into a small smirk.

"Please, make yourself at home," I say, ignoring Bren's threats. "Will you be staying with us tonight—"

"Absolutely not," Bren snaps before I can finish the thought.

Finn looks between the two of us, blinking as if something confuses him.

"Bren, don't be rude. We have spare rooms."

"It's all right, Sofia. I have a room at a resort nearby," Finn says.

Andreas shows up shortly after Finn's arrival with several bags of food and sets everything out on the kitchen island. Carmen helps me fill three plates with meats, cheeses, and olives from a charcuterie board with a handful of grapes for each.

Since Bren will probably want to go out to dinner with Finn later, I give Carmen the rest of the night off. She laughs and tells me how this is the least she's had to work since having this job, but I reassure her it will be our little secret.

I take all the food out to the terrace by the pool, where both men wait for me. I also bring out wine glasses and a couple of bottles of wine I asked Andreas to get from the property's wine cellar. Bren wanted to hire a chef, but I insisted we should order in, and I'd arrange everything. I don't really want a stranger in the villa who could give away Bren's current whereabouts to a tabloid.

Once Andreas leaves for his date with Kikki, the three of us are left alone.

Alone and in paradise.

"Bren won't take me wine tasting," I explain to Finn when he sees the wine bottles and arches a brow in question. "He's afraid of being recognized." I eye Bren with a teasing glare. "So I asked Andreas to get a couple of bottles of the local so we could try."

"Excellent idea," Finn says with approval.

"So, how do you two know each other?" I ask both men.

"We went to college together," Finn says.

"Are you a musician too?" I ask.

"He wishes he were that talented," Bren says before Finn can answer.

"No. I'm an environmental engineer in Germany."

As they finish the first bottle of wine, Finn and Bren reminisce about their time in college together. I am surprised Bren actually graduated while recording the first *Industrial November* album. I can't believe I haven't asked what he majored in—I guess I assumed he had dropped out when the band started. But no. Bren is a college graduate, to my surprise. He majored in literature with an emphasis in poetry.

"But how does an engineering major make friends with a poet?" I ask.

They look at each other and smile. I don't mind feeling like I'm outside of a club when they share a thought telepathically—it's actually endearing. What follows are a series of stories of how Finn turned into a roadie on their summers off, catching the leftover pussy that sought out the band even before they were famous. Finn seems surprised that he can share those stories about Bren's sordid past. Perhaps he expected me to be upset, but Bren's history doesn't upset me. We all have pasts. I sure do. When Bren tells Finn it's okay to share those stories, I could swear Bren looks at me with pride glimmering in his eyes.

We enjoy nibbling at our food and sipping on wine so much, none of us realize the afternoon and evening have passed us by and it is almost dark. All three of us are very slightly tipsy, and I go to the kitchen for a third bottle of wine. I don't realize someone has followed me in until he speaks.

I turn on my heel to find Finn holding some of the dishes and placing them in the sink. I turn the corkscrew in the bottle. "Oh, thanks, Finn. But you're a guest. You don't have to clean up. I'll get those."

"I'm happy to help," he says and flashes me a sexy smile that pops the cutest little dimple on his right cheek. "Do you need help with that?" he asks, looking at the bottle in my hands.

I uncork it expertly and grin at him. "Nope. I got it. But if you want to grab new wine glasses, they're in that cabinet there."

"Sure," he says. I walk around the kitchen island to go back outside, but I halt once again at his voice.

"Bren looks happy," Finn says.

I turn to face him again. "Does he?"

Finn nods. "I haven't seen him that happy since . . ." He trails off, clearly unsure if he should continue.

"Since Emma?" I ask, studying him intently.

Finn's eyes narrow. "You know about Emma?"

I nod. "He told me."

"How much did he tell you?"

"Why?"

Finn sets the glasses down and walks up to me. He tries to caress my cheek, but the moment his thumb grazes my skin, I rear back.

"What do you think you're doing?" Then realization hits. Bren said it was his best friend he found his ex with. My eyes widen. "No." I shake my head. "Please tell me you aren't the one who—"

Finn laughs. "God, no. That was another asshole who is no longer a part of our lives. But I guess he did tell you everything. That's new," Finn says, as he scratches his jaw.

"What was that, Finn?" I ask with fury. "A test?"

He shrugs but says nothing and instead pops a single grape in his mouth.

"Fuck you," I say calmly.

His eyes lock on mine. "Excuse me?"

"I said, fuck you. I wouldn't betray Bren like that."

Finn smiles and nods. "Good. I just wanted to make sure. Please forgive me. Bren's been hurt enough. He seems to be serious about you, so I needed to make sure. You understand?"

He gives me puppy eyes that would melt weaker women than me, and my resolve to be mad at him for giving me a test wavers. "Fine," I say, annoyed. "But don't do it again," I warn.

He pops another grape into his mouth and nods with a grin. "I promise from here on out, you have my complete trust."

"We should get back out there."

I'm horrified when Finn openly tells Bren what transpired in the kitchen only moments ago.

Bren laughs.

"It's not funny," I say and scowl as the two men share a look between them.

"Seriously, Bren," Finn says. "Because you're my friend, I'm warning you, if you're stupid enough to let her go, I'm swooping in."

"I'm right here. I can hear you," I say while seething and sinking deeper into my chair.

"I'm sorry, *Schatzi*," Bren says and lands a quick peck on my lips. "When Finn and I get together, we relive our youth. We didn't mean to upset you."

When Bren says the word '*Schatzi*,' Finn's eyebrow floats up, and he turns his head slowly, slowly to look at Bren. He looks stunned. I still don't know what the word means. I can only assume 'pain in the ass' but refuse to ask Bren. I want him to tell me on his own.

Besides, I haven't yet told him I saved him on my phone as *tonto*. What I don't like, however, is that they are ganging up on me. I don't appreciate being outnumbered, and now I have to find a way to get back at them.

I narrow my eyes at both of them, and they guffaw in response. When their laughter settles, I deliver a question that freezes them both.

"In all your adventures," I say, "did you two ever share a woman?"

Finn blinks at me, stunned. Then he turns his attention to Bren, who sits silently as he studies my features. I raise an eyebrow in a question I know he understands. We discussed this only last night. Bren said no to Andreas because he's around all the time, but he already admitted he and Finn hardly ever get together. Bren smiles knowingly and, after a short moment, nods his approval. I grin like an idiot.

"Yes. We have," Bren answers for both of them, earning him a smash in the arm from Finn. "What was that for?" Bren says and rubs his arm.

"Why are you telling her that? We swore we'd take that to the grave," Finn complains.

Bren only shrugs and keeps sipping his wine. "She asked."

The sun has set behind the valley, leaving a star-speckled darkness above us. The pool lights reflect in waves all around us.

Finn looks between the both of us as Bren and I smirk darkly at each other.

"Oh no, no, no—" Finn says in protest. "I know what you two are thinking and, no. I'm not getting in the middle of that—"

Bren and I roar with laughter at his choice of words.

"I only meant," Finn says, "that when we did that in the past, we were young, stupid, and with a woman neither of us would ever see again. It was different."

"Shame," I say like I don't care my threesome fantasy just slipped between my fingers. I can't deny the heat in my body or the slickness collecting where my thighs meet. I throw Bren one last teasing smirk and stand to kiss him with an open mouth, ensuring Finn can see our tongues playing with each other. I let go of Bren and look over at Finn. "Guess I'm going for a swim. You know, to cool off."

I lock eyes with Finn as I take off my top, then my bra. I shimmy out of my shorts and underwear next and wink at him before turning to walk toward the pool.

I only hear Bren ask Finn, "Are you sure?" before I jump into the deep end.

Holding my breath, I cross my legs underwater, keeping

myself under. The water around me cools the heat on my skin a little, but it also pebbles my nipples even more and is doing nothing to calm the desire inside. I am just devising a plan to kick Finn out so I can have Bren when the water ripples with a splash. I open my eyes underwater as a hazy figure swims my way. Then a second splash follows, and there are three of us submerged.

16

SOFIA

I can't hold my breath any longer, and I kick up with my legs until my head breaks the surface so I can gulp in some air.

I swim to the middle of the pool where my feet can touch the bottom when two heads pop above water next to me. Finn stands in front of me.

Shirtless and in boxers.

They must have ripped their clothes off as soon as I jumped in.

While the water reaches my shoulders, Finn is so tall, his chest is entirely above water, giving me a view of those perfectly sculpted pecs. My mouth waters, and I bite the inside of my lip at all the dirty thoughts running through my head.

The water ripples as Bren moves behind me and leans his chest against my back.

Finn presses his forehead to mine and closes his eyes but won't touch me with his hands—as if I were made of fire. "Are you sure, Bren?" he asks in a husky voice. Finn opens his eyes to search mine, his heavy lids drooping over dilated pupils. The question was addressed to Bren, but I know Finn is asking me if I'm sure too.

Bren's massive hands wrap around my waist from behind. His lips caress the back of my ear as he speaks. "Sofia. It's up to you. Will it bring you pleasure to be with both of us?"

My mouth too dry to speak, I can only nod.

"Only for one night, Sofia. Do you understand?" Bren says.

I nod again and crane my neck so I can look at Bren. He leans forward so I can make out his features. He smiles a sexy crooked smile and nods with encouragement. "Are you sure?" I ask him.

Bren's smile doesn't waver when he nods again. A knot forms in my throat because I know he is doing this for me. Bren is too possessive, too jealous to share, but with this act of self-lessness, Bren is making one thing clear; he will bend to make us work. He hasn't up to this point, but he's willing to try, and that is the message he is sending when he tells Finn he can touch me tonight.

I turn to Finn again, reassured Bren is okay with this.

Bren's voice is raspier than usual when he speaks softly into my ear. "Tell us, Sofia. Do you want both of us? Do you want two dicks inside you at the same time?" One of Bren's hands leaves my waist so he can pinch a nipple and then returns it to my lower body, sinking lower and lower down my middle and past my belly button.

"Yes—yes." I nod again after I find my vocal cords.

Two thick fingers part my throbbing flesh, and I lose my footing, but Bren catches me, letting the back of my head rest on his chest. Finn's lips find my mouth, and my eyes fly open with surprise. He bends his legs so I can straddle them in a seated position, and both his hands drop to my breasts to play with my nipples gently as Bren props my back up so I won't fall under water.

Bren sinks one finger into me, and the sensations are too

much. He flexes his finger and dips it slowly in further—painfully slowly. So slow, I want to cry out, but Finn's tongue is still exploring my mouth, so I can only purr into his.

Bren's free hand wraps around to find mine, and he leads it until I find his erection behind me. My fingers clasp around it, and I stroke it gently. I break away from Finn's mouth so I can catch my breath, and I look down, searching for my second prize.

Finn pulls his length out through the opening in his boxers for me, and while it's true that water magnifies the apparent size of anything in its depths, by the feel of it, Finn's cock is almost as massive in size as Bren's. I work both my hands, one in front and one behind me, the two erections hard against my palms. I don't think I've ever been so turned on before.

Finn's lips come down on my neck, and he growls against my skin as I pick up the pace. While Finn's tongue tastes my neck, Bren peppers sweet kisses in that tender space between my neck and shoulder on the opposite side. The feeling of two mouths on my skin is unreal.

Bren sinks a second finger in me and swirls them in delicious circles. I roll my hips, trying to force his fingers deeper, and water splashes between us.

Finn chuckles. "So eager," he says.

"You have no idea," Bren teases in my ear. He circles his index finger near my clit but never touches it, driving me completely and utterly insane.

"I need you both to please fuck me," I whine.

They both chuckle. "And polite." Finn grins. "She said please."

"She did," Bren agrees. "But Sofia, all the condoms are upstairs," he teases.

Letting go of both of them, I spin around to look at Bren. His white t-shirt clings to his torso, molding into his concrete ab muscles. His lids are low, eclipsing his irises, and he looks at me through long black lashes sparkling with water droplets. "Are you sure you're okay with this?" I ask him.

"I'm okay with anything that will make you happy," he reassures me and grins wide. He really means it, I think.

"We're going upstairs," I declare and quickly get out of the pool. I grab us all towels and dry frantically. Both men peel off the remaining wet garments from their skin and wrap towels around their waists.

I lick my lips staring at them both. I've died and gone to heaven.

Finn bends to pick me up and throws me over his shoulder, making me squeal with surprise. "Finn!" I grab on to his perfect ass—for support, of course.

He smacks my ass playfully. "Lead the way," he says to Bren.

Finn carries me upstairs and lays me down on the bed while Bren rummages through his luggage for condoms. He sets way more condoms than necessary on the bed, and I gulp. I suddenly realize I'm in for a very long night.

Finn twirls one of the small packets between his fingers, and his eyes search mine. "Would you like to do the honors?" he asks.

I glance back at Bren, and he nods with an encouraging smile. I take the packet and open it with my teeth.

"You have a beautiful mouth, Sofia," Finn says as he rubs his thumb over my upper lip.

"Her mouth is mine," Bren says, making Finn chuckle.

I maneuver to take Finn's thumb into my mouth and suck on it. He lets out a small growl, and I let his hand go free so I can sheathe him. I run my fingers down his perfect six-pack and those deep-cut vee muscles and place the condom on the tip of him, which gets wetter as I roll it down his long shaft. He is massive, and veins bulge along the length of his cock.

The bed moves and Bren's hands turn me over to face the other way. His lips find my mouth, and he kisses me deeply, with hunger, need, and desperation to have me. "You're sure you can take both of us, Sofia?"

"I think so . . ." I say but fail to convince anyone, including myself. I talk a big game, but now I'm actually nervous. This might just be more than I can handle.

Finn's hands grip my hip bones, and he scoots me back on the bed, so my ass faces up at him. God, this position is so hot. Not only is this a sublime threesome fantasy, but Finn is practically a stranger, adding to my arousal and making me ache for both of them.

Bren wraps my hair around his hand, and he pushes me down until my face is within inches of his erection. For a moment, I'm glad he didn't want me to go down on Finn because I want to taste Bren, and only Bren, on my tongue. I hold on to his powerful thighs for balance, my elbows propped on pillows.

As the tip of Finn parts my entrance, I take Bren into my mouth. Finn surges through me in one long, deep stroke. "You're so wet, Sofia. You're dripping down your thighs," he says in that throaty, sexy voice of his that plunges me into a frenzy. I suck Bren harder and take him deeper into my throat, forcing Bren to take the reins and fuck my mouth.

I need to scream from the overwhelming pleasure, but the best I can manage is a moan against Bren's cock in my mouth. Both men thrust into me most deliciously, and I am so close to ecstasy that my body tenses.

"Do you want me to prep her for you, brother?" Finn asks.

What the fuck? Prep me? I want to ask, but Bren inside my mouth prevents any words from happening.

"Yeah. Please," Bren says while panting—his eyes glued on me.

My body clenches tighter and tighter until I know release will overtake me soon, and just before my orgasm finds me, Finn rims my other entrance with his thumb. The sensations are all too much. Then he sinks his thumb into that tight entrance, and my entire body shudders with the strongest orgasm of my life.

As I clench, Finn lets out a growl. "Fuck. You're so tight, Sofia." Finn's thumb keeps thrusting in and out of me. He is so gentle at first, it isn't painful. Then he picks up the pace, and I find myself shifting to meet his strokes.

"She's ready," Finn says, and I let Bren out of my mouth so I can look between them.

"Ready?" I ask.

Bren smiles darkly at me while he puts on a condom but doesn't answer my question. He leaves the bed and walks over to the side where Finn stands. Finn leaves me and flips me onto my back. I ache with need at his absence inside me.

His body comes over me, and he finds my center once again. But instead of thrusting out for a second stroke, Finn stands up, taking me with him. I yelp with the surprise, and he chuckles sexily in my ear. This man is having fun—and so am I.

From behind me, Bren grabs my chin, forcing my head to the side so he can kiss me once, deeply, and I clench around Finn's cock, earning a groan in response from Finn.

When Bren's lips leave my mouth, he whispers in my ear. "I'm going to need you to relax, Sofia."

"Wha—" I don't get to finish my question because Bren positions his cock at my back entrance. My eyes widen, and my heart races. There's no way I can handle his size—not back there.

The blunt tip is slick, so he must have put on lube without me noticing while Finn was lifting me off the bed. Even with the lube, though, I'm nervous, and my legs tighten around Finn.

"It's okay," Finn coos in my ear. He rubs the length of one thigh gently. "Relax. You'll enjoy this. I promise."

"You're too big, Bren," I say.

"You can handle it, Schatz," Bren says, "but now's the time to say stop if you don't want to try this."

At first, I shake my head, but another part of me, the insatiable woman I now seem to be, wants two cocks inside me. "Don't stop," I breathe out.

Finn keeps rubbing my leg and peppering kisses on the side of my neck, coaching me into relaxation as he grips me tightly around the waist with one arm.

Bren is gentle, and he surges into me slowly, one centimeter at a time. "You okay?" he asks.

I nod.

The unfamiliar intrusion is uncomfortable—at first. Then he hits a spot, and something relaxes inside me, making way for the rest of him.

"Good girl," Bren purrs in my ear with approval.

Just when I don't think he can go in any deeper, he pushes further until he bottoms out.

With their perfect bodies, both men stand still as statues for several moments while I adjust around them.

Finn grins down at me and dips his head to take my lower lip in his mouth so he can suck on it. "How does it feel?" Finn asks when he lets go of my lip.

I frown, unsure yet. It isn't as painful as I imagined it would be.

"Does it hurt?" Finn asks, studying my tense features.

I shake my head. "No. It's just . . . I'm getting used to it."

I clench experimentally around them, and both men groan. "It feels good," I finally admit, sending them both into a frenzy. They both work together to prop my weight up so they can thrust in and out of me, and the sensation is too much. Too tight. I'm suspended in the air by their two cocks, my legs still wrapped around Finn. They move at a rhythm like they are trying to touch each other inside me, and the visual of that turns me on more than anything.

And it feels . . . fucking amazing. There's no other way to describe it.

I relax my head back onto Bren's shoulder, and that makes room for Finn, who takes the opportunity to bring his mouth to one of my nipples so he can suck and tease it.

That sends me over the edge. I clamp my hand behind Bren's neck and hold on for dear life as I come in waves, clenching around them with each pulse of pleasure, my back arching mid-air. My thighs shake, and I'm grateful both men are propping me up because I can't hold my legs' grip around Finn any longer. Bren pumps in a few more times and stills as he cries out with his climax. He holds me still and in place while Finn keeps going.

"Come again, Sofia," Bren whispers in my ear. "Come with Finn."

My body obeys Bren, and I clench with the building of another orgasm. Finn's lips find mine, and he kisses me, driving into me faster and faster, then freezes just as the man behind me had done only seconds ago. Bren's chest rises and falls, pressed to my back as he catches his breath, and Finn's forehead drops to mine.

"You're fucking fantastic," Finn says.

They both lift me by the ass cheeks up and off them so our bodies can detangle, and my feet can find the ground. My legs are wobbly as I climb onto the bed. Bren and Finn each go into a different bathroom to discard their condoms and join me under the sheets on either side of me.

Thoroughly sated—and let's face it, fuck-drunk—my head rests on Bren's shoulder while my hand laces together with Finn's. I close my eyes and am lost to the world in this perfect sexual fantasy.

Only it wasn't a fantasy. It really happened.

17

BREN

We tucker out Sofia, and she sleeps through the better part of the morning. I watch her sleep, in awe of how angelic she looks despite knowing what a sex goddess she can turn into under the cover of night. I kiss her temple, and her eyes flutter open.

"Good morning," I say and offer her the best smile I am capable of, though it is a small one.

She, on the other hand, smiles wide as she stretches her arms above her. She turns to the other side of the bed, and my heart sinks a little, knowing she's looking for the other man who put her to bed last night. My stomach gets hot, like I want to vomit, at seeing her disappointment when she turns back to me. "He's gone," I say.

"Oh." She purses her lips thoughtfully.

"Do you wish he were still here?" I ask and beg any gods—old and new—that her answer be 'no.'

She thinks for a moment and puts me out of my misery when she shakes her head. "No. I just wish I had gotten to say goodbye. That's all."

My eyes close with relief, and the tension in my forehead

dissipates. "I kicked him out right after you fell asleep," I admit. "I couldn't share you a second longer without pummeling his pretty face into the pavement."

"Oh, Bren," Sofia says, her gaze alert as she studies my face. Her hand drifts to my cheek, where she rests it reassuringly. "We shouldn't have done . . . er, what we did, if you didn't want to. I'm so sorry. I thought you were all for it."

I smile at her, turn my head to kiss the inside of her palm, and then return her hand to where it was before.

How could I tell her that I wanted last night as much as I hated it? My desire to please her—to give her anything and everything she wants—won over my urge to kick my best friend's ass for daring to look at her, let alone touch her.

Then there was that moment when Sofia winked at Finn before jumping in the pool, and I understood deep in my soul that Sofia is a free agent, and me trying to tame her into the idea of what I once thought I wanted in a woman would only dim her light. I'll die before I actively participate in snuffing out the best parts of her—the parts that drew me to her to begin with. How could I ask her to change everything in her I am attracted to?

If she has to be with other people to be happy, then I'd rather be there as an active participant, sharing in her pleasure, than let someone else steal it from under me.

"I wanted to do it, *Schatz*. For you. I wanted to make you happy. Did I?"

"Oh, Bren. You stupid, stupid man," she says, the words coming out honeyed despite their meaning. "*Eres un tonto. I'm happy with just the two of us.*"

I smile at her, finding sincerity in her eyes. "I know. But I want to give you the world, and I started last night. Anything you ever want. It's yours. Just tell me."

"It was amazing," she says. "And no, before you ask, I don't need that again. I wanted to experience it once, but now that I have, the curiosity is gone."

I pray she believes what she is saying to me. While I don't revel in the idea of sharing her again, I will do it every night of my life if that is what she needs.

As our eyes lock, I understand an undeniable truth. I now live for Sofia, for her smiles, her happiness, and her pleasure. I am a slave to this woman, and I happily put on my own shackles, giving her the key to throw away at her discretion.

She tries to move and winces a bit. "Are you okay?" I ask.

She nods. "Just a little sore," she says.

"How about a bath?" I ask.

"That would be amazing."

When I stand to pick her up in my arms, she smacks my shoulder playfully.

"I can walk to the bathtub, Bren."

I kiss her temple. "I know, *Schatz*," I say and carry her to the bathroom.

After running the water in the oversized stone tub for two, I get in first and motion for her to join me. She smirks at me and gets in slowly as she adjusts to the temperature.

When the water engulfs her breasts, she reaches over to shut it off, returning to rest her back on my chest.

She moans in my arms. "I'd kill for a tub like this at home," she says.

"What do you like about it?" I ask, already making plans to make this happen for her. "The stone it's made of?"

She shakes her head. "No. The size. Every girl's dream is a tub that can hold enough water to cover her knees and boobs at the same time."

I snicker, and she wiggles in my arms with her own quiet laugh.

"I never thanked you, Bren."

"For what?" I ask.

"Everything. This trip. Last night. Pushing for time together. Bending so much to give us a chance. I know I'm difficult, and I'm not used to any of this, but I want you to know I appreciate everything."

My heart soars at her recognition and because she is starting to use the word 'us.'

"You're welcome," I say and rest my cheek on the top of her head, squeezing her tight in my arms.

Maybe, one day I'll be enough for her.

18

SOFIA

When I open the door, Lola greets me on the other side. A basket full of cleaning supplies dangles from her hand. "Hello," she says with a smile. "Just finished the bar. Need me to clean your apartment today?"

"Hi, Lola. Um, not this week, thanks."

Lola drops her head.

"Lola, do you need the money?"

She shakes her head but won't meet my eye. "No. Not really."

I would offer to give her the money, but I already know this proud young woman would turn me down. She has to work for it. "Actually," I say, "is Ileana in yet? I have to talk with her about a few things."

"Yeah, she's getting things ready for tonight."

"Then yeah, it will be great if you clean the apartment while I'm out."

The grin spreads across her face so wide, making me stifle a chuckle. I let her in and make my way to the bar. Ileana already has the lobby ready to go, and she is prepping garnish and stocking all the bar supplies we will need.

"Hey," she says. "Lola kick you out?"

"Yeah," I admit.

"Sorry. I tried to tell her she just cleaned your place last week, and you are a neat freak, so it for sure isn't needed. Besides, you were gone most of the weekend. Speaking of, how was your trip?"

Ileana is talking a mile a minute. Though it isn't early morning, it is *my* early morning since I get to bed late on most nights. I pinch the bridge of my nose as I think about what to answer first. "I haven't had my coffee yet, Ileana. You're going to need to slow down."

"Sorry. I'll make you some."

While she makes the coffee, she continues to interrogate me about my trip to Napa. I tell her everything, only leaving out the intimate details. Finn's visit is also carefully left out of any anecdotes I share with her. Those memories are for me and me alone.

The coffee's aroma wafts through the bar, and Ileana props her elbows on the counter dreamily. "That sounds amazing. I'd like to go there sometime."

"It's beautiful," I admit. "I'm sure Lola would be happy to babysit if you wanted to go for a weekend."

Ileana throws her head back with laughter. "Right. A romantic getaway for one? No thanks. I couldn't think of anything more depressing."

She hands me my coffee, and I sip on it, letting the brew wake me back to the land of the living.

"So," Ileana says with trepidation in her voice. "You gonna see him again?"

"Yeah."

She arches an eyebrow. "Wow. He sounds . . . special."

"I think he might be," I admit, and Ileana smirks at me.

"I never thought I'd see the day."

"You and I both," I agree.

It is too soon to tell Ileana everything. I haven't even sorted out my own feelings yet. Bren was fantastic on our trip together, and the picture he's had in his head of what we could be slowly adjusts into focus. The image is distant and blurry, so I can't quite grasp it, but the more time I spend with him, the clearer it becomes: both of us, pursuing our careers and passions, supporting the other while making time to be together.

Could this work? He made one thing clear on our trip: he is willing to learn and adapt to my needs, and not only sexually speaking. He understands now that my business comes first, and he is willing to be second place. I didn't know men could get to that place of understanding, or I may have tried dating seriously sooner.

But as much as I want my thinking to be practical and pragmatic when it comes to Brenner Reindhart, a small corner of my heart beats for him, and nothing has ever been so terrifying. Not going off to college where no one looked like me or had names like mine, not saying goodbye to my only family as they left for another country. All that, I weathered with what I thought was significant grace. Starting my own business wasn't even terrifying. I didn't bat an eye during the entire process as I set it up. But the thought of Bren breaking my heart makes me nauseous. For all of two seconds, I reason it is the fear of the unknown; I've never had romantic feelings for a man, and my heart has never been broken by a romantic partner. I discard the theory because I know already that my feelings for Bren are growing, and I am all in—and nothing could frighten me more.

"Hey," Ileana says, changing the subject. "David Price called again. Left a message for you." She hands me a folded piece of paper, and I roll my eyes. "Again?"

"When is he going to get the picture?"

Ileana studies me. "He is rather persistent. Isn't he?"

"I'll say."

"You wouldn't . . ." She trails off.

"No. I won't sell the bar if that is what you're trying to ask."

Ileana's hands draw up in surrender. "Sorry I brought it up. I'd just hate to see this place sell out and lose its heart."

I smile at her words. I'm proud that's how my bar is thought of in this community.

"Hand me the phone, will you? I'll call him back."

The phone rings twice before David picks up.

"I don't know where you are getting your information from, but I have no plans to sell."

"Who is this?" he asks.

"Sofia Ocampo. I own *La Oficina*. You keep calling, and I'm sorry, but you're wasting your time. I appreciate your interest, though."

"Oh, yes, Sofia! Thank you so much for calling me back. I'd love to set up a time to sit down with you and—"

"I'm sorry, I hate to be rude, but that would be a waste of both our time. I have no plans to sell."

"I like your directness," David says as he chuckles into the phone. "But selling is not the only option. I think the vibe you have going would be very successful in Chicago. Our Latino population is larger. Have you thought about franchising?"

I am not expecting that question. "Um . . ."

The truth is it never even crossed my mind as an option. "No. I've never considered it," I say.

"Look, I'll be in Kansas City in a couple of weeks. Would you please just sit with me to talk? If you don't like what I have to say, no harm, no foul, but I think you'll be interested in what the Price Group can offer."

I rub my temple. I didn't expect to be flipped so quickly, but I have to admit, I am intrigued. "Sure. If you're already in town, swing by outside of busy hours."

"You won't be sorry," he says before ending the call.

———————

ONCE THE HAPPY HOUR RUSH PASSES, I SIT AT A TABLE WITH TWO of my favorite customers. Sara and Mandy show up for happy hour after their shift at the hospital, and both look disheveled and exhausted.

"You two are a sight for sore eyes," I say.

Mandy smiles up at me as I grab a chair and sit down.

"I'm sorry I haven't been by since the concert. And I'm sorry about that night. I can't believe what a jerk Bren was," Mandy says.

"It's all right, Mandy. And he's not so bad," I say.

Mandy cocks her head to the side, and Sara stares between us.

"Mandy said she had quite the night after the concert," Sara says.

"Yes!" Mandy all but squeals. "I got to party with *Industrial November*. I could have died! DIED! And can you believe it? I almost went to bed with the bass player!"

I look over at Sara, raising an eyebrow in question, but Sara only shrugs and sips her drink. "I don't know what she's talking about," Sara says. "Not that I'm bitter about missing it or anything," she adds with a scowl.

"So, if you had the chance to sleep with the bass player, why didn't you?" I ask Mandy.

Mandy shrugs one shoulder and slurps her drink from the cocktail straw to avoid answering the question.

"No." I gasp. "Don't tell me there's someone else?"

Mandy's eyes look everywhere but at me, then she shakes her head. "No. It just didn't feel right, so I ended up not going up to his hotel room. That's all."

"Hey, where's Carolina tonight?" I ask, letting Mandy off the hook.

Sara rolls her eyes. "Still working."

"Do we need to stage an intervention?" I ask.

Mandy roars with laughter. "Probably, but aren't you calling the kettle black?"

19

SOFIA

I text Andreas to pry information out of him about where the band is staying in Seattle. It's been a week since I last saw Bren, and I already miss him. I don't take any pride in admitting I'm needy for a man . . . but I am. Bren seems to be the exception to everything. I'd be a fool to fuck this up, and somehow, deep down, I have the sneaking suspicion that's exactly what I'll inevitably do.

Until then, I can enjoy our time together, and that's precisely what I plan on doing when I surprise him after his next show. Andreas expressed concern about going behind Bren's back, but I reassured him the surprise will be a welcome one.

I'm picking up around the apartment because it's the biggest mess I've seen, and I cringe every time I glance at it. To the average person, this is probably clean enough, but not by my standards. I also like to come home to a clean place after a trip, so I force myself to clean before I even begin to think about packing for my afternoon flight. Midway through washing dishes, Mom video calls me.

"Mami!" I say, and we talk in Spanish. When was the last

time we spoke? A pang of guilt slices through me. "I'm sorry I haven't called—"

"It's okay, baby. I know you're busy."

"How's Nana?"

"She's great. I'd hand her the phone, but she's outside tending to her roses."

I smile, thinking of my beautiful grandma surrounded by rosebushes. She always did love her roses. "I'm glad to hear it," I say.

"How are you, *mija*? We've missed you. I'm hoping you'll come to visit soon?"

"Maybe. I'm training Joe to take on more and more responsibility, so maybe soon. Okay?"

"Okay, baby. I just wanted to check in, but I have to go because I have food on the stove."

"Okay. Love you, Mom."

"Love you."

I almost wish she would stay on the phone longer. I surprise myself when I realize it's Bren I wanted to tell her about.

And seriously. What the actual fuck?

ANDREAS ROLLS MY WHEELIE SUITCASE AS HE LEADS ME TO BREN'S suite. It's a little uncomfortable being in a hotel this luxurious, like I'm afraid to touch anything lest I break it. However, it's ever-so-slightly less extravagant than our Napa trip residence.

"The band has the floor," Andreas says, cutting through the silence in the hallway.

"Oh."

"Adrian is staying down at the opposite end of the floor, and the rest of the band is this way."

"He's trying to avoid the partying?" I ask as the loud music floods into the hallway the closer we get to Bren's door.

Andreas nods. "Here we are." He opens the door, and I take my suitcase back from him, thanking him.

The suite, with tall ceilings and an incredible glass chandelier, is dimly lit and smokey from a couple of people lighting cigarettes. I cringe. Who would allow anyone to smoke in a gorgeous room like this?"

I barely recognize Karl by his blond strands of long hair, though I can't see his face with a young woman attached to it. A second woman in a form-fitting mini dress leans into them, caressing Karl's chest, watching them make out.

Fritz is on the other couch, swirling a glass full of amber liquid in his hands. He leans in while a woman whispers something in his ear, and as he does this, he looks in the direction of the door and tips his chin at me. It almost looks like recognition on his face. Does he recognize me from that first concert when I met Bren? I shake my head because how dense can I be? Of course that's not it.

There are about ten other people in the suite, but I don't recognize any of them. My gaze finally lands on Bren's massively tall figure towering above everyone as he pours himself a drink. He is speaking with a leggy brunette in a leopard-print mini skirt. She tosses her hair over her shoulder, and though the sound doesn't carry over the music, she is clearly laughing at something he said. As she laughs, her red-manicured hand flies up to Bren, squeezing his bicep. Bren stiffens in response, and I know he's discreetly trying to pull away from her grip, though he's smiling politely at her. He leans back and away from her, his posture stiff, his brows creased. I bite back a smile.

And good lord, is this the kind of attention he's used to? No wonder he was so hell-bent on our private little bubble in Napa. I'm beginning to understand.

Bren's still oblivious of my presence as I walk up to the bar. He's clearly trying but failing to avoid the brunette's constant touching. His eyes are turning to annoyance, despite the smile plastered on his face.

"Think you can pour me one of those?" I yell over the music.

Bren's head snaps toward me, and his face lights up with recognition. "Sofia!" his grin is wide until he looks at the brunette, her hand pressed to his chest, and his eyes widen with panic. His big hand takes her tiny one and peels it off his chest. "Sofia, please, this is not what it looks like—"

I try to hold back my smile. I like the sight of him squirming. It's amusing. "It looks like a groupie getting handsy with you despite your clear lack of consent," I yell.

His head cocks to the side, and he just blinks at me. He scratches his jaw. "Yeah. Then it's exactly what it looks like."

The brunette throws me a nasty glare. "Bren?" she says, turning away from me, and trying to get his attention, but Bren's eyes are fixed only on me. She keeps talking. "I thought you were going to give me a tour of the suite?"

I cross my arms and arch a brow at Bren. "Is that right?"

"No!" he snaps. "Absolutely not." He finally brushes past the brunette and walks around the bar to get to me. "I swear I wasn't going anywhere with her."

Bren has a greenish look of panic on his face as he tries to explain himself, though he really doesn't need to. Still, I can't help it when my head tips back with laughter, and I clutch to my belly with the guffaws.

"Sofia, this is not funny. I don't want you to think that . . . that I'd do that—"

"I know, Bren."

"You're not mad?"

I shake my head.

He grabs me by the hand and takes my suitcase in the other as he leads us to the master bedroom. Once the door is closed, the music isn't quite so loud, and I can hear him more clearly.

"Are you sure you're not upset by what you just saw? I swear I didn't give her any indication that I wanted—"

"I'm not mad, Bren."

"Should I be offended, then?"

"Because I'm not jealous?"

He nods.

My brows furrow. He's serious. "Um, no, Bren. For one, I knew you were a rock star when I met you. I'm surprised this didn't happen sooner, but I'd be an idiot to think women don't fling themselves at you."

"I may be a rock star, but I'd never cheat, Sofia. I need you to know that. While I'm with you, I'm only with you."

"Look, Bren. I know what you are. And we are long-distance. I also know you're human."

"What are you saying, Sofia?" he asks, taking a hovering step closer to me, his face starting to contort into something more . . . intense and savage.

I keep my eyes locked on him. "I don't need your body to be faithful, so long as you stay honest with me. Loyalty is more important to me than physical faithfulness."

His jaw clenches. "You're saying if I had slept with her before you showed up, you wouldn't have minded?"

My gaze drifts away from him and fixes on the carpeted floor. "I'm not saying I wouldn't have minded. Only that I would've understood. Your honesty's more important to me than you keeping your dick in your pants."

He grabs my chin firmly and forces my eyes back on him. His glare is stormy and brewing with anger. "Are you telling me you feel free to fuck other people when I'm away?"

"No!" I nearly yell. "I'm just not naive about your lifestyle."

"Sofia, let me make this clear. I want you. I want to see where this can go. But I can only do this if we are *both* exclusive." He runs an exasperated hand through his hair. "Fuck. I didn't think I had to say that."

I'm smiling as his annoyance bubbles to the surface because he's being adorable. "Brenner Reindhart, are you asking me to go steady with you?"

"What?"

"It's an expression. Never mind."

"So we're agreed? We're exclusive?" he asks, his voice softer now.

"Sure, Bren. I can do that. Though, she was kinda cute. If you wanted to invite her to join us, I wouldn't be opposed," I say and bite my lower lip. Heat radiates toward my core at a flashing memory of Bren and Finn together.

Bren's eyebrow shoots up, and after a short moment, he drops his forehead to mine. "Sofia, I don't want anyone but you. I have eyes only for you. I don't want to be touched by anyone other than you."

Be still, my poor little heart. I never thought I'd be so willing to give my heart to this kind of ownership. It goes against everything I've ever felt was right for me, but as wrong as my mind says it is, my heart is fully complicit in letting Brenner Reindhart own this part of me.

I THOUGHT ANDREAS WAS EXAGGERATING WHEN HE HANDED ME the earplugs at the show the following night. Now I have to apologize for the eye roll he got from me. I produce the plugs from my jeans pocket and stick them in my ears because being backstage at an *Industrial November* concert could render a girl deaf.

Despite having already been front row center at one of their concerts, the experience doesn't compare to being backstage.

Midway through the concert, they get to a fast song where Adrian takes over with an extensive drum solo, and Bren sneaks off-stage. His grin is wide, like a little kid showing me a drawing and expectantly awaiting his praise.

"You're fantastic," I yell, and he pulls me in for a painful kiss that bruises my lips, but I can tell he's grinning through the kiss. My hands wrap around his biceps, and I don't recoil at the feel of the sweat he's drenched in. His tank is entirely soaked, and he pulls away long enough to peel it off. He kisses me hard again, then saunters back on stage.

At the sight of a shirtless Bren, the crowd goes wild—as in the true meaning of a crowd going wild. Several bras are flung in the air and land by Bren's feet.

My gaze stays glued to him as he sings, moves, and jumps on stage. He's an expert entertainer, and all his movements are powerful, just like his lyrics and voice.

A woman somehow gets past security and jumps on stage, gets to her feet, and lunges herself toward Bren, but a bouncer catches her just before she reaches him. My heart thumps loud in my chest, and my legs stiffen, readying to lunge me toward the stage until I see the guard catch her. It happens so fast, I am genuinely afraid for Bren for a moment.

The woman struggles in the bouncer's grip, but Bren keeps his cool, continuing the song. He follows the bouncer and outstretches his hand so that the fan can shake it briefly before being hauled out.

I press my hand to my chest and shake my head. Bren has everything under control. There's no need to be afraid.

Is there?

More women fling underwear at my man, and I can't help but smile.

That's right, ladies, I think. *Eat your hearts out.*

Brenner Reindhart is taken.

20

BREN

The tour is finally over, and I have no real commitments with the band for a while, apart from an upcoming charity concert, then nothing until we are ready to record again. Though the guys are all homesick, none of them return to Germany.

Adrian likes the rehab center in Kansas City and wants to be near it should he need it, and Fritz and Karl agree they enjoy having less paparazzi around, so the band is following me back to Kansas City for some R&R before heading home. We plan on writing music and taking it easy for at least a little while.

Over the last month of the tour, I have seen Sofia minimally when I could get away for a few days. We resorted to phone sex and sexting, but it wasn't enough to ease my severe case of blue balls. I need time alone with her soon.

The band has to agree on where we can record next, but already, I am devising an argument for recording in Kansas City. If all goes as planned, I will have at least a year near Sofia with little need for travel of any kind.

Before takeoff, I wrap up two emails—one with my new realtor and the second with a decorator. I have one request: a bathtub for two, big enough so that water can cover a woman's boobs and knees at the same time. I smile at the memory of Sofia telling me that. I hope she likes my new home because I want her around all the time.

"What are you grinning about?" Adrian asks, his face in its customary scowl.

"Nothing," I say and shut off the laptop, placing it back in the side sleeve of my suitcase.

Fritz looks up from his magazine, smirks while shaking his head, and goes back to reading.

Sofia isn't expecting me for a few more days, and I can't wait to surprise her.

MY MOOD SHIFTS WHEN I SEE HER WITH HIM. I ASK ANDREAS to go inside the bar this time and wait in the corner in case all hell breaks loose. Sofia doesn't see me initially as I walk up to the table where she is sitting with a man. I count to ten, forcing my fists to unfurl at my sides.

"Sofia," I say. "Hi."

Sofia looks up, her brow creased with confusion for all of one second before recognition hits her. Her grin spreads wide on her face, and she stands to give me a hug.

"Bren! I thought you weren't getting in until the day after tomorrow?"

"Clearly," I mumble under my breath.

"What?" she asks.

"Who is this?" I ask, looking at the man still sitting.

He stands and smiles at me, offering a hand. I blink, look at his outstretched hand, then look back at Sofia—waiting for an explanation.

Her shoulders tighten under the glare I am sending her way. "I'm sorry," she says curtly. "This is David. David, this is Bren."

David's head tilts to the side, and his eyes narrow before going wide with recognition.

"As in . . ." He clears his throat. "Brenner Reindhart? Oh my god. I'm such a huge fan," he says.

I tip my chin at him, then lock eyes with Sofia. She has some explaining to do, and she had better do it fast. "Sofia?"

She crosses her arms and leans back, building space between us. "David and I are in a business meeting. Can you come back in an hour?"

What the fuck? She's kicking me out instead of him? I haven't seen her in weeks, and she's kicking me out. My nostrils flare as my eyes narrow at her. I don't say it, but I'm sure my features do: Tread lightly, Sofia. This doesn't look good.

"No, no need," David interjects. "Sofia, we discussed nearly everything we needed to. I'll email you the proposal, and we can set up a conference call next week after you've reviewed it." Then he turns to me. "And it was great meeting you," he says.

Then David turns to Sofia, clasps a hand around her upper arm, and leans in to give her a kiss on the cheek. Sofia glares at me through their goodbyes. As David walks out of the bar, I close my eyes and count to ten again.

I follow Sofia as she walks back behind the bar, putting the counter between us.

"What the fuck was that, Bren?" she asks.

"You tell me."

"I think you were being a jealous dick again. We were having a business meeting."

"Do all your business colleagues kiss you goodbye?"

Sofia rolls her eyes. "He's Hispanic. I'm Hispanic. We kiss

goodbye. It's part of our manners. You're European. Don't you know this shit by now?"

"Just a business meeting?" I ask.

"Yes. A business meeting."

"Okay," I say as I relax my shoulders.

"Okay?"

I nod.

"Bren, I know I'm new to the relationship thing, but I meant what I said in Seattle. I consider us exclusive."

"You do?"

"Yes. I'm not Emma. And sure, I've never particularly believed in relationships, but I've always honored loyalty, and as long as you and I are together, I'll be loyal to you. Can you please trust me?"

She is right. I measure her with the wrong yardstick. If I keep acting like the jealous boyfriend, I will only push her to retreat further and further away, like a scared little fawn. I need to take things at a glacier pace with Sofia if we have a shot at what I want—a future with her.

Because I'm starting to suspect she's the one. There can never be anyone else because Sofia was made for me. She's unlike anyone I've ever met, and I'm complete putty in her hands. Life on the road, on tour, jaded me to women and their expectations of me. Then I meet Sofia, who expects nothing from me, needs nothing from me—but I'm the one who needs her.

"I'm doing my best. I didn't yell or say anything mean to him, did I?"

Sofia's features soften, and she offers me a weak smile. "And you didn't storm out like you tend to do. I consider that progress."

She walks around the bar to my side and steps up on her toes to reach for a kiss. "Thank you," she says. "For working on that possessive temper of yours."

I grunt with annoyance, but say, "Anything for you, Sofia."

21

BREN

Though Sofia is an even greater neat freak than me, her apartment is a bit more cramped than what I'm used to. One week there is more than enough, and now that the penthouse condo is ready, we can relocate there.

But first I need to tell her.

"Keep your eyes closed," I tell her as the elevator reaches the top floor. Before the doors open, I decide to play it safe and place my hands over her eyes.

"I wasn't going to open them until you said," she complains.

The elevator doors slide open, and we step into the penthouse. Her high heels click on the black marble floors, and I bring my hands down. "Okay, you can open them now."

Sofia's mouth drops into a small 'o,' but she is speechless, so I grin, proud of myself. The decorator did a phenomenal job with the designer furniture and modern art. The floor-to-ceiling windows display a nighttime Kansas City view as the focal point.

"This is amazing, Bren. Is it yours?"

"I bought it. Yes."

"Wow."

While there is a touch of masculinity to the place, I made sure the decorator understood this wasn't meant to be a bachelor pad, not anymore, so she added some femininity to the main room with sofa cushions, plush carpets, and soft lighting.

Votive candles litter every surface, lighting our way to the dining room.

"Is someone else here?" Sofia asks when the noise from someone moving around in the kitchen reaches us.

"Yes. That's dinner."

Grabbing her by the hand, I lead her to the dining table for her to sit. "I'll give you the grand tour later."

"Hello, Mr. Reindhart. Can I get you started with drinks?"

"Yes, thank you. Sofia, this is our chef for the night, Tristan."

Sofia eyes me with an approving smile, and I have no doubt what she's thinking. She is both glad and surprised I remembered Tristan's name. After our trip and everything that happened with our maid, Carmen, I had some inner reflections to explore. I've had a wealthy lifestyle for nearly a decade and had no idea how far I'd strayed. Luckily for me, the ravishing woman before me does a magnificent job keeping my feet firmly placed on the ground.

"It's nice to meet you," Sofia says. "And thank you for making dinner tonight."

"It is my pleasure, ma'am," Tristan says.

He leaves to fetch our drinks and comes back out shortly with a tray of canapés.

"Congratulations on the new home," Sofia says. "I'd buy you a housewarming gift, but I think you have everything."

"I do." I smile at her. I have everything here that I need, including her.

"When did you have time to do all this?"

"I didn't. I handled it all while I was on tour. The realtor and decorator did all the real work. Do you really like it?"

"They did great," Sofia says as she glances around everywhere. "Since knowing you, I've been to more luxurious places than I would have ever imagined."

I can't stop smiling through our dinner of white fish with capers and lemon because she is pleased with my selection. I spared no costs in making this place as welcoming as possible. I can't wait to show her the tub she requested. This will be her home too . . . soon enough. All she has to do is agree.

As we finish dinner, Sofia grows quiet and pensive.

"What is it?"

"Does this mean you plan on staying here for a while?" she asks.

I nod. "I'm hoping. If you'll have me."

"I'd like that," she says.

After the chef's assistant clears our plates, they dim the lights in the main room. With my phone, I turn up the volume on Karen Souza's rendition of "Wicked Game."

I stand and button-up one button on my suit jacket. Walking over to Sofia's side of the table, I offer my hand. She smiles and takes it, allowing me to lead her away from the table.

I hold her in my arms as we sway to the music. When she leans in and rests her cheek on my chest—it is the best feeling in the world. I want her—no—need her in my arms forever. While a part of me knows she needs to take things slow, another part of me needs to start now. "Sofia?"

"Mmmm?" she moans softly into my chest.

"Do you think I could make you happy?"

She pulls away from my arms enough to look into my eyes. "You do make me happy, *tonto*. What brought that on?"

"This," I say and twirl her away from me. When she lands

the spin, she laughs until she sees the small box now in my hands. Her eyes zero in on it, and she takes a step back.

"Sofia—" I say, but she shakes her head.

"Bren. No."

"Just hear me out. Okay?" I take a single step closer to her. She nods, her hand clasped over her lips.

I get down on one knee and open the small box containing a pear-cut black diamond surrounded by smaller round-cut diamonds on a white gold band—a ring as unique and rare as her. The seconds stretch into years as she looks at me, blinking rapidly. Her chest rises with each breath quicker than the last, and all color drains from her face.

My heart drops to my stomach as Sofia can only shake her head. But I need to convince her that we can make this work. I've waited my entire life for someone like her, and I need her to be mine.

"Sofia, just listen. I know you need to take things slow. We can have a long engagement, but someday, I do intend to make you my wife. I'm not asking for you to marry me today, or even this year or next. We can take it at your pace. But I need to know that in the end, you will be my wife. Please, Sofia. Marry me."

Sofia bites the inside of her lip, still shaking her head. Then she stops moving, and her eyes draw closed. "I'm sorry, Bren. No."

I hang my head for a moment before standing up. I stare at the ring in my hands, watching it turn from the symbol of my future into nothing but an insignificant rock. Placing the box back in my jacket pocket, I ask her, "Why not? It can be whenever you say."

"I'll never marry you, Bren. I'm sorry."

"Did I ask too soon?"

"No, Bren. You could ask me ten years from now, and I'd say no."

I rear back like she has slapped me. "What?"

"Bren, I don't believe in marriage."

"Is this because your dad left—"

"No, Bren. That has nothing to do with it. I don't want to be your property."

"That's not what marriage is."

"Then why the need to secure it now? Huh? Tell me you aren't trying to brand me Mrs. Brenner Reindhart before the world?"

It is my turn to shake my head. "I need to know there is a future. I want us to work. I'm sorry I asked so soon. We've only known each other a few months; I guess I should have waited."

"Bren. Do you love me?"

I blink at her. "Of course I love you. I wouldn't have proposed if I didn't." I scoff, irritated by the question.

"Well, you never actually said, did you?" She takes a deep breath. "Bren, my feelings for you are growing. They have been for a while. I'm not sure I'm in love with you because I don't know what that's supposed to feel like, but—"

"It feels like you can't breathe if the other person isn't in the room with you, Sofia. It feels like you will die if you can't touch the one you love," I say through clenched teeth.

Sofia takes a step toward me, but I step away this time. I fucked up. I fucked up, and I lost her.

"Then, yes, Bren. I'm in love with you. I feel all those things."

I smile up at her, hopeful this could turn my way.

"But I won't marry you. I need to be my own person. I need to have my own name, my own business, my own money, my own home—"

"You can have all those things and be married!"

"Then what's the point?"

"The point is I love you, and I want you to be my wife!"

I'm yelling, and this is not how I wanted my proposal to the woman I love to go.

I don't move the second time she approaches me. She places one hand on my chest and searches my eyes. "If you are asking for a life together, for a partnership, for fidelity and loyalty—those are all things I can give you and things I want from you in return."

"Then you'll marry me?"

"No, Bren. We can give each other those things without marriage."

"Why are you so opposed to the idea?"

"I don't judge married people if that's what they want. But to me, signing a piece of paper sounds cold and clinical, like I'm signing myself over like—like a piece of property. I don't want our love to turn into a contract. I'd rather be with you because I love you than because some contract is forcing me to stay. And I guess I need that reassurance too—that you'll be with me because you choose to be, every single day of your life, not because you have no way out. I've always known I'll never get married, Bren. This isn't some stupid whim out of nowhere."

I take Sofia into my arms once again, wrapping them tight around her slim body. A tear rolls down my cheek because I can't let go of my vision for us. My life was planned out long ago: a successful band, marriage, kids—all of it. I've always been in control of my life and manifested everything I ever wanted into being. A perfect life. That's what I want, and Sofia wants no part in it if it's my way.

I hold her tight for a long moment. The song changes over three times despite the fact that we're barely swaying anymore. I squeeze her tight in my arms, not wanting to let her go because once I do, I'll have lost her forever. I finally find my voice. "I'm sorry, Sofia," I croak out. "But this is it for us if you aren't willing to get married someday."

She drops my hand and steps away from me. Her eyes well with tears, the tip of her nose red, breaking something deep in my chest. She wraps her arms around her middle like she is holding herself from falling apart. "Is this an ultimatum?" she asks.

"I didn't intend it to be, but yes. If we aren't working toward the same future, what's the point?"

"I thought the point was being in love," she says accusingly.

"I wish that were enough."

"Bren . . ." she breaths out.

"Andreas will drive you home."

22

SOFIA

So much can happen in three minutes: a first kiss, an orgasm, a sad goodbye at the airport. Three minutes to decide to let someone into your life, and three minutes to watch them walk out.

Three minutes for your entire life to change.

The longest three minutes of my life comes two days after Bren and I broke up. I stand over my sink, watching the seconds tick on the timer as my foot taps the linoleum tile.

Three minutes for two pink lines to appear out of nowhere and upturn my life forever.

When the timer rings, I grab both tests revealing a total of four pink lines. Two independent tests showing me the same result: I am so fucked.

After realizing how badly I'd hurt Bren, I swore to myself I wouldn't contact him and risk opening up a fresh wound, but he has to know I'm pregnant. The phone rings twice before I'm sent to voice mail. I can't blame him.

"Bren, it's Sofia. I'm sorry to bother you, but we have to talk. It's important. Call me back when you get a chance."

Pregnancy news is best said in person—or so I think. I need

to see him. When he doesn't call me back that day, I try him the next and then the next day. On the fourth day, his number is no longer in service. I try Andreas's number next—also no longer in service.

I resort to the band's social media account and send a direct message: *This is Sofia trying to reach Bren. It's important. Please have him call me back.*

The message goes unread.

And that's that. My life as a single mom started the second two critical phone lines got disconnected.

THE NIGHT STARTS OFF SLOW AT *LA OFICINA*, SO I DECIDE TO JOIN Sara and Carolina at the bar. "What are we celebrating?" I ask.

"An overall state of wellbeing," Carolina says.

I purse my lips. "Sounds like a beer kinda toast then?"

"No," Carolina jumps in. "Tequila!"

"Not all of us can handle tequila as well as you can," Sara says.

"Speak for yourself," I say and give Carolina a high-five.

I grab their drinks, a beer for Sara, and two shots for Carolina and me. "Ileana," I call out. "Can you cover for a bit?" When Ileana tips her chin at me, I settle at the table with my friends.

"Who's the new bartender?" Carolina asks.

I chew my lip. "New bartender? Oh, Ileana. She's been here for a year. You'd know that if you came to visit more often." I cross my arms and arch a brow at Carolina.

"I'm sorry—" she starts to say, looking guilty.

"I'm just messing with you. I mean, she *has* been here for a while, but she works only a handful of shifts a month."

Carolina smiles at me. I can never really give her a hard time.

"You'll be seeing new faces around here," I say, already deciding I want to give them the news. "One is Lola. She cleans up some mornings if I'm in a bind for time. I have a feeling she and Ileana are going to be working more than usual."

"Business picking up?" Carolina asks.

"It is, but that's not why." Sara and Carolina set their drinks down to focus entirely on me. I take in a deep gulp of air and before I can change my mind, blurt it out: "I'm pregnant."

And even though I say it with a straight face, Carolina laughs. When my features don't change into an 'I gotcha,' she stops laughing, and her jaw drops.

Then her eyes grow with horror. "Sofia!" She yells and snatches my empty shot glass away from me. "You can't drink when you are pregnant!"

It's me who laughs now, watching her most scornful expression. "I wasn't drinking. That was water. And please, say it louder. I don't think those guys at the other end of the bar heard your announcement," I tease, and Carolina winces.

"How far along?" she asks, this time in a whisper.

"Eight weeks."

Carolina's perfect, thick eyebrows scrunch up together as she starts thinking. "You need an OB-GYN. Have you started prenatal vitamins yet—"

I place a gentle hand on her upper arm to quiet her. She switched from best friend mode to doctor mode, and right now, I need my friend. "I love you for caring," I say. "But I got it. I already have a doctor, and I'm taking excellent care of myself. You'd kill me if I didn't."

Carolina smiles at me, and after a short silence, Sara speaks up. "And we are happy about this baby?" she asks.

I smile. "We are happy about Spawn," I reassure her.

"Spawn?" Sara asks, her mouth twisted in a scowl.

"That's what I'm calling it—at least until I know if it's a boy or a girl and can name it."

Sara's mouth twists into a grimace. "As in Spawn of Satan?"

"No!" I roll my eyes. "Like fish spawn. Sheesh."

Both of my best friends offer me congratulations and smiles.

"I'm going to be the favorite aunt," Sara says.

"No. That'll be me," Carolina says, and I laugh at the two ridiculous women.

Then my laughter dies in my throat when Sara asks about the father. I shrug. "Who knows? Could be any number of men."

Sara narrows her eyes. "You're lying. You don't want to say."

Carolina blinks as she looks between the standoff Sara and I seem to be in.

I throw my hands up. "Fine. Why do I have to have perceptive best friends? Yeah. I know who the father is, but it was just this guy passing through. Left before I could tell him. Doesn't matter. Don't need him."

"Hear, Hear," Carolina says as she taps her glass on the table twice.

"So long as the baby has one parent who wants him or her, that's all I care about," Sara says, pensive. I give her a side hug knowing she is thinking about her own shitty parents who didn't care about her or her wellbeing.

We linger at the table until business picks up, talking about possible baby names because Sara hates me referring to it as Spawn until I point out 'Spawn' is better than 'it.' They leave when I have to get back to work, but not before insisting on paying their tab and leaving generous tips. Carolina won't hear my protests.

AFTER CLOSING, I LOOK AT MY RAGGED ARMY AFTER A LONG, BUSY shift. Martín and Rubén slouch in their seats at the table. Tracy is texting, and Ileana and Joe sit on either side of her. "Thank you for staying for a team meeting. I know it's late, so I'll make it quick," I say. "I have some news that will probably affect things around here."

Joe's left brow shoots up in question.

"I'm pregnant."

Silence.

Only Ileana smiles. She stands and motions for me to follow so she can take me into a hug. I sink into her embrace, feeling more supported than I have since I found out. "Congratulations, Sofia," she says.

My eyes prickle with tears for a second before I draw them back in. The last thing I need is to cry in front of my staff. I laugh to play off the pain. "Thank you, Ileana," I say.

Martín and Rubén jump up and hug me, offering words of congratulations in Spanish.

Tracy keeps chewing on her gum. "So, like, who's the dad?" she asks.

I keep plastering that smile on when I answer. "Doesn't matter. He's not in the picture."

"Wow," Joe says. He throws me a knowing look, and I shake my head so he won't bring up what I know he wants to.

"But like I said, that'll change things around here. I'll try to work until as close to the due date as possible, but I'll definitely be around less afterward. I'm still going to keep running the business side of things, but Joe, you'll have to find a part-time manager to step in and help. I'm leaving you in charge when I'm out."

"Really?" Joe asks, his face beaming.

"You think you can handle it?"

He nods, seriousness across his face. "Yes. I got you."

"Good. You can start advertising in a few months. Narrow down the candidates to five, and we can interview them together."

"Ileana, I know you don't like to work more than a shift or two per week, but—"

"So long as Lola can babysit for me, I can work extra shifts if you need it," Ileana says.

I let out a long breath of relief.

Since I realized Bren isn't going to be a part of this process, I've been carrying the weight of everything when I don't have to. I know I have Sara, Carolina, Joe, and Ileana in my corner— even Mandy and Lola if I need them. After all, little Spawn is technically Mandy's fault for dragging me to that concert.

And when it comes down to it, I would hate to ask, but I know I can fly Mom up if I really need the extra help. If I do that, though, I'll have to get a bigger apartment with two bedrooms. Though really, I need a house now that a baby is in the picture. I'd love for her to have stability and grow up in the same house.

The list running in my head of all the things I will need starts crashing on my shoulders, piling on that imaginary weight.

"Take a deep breath," Ileana says and places a calming hand on my shoulder.

I smile at her. I dismiss Martín, Rubén, and Tracy for the night and keep chatting with Joe and Ileana.

Joe finally asks what he'd been dying to. "It's—"

"Yep."

"Does he know?"

I shake my head. "And he's not going to know."

"Sofia—" Joe starts to protest.

"No. He will never know. Now, we need to make plans—"

Ileana clears her throat. "Take it in strides. You have months to make plans. Don't make it more difficult than it has to be."

"I'm glad I know at least one mom who knows what she's doing."

Ileana laughs. "None of us know what we are doing. We just do our best, and you will too. Don't forget to breathe and try to enjoy some of your time alone before the baby comes. It'll be rare after that."

"Thank you. Both of you. I'll be leaning on you more than usual."

Joe draws me into his arms. "That's what we are here for."

And it is that tight hug, in those massive Joe arms, that breaks me. I sob into his chest, for I don't know how long until I feel Ileana's hand rubbing circles on my back.

"He's g-gone," I say in a broken voice.

"I'm sorry," Joe whispers and hugs me tighter.

"I loved him," I say.

"I know, honey," Ileana says. "I know."

BREN

"**W**hat the fuck is wrong with you?" Fritz hisses as I get backstage.

"Calm your tits," I say. I'm only twenty minutes late. We've been delayed far worse before.

"You are lucky the opener has enough material to keep going."

"You think the audience cares? They're here to see us. They'll wait as long as we want them to—"

Fritz's teeth are grinding now. "You know that's not how we treat our fans. We have an ethical code for a reason—"

"Okay, okay, won't happen again." What is up Fritz's ass? We aren't getting paid for this concert. It isn't part of the tour. We only agreed to the charity concert as a publicity stunt Roger is making us do so that media outlets refocus on something other than Adrian for a change.

Fritz scratches his jaw. "Bren, you're acting like fucking Adrian—"

"Hey!" Adrian protests. "Don't bring me into it."

"Sorry," Fritz says to Adrian. "All I meant was that if there was one person in the band I never had to worry about, one person I could always count on, it was you. And now you are fucking up, and it's my job to tell you—"

"Fritz. Shut up! I have a massive headache, and I have to get out there and sing in less than two minutes, so give me a fucking break."

"Yeah, that happens when you stay out all night drinking," Fritz mumbles under his breath, but I still catch it.

Roger hands Karl a water bottle and two aspirin. Then, Karl passes it to me while staying as quiet as he did during the whole exchange.

"Thanks, Karl," I say.

WE START THE SET STRONG AND ENERGETIC WITH "FIGHTING Nights." The lyrics are as angry and disillusioned as I feel. That leads to the even angrier "Welded Dragons."

The only thing that could ever cure my hangovers was more alcohol, and luckily Roger knows that; the water bottle he handed Karl was filled with Vodka.

By the time we get to our most popular song, "Metal Red Day," the audience is worked into mania singing all the lyrics, so I don't have to. I am also getting tipsy all over again.

I trip on a cord and fall backward onto the stage, and I stay there, singing from that position on my back. We are playing a stadium tonight, so I just look at the black sky while I sing lying down.

Fritz gets close to me as he continues to play his bass, his eyebrows raised in question or in warning—I don't know, and I don't care. I just close my eyes and keep singing from that spot for the rest of the song.

Once the popular song is over, I stand up for the remainder of the concert. When we go back out for our customary bow, Fritz's hand nearly crushes mine in his grip

from how pissed he is. What a drama queen. I follow the rest
of the band backstage when we are done.

"Fritz," I call out, but all I see is the back of his head as he
leaves.

"Don't, Bren," he yells, not looking back. "Just—fucking
don't."

"Fuck, man," Karl says. "He's pissed."

I pinch the bridge of my nose. "Yeah," I say. "He is."

"Shit, that ain't cool, man. Adrian and I do shit way worse
than that—"

I side glance him, knowing that was nothing but the
truth. I'm a little surprised Karl recognizes it.

Adrian avoids the temptation of an after-party, and since
Fritz abandoned us in his anger, that only leaves Karl and me
to deal with the meet-and-greet post-show. Fucking great.

Roger appears out of nowhere, handing me a beer. "I
think you'll be needing this," he says.

"Best manager ever. Thanks, man," I say.

Then Roger hands Karl the bottle of vodka he has
requested.

"Hell, yeah," Karl says. He takes a big swig from the bottle
then turns to all the groupies in the room. "Now, who wants
to do belly shots?" Karl spreads his arms wide as two beautiful women take a spot under each of his wings. He leads
one to a craft services table, clears it in one fell swoop,
sending food flying everywhere, and lays the woman down.
She raises her top much higher than necessary, revealing a
dainty pink lace bra. Karl pours the vodka on her belly and
licks it up.

I roll my eyes up to the high heavens, making the room
spin for a moment when I bring my gaze back down. I'm too
fucking old for this shit, I think, and snatch the vodka bottle
from Karl's hand. I take it to my mouth and gulp from it like
water.

"Hell yeah!" Karl shouts. "Now, that's what I'm talking about. Who wants to party with Brenner Reindhart?"

Two girls jump up and volunteer, getting to my side in ten seconds flat. One is a blond, one a brunette. I shake my head. This won't do. I scan the faces in the room until I find one woman with raven-back hair.

"You." I point, and she perks up with a huge grin. "Come here."

She walks over to me sexily, and I gulp more of the vodka in an attempt to forget that the woman now at my side isn't Sofia.

When she gets to me, I wrap my arm around her tiny waist, bringing her body close to me. That is the last thing I remember before everything goes black. The next hazy memory I have is of Roger and Fritz on either side of me, carrying me to my hotel room.

With a grunt, Fritz lies me down on the bed. "What the fuck, Roger?" I hear him say through the haze.

"Sofia," I whimper and try to get up, but Roger pushes me back down. I shake my head, the belligerent drunk that I am. "No. Sofia's waiting. I have to go."

"You'll go in the morning, buddy," Fritz says, and he no longer sounds mad.

"Okay," I say, hugging a pillow to my middle.

"Fuck, man," Fritz says.

"Yeah. Fuck," Roger agrees.

I drift off again to dreams of Sofia.

SOFIA

"Davced?" I say when he picks up the phone.

"Hi, Sofia. Great to hear from you. Have you come to a decision about franchising?"

"No, um. I was wondering . . . if you still wanted to buy, would you be willing to be only part owner?"

"Yes! I didn't include it in the proposal because you seemed pretty set on not selling."

"I know—"

"Listen, I'm in town. Why don't we sit down and chat in person?"

"You're here?"

"Yeah. KC is a booming market with tremendous growth potential. *La Oficina* isn't my only interest in town. I'll be over in an hour."

That surprises the hell out of me. After looking him up, I know David Price is a wealthy and important restaurateur and club owner with business interests from coast to coast. And now he has his eye set on the heartland.

"Actually—um, I don't want my staff to see you just yet. Can we meet elsewhere?"

"Sure."

"There's a café on Westport Road I really like. I'll see you in an hour."

DAVID LOOKS EVERY BIT THE RUTHLESS BUSINESSMAN HE IS WHEN he shows up. He wears a blue pin-striped suit, is clean-shaven, and keeps smiling like he has already won—though the single diamond stud on his ear seems out of place. For the first time, I'm unsettled about a business deal. What am I getting myself into? Is he as nice as he seems, or am I about to sell half of my bar to the devil? My hands get clammy, and I wipe them on my jeans under the table.

Suddenly, my stomach warms up into a wave of nausea that I am sure isn't Spawn's doing. *Breathe, Sofia*, I coach myself. *You'll be able to buy a house. Spawn can have a yard and a dog, or whatever it wants.* I want Spawn to have the stability of growing up in the same house, not moving around like I did all my life growing up. I can do this for him or her. I just have to get through this meeting.

David sips his coffee, all while studying my face. "So, what are you thinking?"

"I, um—" I clear my throat. "My circumstances have changed. Would you be interested in part ownership?"

"Yes. I very much would, though I'd still like to franchise on top of that."

I smile. That is a good chunk of change on its own. This could work. "Amend your proposal and email it to me. We can negotiate from there."

"It'll be in your inbox by the end of the week. I'll even throw in a sweetener," he says and flashes me those shiny pearly whites. "I'll only propose a 49% buy. You can retain control over everything, and the Price Group can include *La Oficina* in its roster."

I tilt my head to the side as I take in his features, trying to read him. His posture is relaxed, his smile natural as it spreads to his eyes. The offer for me to retain control is unexpected. My greatest fear in selling is having corporate goons sucking the soul out of the place, but he is giving me reassurances that none of that will happen.

"It's sounding too good to be true, David. I'm not sure that reassures me—"

He sets his mug down and leans in closer, his tone lowering as he speaks again. "I'll come clean, Sofia. It's a sweeter deal than I'm used to offering, but I like you. Usually, I wouldn't dream of offering so much on a first offer."

"Oh," is all I can manage to say.

"In fact," he says, "I was hoping once we were done talking business, you'd agree to go to dinner with me."

"Done with business? Like on a date?"

He nods, and his eyes tighten a bit at the corners as he waits for my answer.

"I'm sorry, David. But I can't go on a date with you. Does that change your business offer?"

His face falls for only one second before he recovers and smiles wide again. "No, Sofia. I'm a man of my word when it comes to business. But can I ask why you won't go out on a date with me?"

"To begin with, it's a terrible idea if we're considering being business partners—"

"I can assure you our contract would protect you in any possible outcomes on the personal front."

I smile at him. Before Bren, I may have considered something with this handsome restauranteur who knows my business inside and out. In the end, I shake my head. "I'm sorry," I say.

"Can I ask what else is stopping you besides the business angle—for which I have already provided a solution?"

I chuckle. "Oh, you are a smooth one, aren't you?" David only shrugs as he throws me a sexy smile. "I mentioned my circumstances have changed. That's why I'm considering selling part of the bar."

"Right."

"I'm expecting a baby," I say. Without realizing it, my hand drifts down to my lower belly protectively. I smile at him, not breaking eye contact. "I need the hard cash to buy a home. My apartment is hardly suitable for a child."

As prepared as David was for this meeting when he first sat down with me, he can't hide the shock plain on his face as his jaw drops before he shakes his head and chuckles nervously.

"So, you see? Dating won't be on my radar for a long while."

"I understand. And if you don't mind me asking . . . the father? Is he in the picture?"

My smile erases from my face. "No," I say, resigned.

"I see. Well, none of what you've told me changes things. I'm still very interested in being in business together."

"Good. I need to give my bar manager a raise because he will be taking on more responsibility, and we'll need at least another part-time manager. We were going to start interviewing in a few months, but if you'd like someone from the Price Group to be involved in the process, I would be fine with that."

"Oh, I definitely want to be involved," David says with a smile so devious it sends goosebumps down my arms. Somehow, his words don't seem to apply to the topic at hand.

"I'll be in touch after my lawyer reviews your proposal." I stand up and shake his hand. "Oh, and David? Make it a good offer. I need this to work."

BACK AT HOME, I GO TO BED, MY LAPTOP IN HAND, TO LOOK AT houses as close to the bar as possible. When I get tired, I lie down and stare at the ceiling as music blasts from the laptop.

The first song in Brenner's first album is "Industrial Thoughts." It is a vicious heavy metal song, but his voice as he sings manages to carry some soul that seems out of place. "Do you hear that, Spawn?" I say as I rub my belly. "That's your daddy's voice. He'll sing you a lullaby every night."

We listen to the entire album that night, and I whisper a promise to my child that one day when Spawn is old enough to understand, he or she will know who his or her father is.

SPAWN IS ABOUT THE SIZE OF A BOTTLE OF JÄGERMEISTER—AT twenty-one weeks—by the time I finally close on the house and start moving in.

The one-story cottage-style house is small but picturesque. Nestled in the Brookside neighborhood center, it is farther than I would have liked from the bar, but the place is perfect for us.

The outside isn't anything to write home about, but the inside is updated and clean, so I don't have to do too much work before Spawn comes. It only has two bedrooms, but we don't need more. The best features are the farmhouse kitchen sink, hardwood floors, the walk-in closet in the master bedroom, the fenced-in yard, and the walking distance to shops and a park. The outside I can fix later with a coat of paint and some flowers. Spawn will be happy here.

Though I hired movers, both Mandy and Lola insist on showing up to help unpack. I tell them it isn't necessary, but it falls on deaf ears. They both like the house, and in the end, I am glad they are around. Having a familiar face in a new home is comforting, and once again my thoughts drift to Mom and Nana and how much I wish they were here.

I walk out into the garage where Bonnie stands proud. I kiss my fingers and run them over the leather seat slowly. "This is goodbye, old girl. You were great, and I'll always love you," I say before putting the protective motorcycle cover over the bike— retiring my first baby forever.

As I part ways with my first love, I pat my belly gently. "You are NEVER allowed on a motorcycle. You hear?" Spawn kicks me right in the liver. I roll my eyes. "I hope you are not my karma for the grief I gave Grandma."

I shut off the lights to the garage and go inside my new home.

AT TWENTY-NINE WEEKS, SPAWN IS ROUGHLY THE SIZE OF A SMALL pumpkin. I should have nicknamed Spawn 'parasite' instead because she turned into a black hole for all of my energy. I spend most of my time on my back, with my feet raised, and check in on the bar only minimally. Joe is doing a great job.

Carolina texted a week ago about having a baby shower at my place, but I never finished unpacking, so I declined. I should have expected she would send the cavalry, but I didn't.

I am content in my lazy time that keeps Spawn happy, which is why I am surprised when Lola and Mandy show up unannounced at my door. When I don't get up to open the door. Lola texts.

Lola: *You home? Open up.*

Me: *You have a key. Come in. I'm in my bedroom.*

When Lola and Mandy take me and my room in, they have to do a doubletake. I have a bowl of popcorn on the bed, and stray popcorn litters the duvet. I also have a Banderilla in my hand—one of those tamarind candy sticks covered with *chamoy* and chili pepper—one of Spawn's favorite snacks that I became addicted to those first few weeks when it was the only thing that didn't make Spawn push the food out. The wrapper lies carefully over my belly.

The mountain that is my belly peeks out from under my black tank top because I never bothered to buy maternity clothes and nothing fits, so I've just resorted to a uniform of yoga pants.

The worst part is that Lola knows what a neat freak I was in a previous life. Everything has changed, and my life is no longer my own.

As I stare at their horror-stricken faces, I start to bawl. Just ugly crying my eyes out.

"Hey, hey, what's wrong? Why are you crying?" Mandy asks.

"Because she's so pretty," I wail, pointing at the television screen.

Mandy and Lola blink at each other and then look at the TV. "Uh," Mandy says, "that actress?"

I nod, my eyes still glued to my telenovela that I only started watching hoping that's how I'd get Spawn to come out understanding Spanish over English.

"Yes!" I cry out even louder. "Erica Moran is so pretty!" I sniffle and tug my shirt to cover more of my belly, but it springs back up, forcing another cry out of me.

Lola scratches her head, unsure of what to do or say. "Why is that a bad thing?" she asks.

"Because I'm a whale!" I cry out. "I can't move without Spawn kicking my bladder or my lung. Everything hurts. None of my shoes fit . . . and —and . . ." I sob harder. "And all I want to do is ride Bonnie, but I can't because it's not responsible," I whine even louder.

Mandy maneuvers around the stacks of boxes and dusts off some of the popcorn from the bed so she can sit next to me and take me in her arms. "Oh, honey," she says. "You're still so beautiful."

"You're the hottest pregnant lady I've ever seen," Lola adds.

"You're lying! I'm a mess. This place is a mess. Look at it!"

"It's okay," Mandy says, rubbing my arm. She peels the candy wrapper from my belly, balling it up in her fist. "Why don't you go take a shower? Lola can start cleaning the room here, and I'll unpack some of the boxes in the kitchen. How does that sound?"

"Yeah," Lola says. "Between the two of us, we'll be done in no time."

I look up at both women and wipe my eyes. Fuck, I'm emotional. "Really?"

"We got you," Lola says.

AFTER LOLA AND MANDY'S INTERVENTION, I KNOW SOMETHING has to change. I need to take control of my life and get my shit together. Spawn is going to need a strong mom, especially with her dad out of the picture.

So I call reinforcements.

I pick up Mom at the airport, and after hugging me, she brings her hands to my enormous belly, feeling around for movement. Spawn obliges with a little kick, and one of my mom's hands flies up to her mouth. Her eyes well until the dam bursts, and we are both crying in the airport like a bad nineties movie. I haven't hugged her in years. I don't even care if I am a grown woman because damn it, I need my mommy!

"Oh, Sofia," she whispers, looking at me with awe. "I can't believe my baby is having a baby."

I scoff. "I'm not a baby, Mom. I'm twenty-eight."

"You'll always be my baby."

I look away from her and dare to ask, "So you're not mad at me?"

"What on earth for?" she asks, confused.

"Because the dad's not in the picture."

"*Hay, mija.* Of course I'm not mad. No matter what, this baby is a miracle."

I sniffle a little and lean into another hug. "*Gracias,* Mami."

I wish my nana could be here too, but traveling just wasn't an option for her, so instead, we hired a stay-at-home care service during my pregnancy and for the first few months after Spawn is born.

Mom wants to help, and I'm so glad for it. But mostly, I'm glad she'll get to meet her grandchild. I wish we could live together, but Nana has earned the right to spend the last of her days where she wants to.

That first night with Mom home, she tucks me in like I'm a little kid, and I take her hand and kiss the back of it. And I have to ask once again, "Mom, are you sure you're not mad at me?"

She shakes her head. "Should I be?"

I shrug. "I don't know. The dad's gone and—"

"And what? What does that have to do with anything? Your father wasn't around, and you turned out great."

I smile at her, relieved she isn't upset that I'm unwed and pregnant. She also reassures me that she won't be mad if I don't want to say who the father is. She understands the need for a single mom's privacy, and it is nobody's business but mine unless I want to share.

"I love you, Mom," I say.

She shuts off the lights. "I love you too," she says before closing my bedroom door.

BREN

I'm staring through the back porch window at the lake past my backyard. It is serene and peaceful—and fucking pissing me off. Every time I look at it, it accomplishes the exact opposite of its intended serenity.

This house is my vacation home away from the city. I bought it so long ago, knowing even then in my youth, with fresh *Industrial November* money, that one day, I'd bring my family here to vacation in the country every summer. We'd escape the city and the noise and just be. It's supposed to be a quiet place for reflection and relaxation, and yet I've done nothing but work myself to death since coming here the day after proposing marriage to Sofia a year ago.

My stomach churns every time I picture her beautiful face and her horror at the very word 'marriage.' We weren't meant to be after all. Not like I'd thought. But not a day goes by that I don't think of that night and wonder how she's doing and who she's with.

But I don't let myself check in on her. Anytime I'm tempted to ask Roger to check in on her, instead, I pull from the whiskey bottle and grab a piece of paper to write a song.

The table in front of me is littered with stacks of paper full of chicken-scratch penmanship and sticky whiskey rings from the many glasses on the table that I never took to the sink. When I ran out of clean glasses, I started drinking straight from the bottle, and that system works infinitely better.

I bring the bottle to my lips and take a pull, thinking of the following line of lyric I want to write, when the doorbell rings. I glance at the clock on the wall: two p.m. I'm not expecting anyone, and I glance down at the robe I'm wearing over my pajama bottoms and try to remember when my last shower was. If it's reporters or media of any kind, I can't be seen like this.

I grab my phone and look at the door-cam before making a move to answer it. My eyes roll at the sight of the top of Fritz's head. He says something, and I read his lips to see what I'm pretty sure is *open up, asshole*.

When I open the door, Fritz's nose scrunches up.

"What do you want?" I ask, not making way for him to come in. I don't care if he drove three hours to get here from Berlin.

"You can't pull off a beard like that, mate."

"Is that what you came to tell me? Because you can fuck right off."

"No. No one's heard from you in months, not since Roger's last check-in when you said you wanted to write and that you needed to be alone."

"I still want to be alone, and I'm still writing."

"Can I come in?"

"No."

But Fritz pushes past me, breaking my iron grip on the door, and walks inside. I'm not in the mood for this today.

"You stink, Bren." He says while stacking loose papers from the couch so he can sit. He starts reading through them, not looking up at me. "If you want to keep writing, that's fine and all, but give us your finished songs so Adrian and I can start making some of the music at least. We can have some demos for you when you come out of your cave."

Fritz is pissing me off, but I say nothing because these days, everything pisses me off. I even scared off my cleaning staff, so this place has turned into a pigsty over the last several months.

"I'm going to go shower." Fritz peers up at me from his reading. "And stop reading that trash. The good stuff is in piles on the kitchen table."

Fritz stands and walks to the kitchen as I go upstairs

After my shower, I come into the kitchen, and Fritz stands. He looks at me, and he runs both hands through his hair. "What?" I ask, annoyed at the funny look in his eyes.

"Bren . . . these are . . ."

"Shit?" While the songs here are better than those in the living room, I doubted every last syllable I wrote.

Fritz shakes his head. "No. They're phenomenal, Bren. We have enough here for the next three albums. We can start recording next month—"

"No," I roar. "I'm not fucking recording next month."

"Bren. It's time to move on." Fritz takes a step back, no doubt finding murder in my eyes.

My fists are clenched at my sides. "I'm not done writing," I hiss. I grab a stack of songs I've revised to within an inch of their lives and hand it to Fritz. "Take those. Entertain yourselves for a while making some music. Have demos for me when I'm done writing."

"When will that be?" Fritz asks.

My lip curls in distaste. "When I'm done," I say.

"And who is going to sing in the demos?"

"Karl has a good voice. Use him."

"Are you kidding? With his pre-pubescent-sounding voice? We're not a boy band, Bren."

"Just for the fucking demos. Fuck, Fritz. I don't want to talk. Take the songs and call it a win. Record music, sneak off to Mexico like you tend to. I don't care what you do as long as you get the fuck out of my house."

———

A MONTH LATER, ON THE DOT, SOMEONE ELSE IS AT MY DOOR. THIS time, it's Karl with two women on either side of him.

I open the door and want nothing more than to punch his pretty little face and that happy little smile. "What do you want?"

"I brought you gifts." His smile is broad, and he shoves the two women forward. They are both wearing trench coats, and they unbelt them seductively, revealing lingerie underneath. The brunette on the left is wearing a crimson lace bra that only makes me think of Sofia in Napa Valley. My dick twitches for the first time in weeks. I look back at Karl, who believes he has found a way to get me out of my anger, and I laugh bitterly.

"Hookers, Karl?"

Both women close their coats and pout, looking at Karl for instruction.

"Gifts," Karl corrects.

"Get the fuck off of my property," I growl and shut the door in their faces.

I'm so fucking angry at Karl for that little stunt, and hard as steel at the thought of Sofia that night we had tapas and champagne. I stomp upstairs and get in the shower, letting the hot water roll down my face. I need to stop thinking about her.

But I can't. I roll my time with her on a loop in my mind.

That night I took her back to the villa after dinner, her red lipstick smeared down my shaft after I fucked her mouth. I squeeze my dick and pretend it's her hand on me and not mine.

I haven't been able to get hard at anything except memories of her. Not porn, not other women. Not the hookers Karl just brought for me. I'm starting to wonder if I'll ever be able to be with another woman who is not her.

OVER THE NEXT SEVERAL WEEKS, EVERYONE CHECKS IN ON ME periodically on a rotation. I was surprised when Adrian even showed up. According to him, the band thought that since he had the most experience with depression, maybe we could commiserate together. The gloomy fuck just made me sadder, and he ended up excusing himself when he realized he was having the opposite effect.

So when the doorbell rang today, I think it is Fritz's turn again, and instead, I hang my head in shame when I open the door.

The woman outside my door takes off her sunglasses so she can give me a good look, but she has the decency not to react. Instead, she takes a step forward and takes me in her arms, rubbing my back.

"Hi, Mom."

"We need to talk," she says.

Scheisse. "I know."

I WASH A COUPLE OF GLASSES AND POUR MYSELF A GLASS OF whiskey. "You want one?" I ask Mom.

"You have any tequila?"

I take a deep breath. Why do all the women in my life have to like fucking tequila? "No," I say and hand her the glass of scotch.

"Roger says her name is Sofia," Mom says. She's never been one for mincing words.

I smile sadly into my glass before my sip. I nod.

"Tell me about her."

"Not much to tell. Thought she was the one, but clearly she wasn't."

Mom cocks her head to the side to study me. "Why do you say she wasn't?"

"She didn't want to get married."

"I don't see the problem," Mom says, and I gape at her.

Is this woman kidding me? "I wanted to get married."

"Why?"

I narrow my eyes at her. What does she mean 'why?' Because I do.

"Bren, sometimes I think you'd make a better engineer or mathematician than you do an artist."

"What do you mean?"

Mom folds a napkin neatly onto her lap after dabbing the corner of her mouth. "Your personality. It's too incongruous. Your mind needs things to be just so, but that's no way to foster creativity."

I suck in air through my teeth. "What does any of this have to do with Sofia?"

"You only want to be married because it's what you think you're supposed to do. The next logical step in your life. You make these rules for yourself, and they are so confining, Bren. Can't you see that? No one is making the rules for you. You get to make them yourself." She pauses then adds, "So fucking change them."

I laugh. It's not quite as black and white as that.

"I want it all, Mom. And I want it with her. I want the

wedding, the marriage, the kids." I swirl my hand in the air around us. "The vacation home in the country. That's the life I want for myself and my family."

"So have all that minus the wedding. Why are you being so uncompromising about this? What are you afraid of?"

"Something Sofia said."

Mom stays quiet while I form words.

"She said she wants us to be together because we choose to every day, not because we have no way out." I pause to take a deep breath. "I guess I feel like without the marriage, she'll want to leave at the first sight of someone better. And at the end of the day, I want what you and Dad have. That's the bottom line. Something everlasting. Reassurance. Comfort. Knowing it's for life."

"Brenner, I could leave your father tomorrow if I wanted to. Or he me, for that matter." My eyes snap to her, and she nods. "Our marriage certificate is no reassurance of that. Divorce wouldn't be all that difficult for us if that's what we really wanted."

"Please don't tell me you are separating. I don't think I can handle it right now."

"No," she laughs. "That's not what I'm saying. Marriage is no guarantee of forever. Love is."

I let that thought sink in. I do love her. And she loved me back. I wonder if she does still.

"Besides," Mom says. "If it were today, I'm not sure I'd marry your father—"

"What?" I gasp.

"It's all so terribly archaic, don't you think?" she asks. "We're not chattel."

"Mom, I can honestly say you would love Sofia. Two peas in a pod. Seriously." I shake my head.

Mom sets her empty glass on the table and hands me one

of the pieces of paper. "This one's good," she says, looking down at the song.

I smile at her. "Thanks, Mom."

"This has got to stop, Bren. I thought you'd lost over a year of your life, but I see you've been working, so that's good. But I need you to move on. It's up to you if that's with Sofia or without, but whatever you decide, you will take this week"— she runs a hand through my long beard and tugs on it— "shave this god-awful thing, call Roger, and set up some recording sessions. Work on your next album. Take it slow and make it good. But start seeing people again. Understood?"

"Yes, ma'am."

"And get a housekeeper for this place."

I wince. "I will, Mom. I promise."

"And you'll think about what I said?"

I nod and watch her leave. I sit in the kitchen alone for an hour thinking about what she said. She's fucking right. Why is she always fucking right? It's so annoying.

I run upstairs to shave my beard. I'm looking at myself in the mirror, watching my transformation back to my former self, and I know one thing for certain. I'm going to get Sofia back.

But first, the album. She needs to know I never stopped thinking about her, and I need to apologize. I will record and dedicate the album to her and let that be my apology.

MONTHS LATER, WE'RE ALL IN THE STUDIO LISTENING TO THE mastered cut of the last song. Fritz is like a little kid at Christmas. Karl is smug as fuck, as if this album were a given, and even Adrian has surprised us all by cracking a smile.

The album is good.

I told them I'd agree to record so long as we don't tour. Not for a while. As soon as the album releases, operation Get Sofia Back commences.

"Since we're not touring, why not start writing music for the next one? We have enough songs for at least five albums," Fritz says. Roger's eyes sparkle with greed.

"Nope," I say. I'm going away for a while.

"Not this again," Roger says. "You can't stay in your country house. There will be press for the album—"

"That's not where I'm going."

"Where then?" Fritz asks.

I just look at him and tip my chin.

"Oh, shit," Fritz says.

Karl looks between Fritz and me, trying to piece it together. "What? What am I missing?" he asks, annoyed.

Adrian laughs darkly. "He's going to Kansas City."

26

SOFIA

Spawn shed her nickname on the day she was born at seven pounds three ounces. When they placed that disgusting-looking little bundle, head smeared with blood and white goo, in my arms, she turned into Audrey.

Audrey Ocampo Reindhart cried as she was forced into the world, but then the cry stopped, and she cooed gently in my arms. Ever since, Audrey has always cried for legitimate reasons and legitimate reasons only. If Audrey protests, she needs a diaper change or my boob.

Mandy calls her a miracle baby because otherwise, Audrey is pretty chill, and you wouldn't know there is a baby in the house apart from bath time when she screams at the top of her lungs.

Mom left to be with Nana again two months after Audrey's birth, and honestly, I don't know how I would have managed without her—and Ileana and Mandy—those first few weeks.

Today, Mandy is coming over with baby Lucas, the son of a man she is babysitting for some reason. She already has two jobs, so I am not really sure what is happening apart from the fact that Lucas is the exact opposite of Audrey.

Now that Audrey is eleven months old, Lucas is closer to a year old, and he is running Mandy ragged.

"Make it stop!" Mandy begs the minute she steps inside the house.

Since having Audrey, my energy has returned a little, and my home is now as clean and neat as my apartment always was before I moved into this house.

Lucas is in Mandy's arms, looking gigantic against Mandy's small frame, screaming at the top of his lungs. "Nothing works," Mandy yells as she tries to soothe the bundle in her arms. "He has a clean diaper; he just had a bottle; I burped him. I don't know what to do!"

I am holding Audrey over my chest, patting her back gently because she finished eating only moments before Mandy arrived.

"Here," I say. "Trade with me."

Mandy sets Lucas down on the couch so I can hand her Audrey, and Lucas turns red in the face with his cry.

"This is the most unhappy baby I have ever seen," I say, and Mandy sinks into the sofa, holding a perfectly quiet Audrey in her arms.

"Can we trade?" she asks with a pathetic little chuckle that sounds more defeated than humorous.

I laugh. "Absolutely not," I say.

I take the red-faced Lucas over to Audrey's baby swing and lay him down. I buckle him, place a pacifier in his mouth, and put a blanket over him. He squirms, trying to get back into human arms for a moment, until the swing begins to sway. He rejects the pacifier three times before the swing lulls him to calm down, then successfully keeps it in his mouth.

Mandy walks over to us, Audrey still in her arms. "How did you do that?"

"Baby swing," I say. "Best investment you could make, though he's probably getting too big for one."

"I'll tell Lulu's dad," Mandy says, and I smile at the nickname she has given the baby.

I take Audrey back in my arms so that Mandy can sit down and relax. I sit opposite her on the other couch.

"Are you ever going to try to reach out to Bren—"

"Mandy, stop it," I say, tired of the same conversation.

Mandy learned about Audrey's father in the most dramatic way possible—in the delivery room. Apart from Mom, she's the only human who knows my daughter's last name.

"Fine, fine. I won't say anything," she says.

During my pregnancy and since Audrey's birth, Mandy and I have become almost inseparable. Carolina and Sara became workaholics while they nursed broken hearts, so I leaned on Mandy and my bar team. Even David turned out to be a fantastic guy, in the end, and a surprising source of support.

During that time, Lulu and his dad came into Mandy's life like a bulldozer, and she learned all the baby stuff with me. We were both clueless at the start, and Ileana is often a source of information. She is our ultimate life hack, and we treasure her dearly.

"She looks like him, you know," Mandy says.

I look down at my daughter, who stares up at me with her father's same chocolate-brown eyes. She yawns the cutest little yawn, and I smile because those full lips of hers are a duplicate mini-version of mine. She is the best parts of both of us, and he will never know.

"I know," I say, but my voice cracks.

"I'm dropping the subject, I swear, but I also came over for a reason."

My eyes snap up to her. "What?" I ask.

Mandy averts her gaze. "You haven't seen the news today, have you?"

I shake my head.

"There was a press release about *Industrial November*. They dropped a new album and released a music video for one of the new songs."

"Oh, yeah?" I try to sound as disinterested as possible, but my heart is beating hard against my chest.

Mandy nods. "And it's fascinating," she says. "The song in the video is called 'The Girl from Kansas City.'"

I grip tightly to Audrey because I don't want to drop her. "What?"

Mandy's mouth quirks up into a teasing and smug 'I got you' smile. "I wonder who it could be about?" she asks, her arms crossed. "All I'm saying is, it doesn't look like he got over you."

"Mandy—"

"I know. I know. I'm butting out. I just thought you should know."

AFTER MANDY LEAVES, I PUT AUDREY DOWN FOR A NAP AND TAKE a deep dive on the internet, reading article after article.

"*Industrial November* released a new music video in promotion of their new album. Band manager Roger Kemp stated in a press release today that the band has no plans to tour at the moment. The album aptly named *Breaking This Way* breaks away from Brenner Reindhart's usual style of lyric. As the primary lyricist, Reindhart has always gravitated toward simple yet powerful songs about anger, women, lust, and other rock and roll themes. In their last album, he also included the surprisingly popular revenge ballad, 'Late Night Legs.'

"For fans of the ballad, they'll be happy to know *Breaking This Way* is full of equally powerful ballads. In a surprise pivot for the band, the ballads croon all about heartbreak. Two of the songs include the name Sofia and given the music video release of 'The Girl from Kansas City,' we can only assume the elusive Sofia is from Kansas City.

"Both songs, 'Dreams of Sofia' and 'Sofia is Waiting,' will undoubtedly break many hearts. It is no mystery that Brenner Reindhart's heart has been broken. The only question now is: Who is the mysterious Sofia?"

My pulse quickens as I read on. The album isn't available yet, and all the criticism is from early reviewers of the album, so I can't have a listen for myself apart from the song in the video.

"The Girl from Kansas City" isn't about heartbreak, though. It is almost upbeat, with a touch of nostalgia, and includes references to our first meeting, one line about passionate tequila nights, and a line about swimming in the valley. Finn would understand what that meant, but most of the lines would only mean something to me.

Fuck.

Guilt for breaking Bren's heart washes over me anew. I can't believe he would write about us, about me—about me breaking his heart, specifically. I have to get my hands on the rest of the songs. I run a hand through my hair, which now hits below my shoulders, and I pull on it once. It was hard keeping up with the maintenance of my short, asymmetrical bob once I became a full-time mom, so I let it grow wild, more like Mandy's witchy hair.

Then, for the most shameful second of my life, I dare to let a glimmer of hope enter my tattered old heart. I hope Bren still thinks about me. That he will come back to me—to us.

I let myself envision a future where he meets Audrey and falls in love with her as much as I have. A collage of scenes flashes through my mind. Her first birthday party, her dad holding her for pictures. Dance recitals and a giant rock god in a moto jacket holding the hand of a little girl in a pink tutu. Sunday morning pancake breakfasts—all of us in pajamas.

But I snuff out all of those ideas as I keep on reading and watching tabloid 'news' videos online.

One perky, young reporter for a gossip site smiles through her reporting on the band.

"In other news, Brenner Reindhart was spotted with his old flame, Swedish supermodel Emma Johanssen, in Berlin earlier this week before the announcement of their new album. This, even after much speculation about the mysterious Sofia who broke his heart.

"I don't know about you ladies, but if this Sofia was dumb enough to let Brenner Reindhart go, she deserves for him to rekindle the relationship with the stunning Emma Johanssen."

Get it together, Sofia, I think to myself. He wrote those songs over a year ago and probably didn't think about the ramifications of having to go on singing them for a long time. He isn't thinking about me anymore. Clearly, he moved on, and he did so with Emma. Maybe it's time for me to move on as well.

Then I get angry. How dare he use my name in his songs? Was he that mad at me to risk bringing me into the media's insanity if my identity were to ever be revealed? I mean, even in "Late Night Legs," he never mentioned Emma by name.

Now I have Audrey to think about and protect. If paparazzi start buzzing around me or my daughter, Brenner Reindhart had better be prepared for my wrath.

27

SOFIA

When I take Addy out of the car, I grab the car seat base and hand it to David. "Thanks," I say. We'd bumped into each other in the parking lot, and he'd offered to help. David also grabs the massive diaper bag and trails Addy and me—as we now call her, because her grandma had a hard time pronouncing 'Audrey'—into the bar before opening hours.

"She's getting big," David says.

"She is," I say and look down at Addy in the car seat as she says the second word-like thing she has learned: "Gah." The first word she learned was 'ma.'

"You turn around for one second, and she's a little bit bigger when you look again."

David unlocks the front door and holds it open for me. "Thanks. You're my savior."

He smiles wide.

"What brings you to our neck of the woods?" I ask him.

"Business. I have a meeting with Joe today to go over some numbers. And I wanted to see you."

"Ah. I don't know if he's in yet," I say, ignoring the last part of his answer.

"Sofia, are you ever going to let me take you out on a date?"

The truth is, David is persistent in a gentle way, and he is starting to wear me down. I haven't seen or heard from Bren since he proposed. And it has been so damned long since I've been out that my collection of new sex toys is my only company.

"Maybe," I say, and David's big, hopeful eyes snap up to mine.

"Really?" he asks.

"When do you leave?"

"I don't have a timeline."

I chew the inside of my lip. There is really no better candidate. He already knows I have a baby and doesn't seem to mind. I don't envision much of a future with him, but a nice night out with some male attention sounds fantastic. "If I can get a sitter tomorrow, and the expectations are nothing but dinner and good company—"

"Of course," he hastens to reassure me.

"Then maybe dinner tomorrow night?"

"I'll take it," David says with enthusiasm.

I take Addy out of the car seat, leaving it on the table where I'd set her. She reaches her arms out to David before he can leave for the back office. "Gah," she says and starts giggling.

David outstretches his arms to take her.

"You don't have to—"

"I want to. Besides, Joe isn't here yet," David says.

He takes Addy in his arms, and she huddles close to his chest, transfixed by his silvery tie.

"You're getting so heavy, Addy," David says. "My old man arms may not be able to carry you much longer."

At his voice, Addy looks up at his face. She giggles, and before I can stop her, she reaches up for David's left ear.

"Addy, no!" I yell and try to grab her again, but her chubby little hand latches onto the single stud earring.

"Ow-ow, ow!" David complains, his head tilting toward Addy's hand as she pulls on his earlobe.

"Addy, no!" I scold again as I pry her tiny fingers until they unfurl, then take her back in my arms.

David's now-free hand flies to his ear to make sure she hasn't yanked it right out. He checks his hand for blood, but luckily there is none.

"I'm so sorry, David," I say, completely mortified. "We're in the 'loving shiny things' stage."

He laughs. "Girls and their diamonds," he teases, and we both laugh, Addy joining us with her own little giggle.

I shift into a baby voice when I talk near Addy's ear. "You're going to buy your own diamonds when you grow up, aren't you, Addy? You don't need a man to get them for you, do you?" I tease, arching an eyebrow at David.

"Or steal them," David jokes, palming his ear once more.

"Gaaah," goes Addy again, and we all laugh.

"Are we going to see you tonight at the party since you're in town?" I ask David.

"Wouldn't miss it," he says. "Got her a present and everything." Then David grabs Addy's tiny hand, and she wraps it around two fingers. "Sorry it's not diamonds, kiddo."

Joe and Lola arrive at the bar within minutes of each other. Joe greets Addy with a gentle squeeze of her chubby cheek, and David excuses himself for their meeting.

"Addy, girl," Lola coos as she takes her into her arms.

Addy says something that sounds like 'ia,' which we are thinking is her way of picking on what I use to reference all her aunties: *tía*.

"Thanks so much for watching her until the party. I have so much to do, and there's just no way I could get everything done with her."

Lola bounces Addy in her arms. "I'm happy to. She's the least troublesome kid I sit for," she says, not so subtly jabbing at Ileana's son Isael who she also babysits.

I laugh. "All right, everything you need is in the diaper bag; if you could have her back by six, that would be great. Guests start arriving at six-thirty."

"Yeah, yeah, we got it. Right, Addy?" Lola says in a baby voice way more ridiculous than mine.

I walk behind the bar to take inventory of the party supplies I stored under it and make sure I didn't miss anything.

"Can't believe she's a year old today," Lola says.

"I know. Time flies. Oh! Thanks for reminding me; I couldn't find a candle with the number one in the color I wanted, so I have to stop by the party store too. Do you need help getting to the car?"

"Nope. I got it."

I duck behind the bar to organize some of the party supplies and take inventory when the doorbell rings. Assuming it's Lola leaving, I yell out a 'see you later.'

"Um," Lola says. "We're still here."

"Oh?" I stand to see who came into the bar, and a ball of lead settles in my stomach.

———

MY MOUTH DRIES AS I SIZE THE MAN UP AND DOWN. IN THE roughly one year and eight months since I've seen him, nothing about Bren has changed.

"Hello, Sofia," he says.

I have to be imagining things because he can't be here. Can he? Not after all this time.

"Um," Lola says to break the silence. "Hello, Bren. It's Lola— we met a while back," she says, offering him her hand.

"Right. Hello." They shake hands while Addy is still in Lola's arms, playing with her long, curly, blond hair, but Addy never turns to look Bren's way. Bren's eyes fix on the back of Addy's head for one second, then he smiles and returns his attention to me. "Can we talk?"

My breathing starts to come in shallow, and I break out into a cold sweat as I stand there looking between father and daughter in the same room—breathing the same air. I never thought I'd see the day when that would happen.

"I guess I'll get going," Lola says. "I'll bring—"

"Thanks, Lola!" I cut her off before she finishes the sentence. Bren seems to think the baby is Lola's, and I need it to stay that way, at least until I collect myself. "I'll see you later."

Lola throws me a questioning look and mouths an 'are you okay?' at me. I nod, and she secures Addy back in the car seat. I watch her go past Bren as she leaves through the front door. I track them both as she walks past the bar, and only when they are out of sight does my heart calm down to a regular beat again.

"I, um—have some errands to run," I say stupidly.

"You don't have five minutes for me?"

I let out a breath. "Yeah, Bren. I have five minutes for you."

"You look well," he says and offers a small smile.

"That's a lie, but I'll take it. You, on the other hand, haven't changed a bit." He is wearing jeans and a forest green hoodie that makes his brown eyes pop. He is more handsome than ever, and I inwardly kick myself for letting this perfect man get away. We could have had it all if I could have just gotten over my fears.

Now things are different, and I can't lie to myself and pretend my anger toward him hasn't been building since the day he left.

"How've you been?" he asks.

I pause to examine him, my head tilting to the side. "Why are you here, Bren?"

His slow smile starts building. "I wanted to see you. Check in. See how you're doing."

"You're not touring . . . wait." I narrow my eyes at him. "Did you fly in from Germany to 'see how I'm doing?' Because you could have picked up a phone and saved yourself a trip."

"Sofia—"

"I, on the other hand, couldn't call you to 'see how you were doing' because you disconnected your phone—"

"I'm sorry about that. I was hurt. Being around you hurt. And I knew hearing your voice would hurt. I couldn't . . ." He trails off and averts his eyes.

Despite my best efforts to stay angry at him, the tension on my face relaxes. I am still mad at him for missing out on Audrey, even if he didn't know about her. Looking at him now, so vulnerable, softens my anger. But mostly, I also understand I broke his heart when I refused to marry him.

"I know you're busy. Maybe we can have lunch tomorrow?" he asks.

My gut is telling me to say no. To deny him any time and send him on his way so I'd never see him again and he'd never know about Addy. As I stare at the man who so clinically cut me out of his life, a new fear slithers into my heart. Would he want custody? Of course he would want at least *partial* custody. With him so out of my life, I never had to think about that before, and the very thought of it churns my stomach.

I can't keep this from him, though. Not only am I not that person, but I couldn't do that to Addy. If he wants to be in her life, I can't deny her that. I know what it is like to grow up without a father, and though my mother did a fantastic job on her own, I missed out on a lot from his absence.

I have to tell him.

"No strings?" I ask before agreeing.

"No strings. Just two old friends catching up." He smiles

sexily—his eyes full of mischief and intent—and I don't buy he's being sincere for even one second.

We were never friends, but I don't tell him that. "Then sure, Bren. We can have lunch tomorrow. It will be nice to catch up, and I have something I'd like to talk with you about as well."

His smile is so wide, it is like having the old Bren back—my Bren. "We've had some paparazzi trailing us, so Andreas and I will pick you up tomorrow."

Paparazzi? My stomach unsettles all over again. Before, we were so careful that I never got to experience the total paparazzi insanity, but now there's Addy to think about. I feel my heart all the way in my throat. I recover and force a smile.

"Sure. I have a new address, though." I give him the address, and he is writing it down on his phone when Joe and David's voices filter into the bar as they approach us from the back office. Then Joe goes dead quiet.

Fuck. I forgot they were back there, so caught up I've been with the emotional rollercoaster of the last five minutes. Joe blinks, then gapes between Bren and me. I shake my head at him as discreetly as possible, begging him with my panicked eyes not to say anything.

Then Joe's fists clench at his sides. In his mind, Bren abandoned Addy and me when we needed him the most. He's been dying to sock him in the jaw since he learned about the pregnancy.

"Joe, can you get started on inventory, please?" I say, breaking his concentration. He throws me one last wary look before he leaves, shaking his head the entire way.

"Hey, man," David says as he tips his chin at Bren. I am not surprised he doesn't offer his hand for a shake this time since Bren left him hanging when they first met.

"Hi," Bren says coolly.

"How was the meeting?" I ask David, if only to break the tension in the room.

"Good. Joe will send you the report tonight. Third quarter exceeded targets. So did the Chicago branch."

I smile wide. Since going into business with David, *La Oficina* has boomed. I have to admit, he has great ideas and all of us at the bar have adapted well to the new split management. "I'm glad," I say.

Before I realize what's happening, David steps in closer to me and wraps a hand around my waist, following it up with a kiss on my cheek. He smiles down at me, his arm still around my middle. "I'll see you tonight?"

I chuckle nervously. "Yeah. See you tonight."

David leaves us alone, and Bren's eyes darken as they spear through me. "I thought you said that was only business," he says when we're alone.

"It was," I say, crossing my arms, sure of where he's taking this.

"Was? As in past tense? It's not only business anymore?"

"Bren, if you really want to catch up, we can do it at lunch tomorrow. It'll give you time to cool off and rethink if you want to interrogate me like you have any fucking right to do so. Now, I really have to run those errands." And for once, it is me who storms off, leaving Bren stunned and alone in the empty bar.

"Hey, are you okay?" Mandy asks. I didn't realize that she trailed me out of the party room.

So far, I have spilled a total of three drinks and almost dropped the cake when I was bringing it in from the car. Addy, thankfully, spends her time bouncing from Carolina to Sara to Ileana, and even to David in the party room—David thoughtfully showed up to the party minus one signature diamond stud. I am glad they can all take turns holding Addy so I can do the

other million things I need to—the million things on top of
freaking out about Bren being back.

"Yeah. Fine," I lie. "Why?"

"You seem . . . on edge," Mandy says.

"Just a tad haggard. It's been a long day. You know how it is."

"I do!" Mandy says. She squeezes my forearm gently. "You'd
tell me if anything was wrong?"

"Of course," I say, then change the subject. "Need another
drink?"

"I'll get it."

"Okay, then get back in formation. I'm about to bring the
cake in. Can you make sure to record?"

"Always do," she says with a wide toothy smile, and I roll my
eyes. Her and her stupid phone camera. At least this time, it will
be put to good use.

I light the candle on the cake, shielding it with one hand as I
walk into the party room as we all sing: *"Feliz cumpleaños a ti,
feliz cumpleaños a ti, feliz cumpleaños a Addy . . .*

THREE PAPARAZZI WAIT OUTSIDE THE GARAGE ENTRANCE TO THE
same building where Bren bought his penthouse condo. Had he
not sold it after all this time? I know the men with cameras are
shouting something, but I have no idea what they want with the
windows completely shut.

My legs become unsteady as we enter the building and get in
the elevator. I keep my eyes glued to the changing numbers in
the elevator as we ascend to the top floor.

"Are you okay?" Bren asks. "You seem nervous."

"I guess I am a little," I say, not glancing his way.

28

BREN

I run the back of my hand over the span of her naked arm, and she shivers under my touch. She takes a step away from me in the elevator, as if that keeps her out of my reach. I smile inwardly. Her body still reacts to me. Whether she is with that fucking guy from the bar or not, her body tells a story: she belongs to me, even after all this time.

Sofia gets out of the elevator first, and I trail her out. Her hips are a bit rounder, but she wears the new curves in an incredibly sexy way. Even if she tries to hide these new curves under an A-line dress instead of the second skin dresses that are seared into my brain from before.

Her hair, too, is longer, making her face look a bit softer. She's changed outwardly, and I'm now wondering what else has changed in the woman I still love. The woman I couldn't slice out of my heart without removing the entire thing.

After offering Sofia a seat in the living room, she crosses her legs and stiffens her posture. She's adorable when she is nervous. She clasps her hands on her leg, then brings them to her sides, then back again to her leg like she doesn't know what to do with them. "Do you have something to drink?" she asks.

I try and fail to hide the smirk building on my face. "How about tequila?" I ask.

Her mouth parts slightly as my eyes search hers. My dick twitches as I wait for a reaction from her body. Yes, Sofia. I remember. I know I'm invoking that shared memory in her.

"No. I meant, like coffee," she snaps, clearly annoyed.

"Yeah. I can make us coffee. I have sandwiches and fruit whenever you're ready to eat," I say.

"Let's chat first," she says, but there is something off about her. It's in the way she fidgets in her seat and keeps biting that lower lip of hers; she's clearly more nervous than anything.

Where did my reassured badass Sofia go? I guess a lot can change in over a year and a half. I sure have. As I make the coffee, I wonder why she declined a cocktail, even if it weren't tequila. It would certainly take the edge off, but if she's not drinking, neither am I, so I stick to coffee too.

I set a mug with coffee in front of her, and I take a sip of my own. She picks it up in her hands but doesn't drink it. She just twirls the mug slowly in her hands, focusing her eyes there. She can't even look at me. God, I hate this.

"I'm sorry," I say abruptly, and her eyes finally meet mine.

"For?"

"Yesterday. I mean, I do want to know if you're with that *hundesohn*, but that was no way to ask."

"Thank you," she says—not offering more.

"So, are you?"

"That's where you want to start?"

I narrow my eyes at her. Why is she so damn evasive? "Where would you like to start, *Schatzi*?"

"Okay, let's start by not using your little pet name for me.

How about there?" Her eye roll is so deep, I don't know how I keep my laugh inside.

I chuckle. "Okay. I'll stop calling you *Schatzi*." *For now*, I add mentally. Because I'm determined to get her back. I tried stopping my love for her until I realized that would never happen—not in this lifetime. She'll always be my *Schatzi*, even if she's not with me.

She sets the mug on the table and crosses her arms. "I'd actually love to hear an explanation about your last album, Bren." Her eyes are accusing as she pins me with an icy glare.

I rub my hand over my face and look up to the high heavens before bringing my eyes back to my beautiful Sofia.

"Of course that's where you want to start. What do you want to know Sch—Sofia?"

"You used my real name, Bren. What the fuck was that about?"

I shrug. "I write about what I feel. All the best writing comes from the most vulnerable places. I'd never been so vulnerable, and it paid off. Best critical reception in the band's history."

"At my expense!" she snaps.

"No one knows who you are."

"You and I both know it's only a matter of time. Especially now that you're here," she says.

I shift in my seat. She's right. Returning to the city named in the two Sofia songs certainly has raised some eyebrows already. "Are you looking for an apology?" I ask. The album is meant to be my apology. I need her to understand that.

"No," she huffs. "I'm just annoyed. And if my identity is revealed, there will be hell to pay, Brenner Reindhart."

"I can live with those terms," I say with a low chuckle. She is not amused.

"How come you included my name? You didn't have to do

that. You didn't reveal Emma's name. Why couldn't you offer me the same courtesy?" She's angry now.

"I didn't love Emma," I say simply.

She studies me for a long, silent moment. "You told me she broke your heart."

I shake my head. "I didn't know then what heartbreak really was. I thought what I had with Emma was love. But I didn't know love. Not until you."

Sofia's hand drifts to press on her heart as her eyes start glistening. I have her now.

Then she composes herself. "Why are you back?" she asks with a sharp tone.

"I'm sorry. I thought that was obvious. I'm here to get you back." I smile wickedly at her.

She sets down her coffee, then laughs. Right in my face.

"What's so funny?" I ask, more than a little annoyed.

"You are!" she says then mocks me in an attempt to imitate my voice, "I'm here to get you back. Hah!"

"I'm serious," I say.

"Bren, come on."

"Come on, what?"

"It's been over a year. What we had—it's gone."

"I'm not so sure it is. I haven't moved on. Have you? With your business partner?" I ask as calmly as I can muster because the question tastes like battery acid.

"How about you, Bren? Haven't you moved on with Emma?"

My eyes widen with the surprise of her rebuttal. "Why would you think that?"

"There was a report about you two being back together."

"There was?"

Sofia nods.

"Don't know what you are talking about, but no. We never got back together."

"You didn't?"

I shake my head.

"You were seen together in Berlin."

"So?"

"That's proof—"

"Were we kissing? Holding hands? On a romantic getaway?"

Sofia's eyes narrow. I got her. "We met for dinner. Once. She wanted closure. I'll admit we parted ways more amicably than the first time, but no, Sofia. We never got back together. Now. It's your turn. Stop dodging the question. I'm asking nicely now. Are you with him?"

She shifts in her seat and drops her eyes to her hands as she answers me. "We're dating. Yes. It's new."

That sends me lunging from my seat and into pacing. I don't want to explode and push her away like my temper always did back then, but fuck, this is not how I wanted this to go.

But really, what the fuck was I thinking? A woman that perfect? Of course she would have moved on.

"Bren . . ." She trails off as I keep pacing.

"How long?" I snap.

"How long what?"

"Stop being obtuse. How long have you been together?"

"Does it matter?"

I stop in my tracks to stare at her. Then I sit next to her, taking her hand in mine. "Tell me I'm not too late," I plead.

She pulls her hand out of my grip. "Why now, Bren?"

That is a more complicated question to answer. How could I explain why it took me so god damn long to get my head out of my ass? How do I tell her about that grim period in my life? I became a recluse, saw no one, spoke to no one. All I did was work. I wrote, and I wrote some more. I wrote until my fingertips felt like they would bleed. My feeble attempt to stop thinking about her only resulted in all my writing being about her.

"I tried to stop loving you. I thought time would . . ." My voice cracks. "But it didn't, and here we are." My smile is weaker now as I reveal my vulnerability to her.

"Bren, there's—"

I'm not sure I'll have the courage much longer, and I have to say it while I can, so I interrupt her thought. "I still love you," I stammer. "Please tell me I didn't run out of time—that you still love me."

"It doesn't matter what I feel—"

"Yes, it does. It matters to me."

"No, Bren. It doesn't. You still want something I can't give you."

"I'm okay with that," I say, closing my eyes.

"I'm not," she says. "I don't want to be the reason you give up on your dreams."

I smile at her. "*Schatzi* . . . you are my dream. I'm just sorry it took me so long to square that with what I thought I wanted."

"No. You want to be married. You want a wife, someone to take your name—all of it. I haven't changed my views on marriage. And if you're thinking you can one day change my mind, you have to understand I never will. Not on that front."

"I'm okay with that. What I thought I wanted . . . it's nothing without you. I'd still like to have children one day, but even then, I'd give that up if you truly didn't want any. All I need is you."

She doesn't say anything for a long moment. "You want children?"

"Not if you don't, but yeah. I'd love at least one kid."

"You'd be happy with just one?"

"That's an important question, Sofia. We should figure that out together if you are saying yes to trying again."

"I'm not saying that."

"Is it because of that guy?"

"That guy is David, and he's been my rock since you left. You really need to start being nice to him."

I suck in air through my teeth. "I'm sorry. I have a lot to apologize for, don't I?"

"Bren. David really is just a business partner. He has asked me out for a long time, and for a long time I've said no."

I let out a long breath of relief.

"But," she continues, "before you showed up yesterday, I said yes. We're having dinner tonight. It will be our first date. I'm just trying to be transparent here."

"Don't go," I beg. Like a fucking dog.

"I have to."

"Please, Sofia. Don't go on a date with him. I don't even want to hear about any men you've dated since I left . . ." I trail off when a small smile spreads on her face. "Is this funny?" I ask.

"A little. Yeah. You broke up with me, Bren. Not the other way around."

I hang my head with the shame of it. "And that was the biggest fucking mistake of my life." I look up at her again, and her nose is red like it was the last time I saw her, when I proposed and she was about to cry. "Please don't go. Not if you still love me. Not if we have a chance."

I caress the side of her face, and her lips part. When she doesn't flinch away from my touch, I lean in closer until my lips press flush with hers. Her eyes drift closed, and she leans into the kiss, opening up an invitation to me. She doesn't say the words; she doesn't say she loves me back. She could hardly say it then, and she isn't saying it now. She still has trouble with the concept of love, but she doesn't have to say it.

I know she loves me by the way she kisses me—by the way she touches me. It is tender and hungry, and all of it is Sofia. The kiss is gentle, sweet, and short. Then I pepper kisses down her jaw and down her neck. My hand drifts down the skirt of her dress, and when I get to the hem, she doesn't push my hand away, so I trail it up her thigh until it meets with the cloth of her underwear already starting to dampen. I press with my thumb over the cloth, searching, searching, until I find her clit, and she whimpers out my name. "Bren . . ."

I smile against her neck. "I missed you." I rub the bundle of nerves in a circle. "Did you miss me?"

She nods. "Yes," she says with a breathy voice. Her chest rises and falls more rapidly each second. As she opens her legs for me, I maneuver in front of her so I can kneel at her feet. I am not beneath begging for her to take me back, and that is precisely what I am doing—on my knees.

Her head falls on the backrest of the sofa as I pull her underwear to the side, making room for my tongue. I spread her flesh with two fingers, and the sight of her beautiful swollen clit earns a twitch from my cock. Fuck, I forgot how beautiful she is.

I circle the bundle of nerves with my tongue, slowly at first, enjoying Sofia writhing in her seat, then pick up the pace, lapping it like a starving man. Her hands come to my head, and her fingers run through my hair as her legs start to shake. I lick faster until she is a shuddering puddle under my touch. When her spasms fade, I look up at her, damn pleased with myself and what I can still do to her.

"You're not playing fair," she breathes out, looking down at me.

"I never have." With one last gentle flick of her clit, I cover her again with her underwear and set her skirt straight so I can retake a seat next to her. I scoot her into my arms, and she pants there for a long moment while she catches her breath.

"Now, will you please say we can try again?" I ask her.

"Bren, I—I'd like to, but before we go there, there's something you should—"

"Shhh," I say. "Just think on it for a couple of days, okay? Don't give me an answer now." If she is still on the fence, I don't want to risk her giving me the wrong answer right now.

She nods in my arms. "I have to explain to David why we can't date just after I told him we could. Can you trust me?"

"Of course I can trust you."

"I have to go to dinner tonight. I have to explain what happened."

"Okay."

Sofia leans back to look up at me. "Okay?" Her eyes narrow, not buying my calm tone.

"Yeah. Okay."

"That was too easy," she says and arches a brow.

"If the poor bloke gets anywhere near where he shouldn't, he'll pick up the smell of me on your pussy," I say and grin at her because really, she wouldn't be romantic with one man hours after another one already ate her.

"He's not a dog, Bren."

I roll my eyes.

29

SOFIA

"You're home early. Bad date?" Lola asks from her spot on my couch. She's wearing her beloved Television *Marquee Moon* album cover t-shirt over ripped jeans, which is hilarious in contrast to her curvy beach-babe body and blond hair.

I crumple on the seat next to her and toss my purse on the floor. "Not really a date after all. But bad day."

"Sorry," she says, handing me the remote. I shake my head, and she shuts off the TV. Addy is nowhere to be seen, so I can only assume she's asleep in her room. "Wanna talk about it?" Lola asks.

I rest my forehead on my hand and peek at her through my fingers. "Umm . . ."

"Or do you want to talk about why Brenner Reindhart was at the bar yesterday?"

Everything is going to come out. I need to vent, to tell someone, but it feels wrong for anyone else to know Bren is Addy's dad before he even has the chance to hold her in his arms.

I take in a deep breath. Twice, I managed to start to tell him, but each time he cut me off. Then his stupid, stupid declaration of love sent everything into a tailspin, and I couldn't process anything, least of all, how to deliver devastating news.

"You know, when I met him that first time, what was it, over a year ago? I totally freaked out," Lola admits, and I sit up to look at her.

"You did? I don't remember that," I say.

"Oh no, inwardly, I was freaking out. You don't remember, but I was a mess in my work clothes, had rubber cleaning gloves on, and held a bottle of cleaning spray. I tell you, I'm cursed . . ."

Lola always claims to have been cursed with bad luck ever since her parents named her Dolores, the translation of which is pain or sorrow.

I roll my eyes. "Lola, you're not cursed," I say.

She nods. "I am. How else can you explain why on the day I got my chance to meet a member of *Industrial November*, I'm elbow-deep in a toilet?"

We both burst out in laughter, and Lola nudges me on the arm with her shoulder. "See?" she says. "Nothing can be worse than that. Now, tell me what happened with David."

"Nothing."

"Nothing?"

"Nope. I felt awful stringing him along. I finally agreed on a date only to back out on the first try."

"Was he mad?"

"No. David's a prince. He was maybe more . . . disappointed?"

Lola chats for a bit before heading home. I pay her for the night and go into Addy's room to take a look at my angelic sleeping daughter. I have to roll my eyes because Lola has *Marquee Moon* playing softly on a loop in her room. According to her, a musical education can't start early enough. I don't disagree, though my choice wouldn't have been Richard Hell's band quite so soon. She should be older to appreciate that shit.

"You're going to meet your daddy very soon," I whisper and

brush Addy's wispy black hair away from her forehead. "He told me today that he wants kids. I think he'll be delighted to have a daughter, and when he sees you—oh, Addy, you'll have him wrapped around your chubby little finger."

THE FOLLOWING DAY IS BEAUTIFUL AND ENTICING. I ALSO HAVE A lot of thinking to do, so I decide some fresh air will do Addy and me some good. I wrap my baby sling around me and stuff Addy in. She loves being pressed close to my chest.

I walk us over to the park, thinking out loud in Spanish so Addy can pick up my first language too.

Mostly, I worry about Bren's reaction. He may want to take everything he said last night back when he realizes I've been keeping his daughter from him.

Then I will have lost out on both Bren and David. *Como el perro de las dos tortas,* I say to Addy in a funny voice, earning me a giggle.

When we round the corner on our street to get home, I frown. A white van is parked in my driveway, and I can make out two figures standing on the sidewalk by my house. I don't recognize the car or who they are from a distance, but as we near the house, I see the camera and the microphone in the hands of a man in a suit.

"Sofia, hello. I'm with Channel Seven Evening News. Do you have a moment?"

"I'm sorry, no," I say, pushing past him but not missing the camera following me—following us.

"Is it true that you're the Sofia referenced in *Industrial November*'s latest album?"

"No comment." I fumble for my keys in my jeans pocket and can't open the door fast enough.

"Is that your baby?" the man asks just before I shut the door behind me.

Once inside, I set Addy down in her baby swing and rush to grab my phone out of my purse. I have to call Bren. My heart is pounding out of my chest.

After several rings that last a lifetime, I get his automated answering message.

"Bren. We have to talk. It's urgent. Can we move our meeting to today?"

As I wait for his call, I pace my living room, biting my thumbnail. *Call me back, Bren. Come on.*

He has to hear this from me.

30

BREN

Fritz looks over the binder I handed him. Over the last year, I've written enough decent songs for five albums—at least. We carefully curated the previous album from that binder, and now we're starting to catalog the rest of the songs.

Fritz and Karl are critical to the process because the lyrics have to inspire music out of them, so they effectively choose the order in which we produce each song and album.

"You could have done this from home, you know. You didn't have to come to KC with me," I say to him as I hand him a beer. He is reading a lyric, deep in thought, then looks up.

"What?" he asks.

"I was just saying you could've done this from Germany—or Mexico."

Fritz shakes his head and ignores the Mexico comment. "You know it's better in person. Besides, with the album out now and the media frenzy back home..."

We both smirk because neither one of us is saying what we're thinking. To Roger, Karl, and Adrian, we escaped the grueling press responsibilities, leaving them to take the brunt of it.

Glancing at the coffee table, Fritz already has a separate pile going.

"Which are those?" I ask, and he grabs the two pieces of paper, handing them to me.

"They are some of the stronger ones. The first one has Adrian all over it. We should make room for a hefty drum solo."

"Yeah. I was thinking he'd like that too. I'm pulling the songs I think are strongest and dividing them up. We shouldn't include all the best ones in the first few albums and start going downhill in the later ones."

After a few hours of arguing about song lineups and music ideas, I throw my hands in the air. "I can't keep looking at these songs anymore today. Wanna take a break? We can catch the game."

"Yeah. We should step away. Come back when we can be more objective," Fritz says.

I hand Fritz the remote then stand to grab us a couple more beers. I am holding on to both bottles while I look for the bottle opener when the band name on the TV turns my attention.

"Both front man Brenner Reindhart and bass player Fritz Hartmann were spotted at the Kansas City international airport earlier this week, not one week after releasing the record-breaking hit single 'The Girl from Kansas City.' While two of the other songs in the album mentioned a woman named Sofia, no official link had been made to the popular music video until today.

"Yesterday, Reindhart was spotted going into this bar—" The camera pans to the outer face of *La Oficina*. "We have confirmed that the bar is a shared property with the Price Group based out of Chicago and Sofia Ocampo, a Kansas City local. Could this be the same Sofia whom Reindhart sings about?

"Sofia Ocampo declined to comment early this morning outside her Brookside home."

I close my eyes. Fuck. She'll have my head on a platter for this. Why hasn't she called to chew me out yet?

"Are you hearing this?" Fritz asks as the reporting on Sofia's background continues, but Fritz keeps his eyes glued to the TV.

"Fuck," I say. "I'm so fucked."

Then it happens. A camera shot, only three seconds in length, of her going into her house, and all the air leaves my lungs.

Some type of scarf is wrapped around her chest as she carries a baby.

The reporting continues. "Speculation on the father's whereabouts has many heads turning—"

Fritz shuts off the TV.

"Bren? Mate?" He approaches me, but it is in slow motion. His phone is to his ear. "Roger's been trying to call you. He says your phone is off."

The room spins, and I lose my grip on the beers that fall to the floor, shattering on impact.

31

SOFIA

"**G**o to Channel Seven! Now!" Mandy screams into the phone when I pick up.

A ball of lead lodges in my throat as the report unfolds before my eyes. I take a deep breath, closing my eyes. Fuck. It's out.

"Please tell me he already knows," Mandy says.

I shut off the news. "No. I've been trying to get away for hours, but the reporters parked outside keep increasing in numbers. I can't leave the house!"

I damn Bonnie then. If she weren't taking up the only space in the garage, my car wouldn't be in the driveway, and Addy and I could have escaped hours ago, before the news broke, so we could find Bren and explain everything.

"Fuck," Mandy says. Yeah. *Fuck*, I think.

"Hey, Mandy, I gotta go. I have another call. It's Bren."

"Good luck—"

I press the phone to my chest and take a deep breath before taking the second call.

"Bren. Hi."

"Were you going to tell me?" His voice is low . . . and calm. Too calm.

Twice I'd started to tell him, but he won't buy that. Not now. Not after the news report. "Yes. Since I saw the reporters, I've been calling you. When you weren't picking up, I wanted to come to you, but we're cornered by paparazzi."

"Andreas and Fritz's security guard will pick you up in ten. Bye—"

"Bren? Wait."

"What?" he hisses, his anger rising.

"I'm alone with, um . . . tell Andreas he needs to get a car seat."

A long breath from Bren filters through the call. "Right. Make it thirty minutes."

THE OPERATION TO GET US OUT OF MY HOUSE IS SWIFT. ANDREAS and the second security guard do their best to shelter us. Andreas shields us from the cameras with his body as much as possible while the other guard pushes people back, making a line for the car door. But the shouting and chaos are too much for Addy, and she starts crying in my arms. I want to claw some eyes out for scaring her, but I just keep my head down, saying nothing.

My heart races as I look out the back window at the trail of vans and cars following us now. Luckily, the garage in Bren's building is secure, and we won't have to be shouted at again.

Addy is back in her sling on my chest as we ride the elevator up to the penthouse. I start bouncing a bit on my feet as I pat her back, but really, the fidgeting is more for my nerves than to soothe her.

Bren stands in the main living room, watching me leave the elevator. He tips his chin at the guards behind me, and the elevator doors shut, taking away my two protectors and leaving me more nervous than ever.

Bren's eyes are cold, his brows knitted together firmly, but his eyes freeze on that tiny bundle strapped to me.

Someone clears their throat, pulling my attention past Bren to Fritz. He is leaning on the back of the couch, his legs crossed at the ankles, hands in his pockets. "Hello, Sofia," he says.

"Hi—"

"Fritz, you need to leave," Bren says, his voice stern.

"I'm not going anywhere. Don't want you to do anything you'll regret."

Bren turns to his friend. "You think I'd hurt a woman and a baby?"

"No. I don't think that. But you're really angry, Bren. Don't do or say anything stupid. Get all the facts first."

"Get the fuck out of my house," Bren hisses with such anger, I tighten my grip on my daughter.

"No can do." Fritz shakes his head, standing there—cool as a cucumber—and I desperately want some of his level-headedness right now. "I'll go to the guest room so you can talk. Sofia? Call for me if you need me."

"Thank you, Fritz," I say with a weak smile.

His footfalls disappear down a long hallway, and the sound of a door closing brings Bren's eyes back to mine.

He swallows hard, his Adam's apple bobbing. "How—how old is—is . . ."

He can't get the word out. "She just had her first birthday."

"She?"

I nod and smile as I unwrap the sling from me, revealing her straight black hair. A sprig of hair shoots straight upward from a blue sunflower clip I used to try to gather her hair into some sort of ponytail. The result is comical but adorable. No way Bren won't fall in love with this sweet little thing. "Would you like to meet her?" I ask.

Bren takes a scared step back. I look down at Addy, who is awake and alert, looking up at me, her pacifier twitching slightly. I smile down at her. She's acting as a buffer. Her presence alone placates Bren, and he wouldn't dare shout with her present, even though everything about him tells me he wants to. From his taut muscles, veins popping over his forearms, all the way to the fisted hands at his sides as he clenches and releases them over and over.

"Were you going to tell me?" he asks, accusing.

"Yes. I started to so many times yesterday, but then . . . I have no excuse, Bren. I decided to tell you tomorrow when I'd had time to think, but then, well, those jerks beat me to it."

Bren takes a step forward then stops. His hesitation is almost funny, the way he approaches us like some scared little animal.

I take several long steps to get close to him, not faltering, hoping my confidence will bring out his. "Here," I say and hand Addy to him before he has the chance to voice any protest. "Her name is Addy."

He holds her away from his body at first, looking her up and down. Addy squirms a little in his hands. "Uh, she doesn't like me," he says.

"She's not used to strangers. Give her a minute."

He brings her closer to his body and then looks up at me. "Am I doing this right?"

I smile. "Yeah, Bren. You're doing great."

My body isn't prepared to watch this handsome, strong, hot beast of a man cradling his daughter in his arms as he looks down at her in awe. My heart squeezes a little at the sight of it. Then Bren's eyes find mine once again.

"She's mine?"

I nod. Addy must sense the change of mood in her dad because she starts fussing. The pacifier clinks to the floor, and though she doesn't cry, she grunts, trying to get out of this stranger's arms.

"Uh, here." He hands her back, and I can't push him any more than I already have, so I take her back in my arms.

His jaw clicks as I look at him again. Bren nods. "And her name?"

"Audrey Michelle Ocampo Reindhart. But we all call her Addy."

Bren's features soften. "You gave her my name?"

"I thought you might want that . . . one day."

Addy starts nodding off in my arms after a long moment of silence. "You think I can set her down for her nap?"

I walk Bren through the procedure as he takes the cushions off his couch and sets them on the floor. When he comes back from his room, he has a blanket, and we make a makeshift bed for Addy on the floor where I can watch her while we talk. And aw, hell . . . watching him tuck her in for the first time in his life is one of the best days of my life.

We walk over to the dining table so we are less likely to wake her. We speak in quiet voices for that very reason, and I thank the stars Addy is here to calm her father for the most difficult conversation of our lives.

"You should have told me," he says.

"I tried—"

"Bullshit."

"You disconnected your phone, Bren. You disappeared. I had no way of contacting you. I called Andreas, and his number was disconnected too. I'm guessing you ordered him to do that?"

Bren looks away and out the window at the Kansas City skyline. "You should have gotten lawyers involved. You should have . . ."

"Bren. Look. You'd made it clear you wanted nothing to do with me after . . . well, after everything. You didn't seem to want to be found by me, and I decided to respect that. Maybe I didn't handle it the best way, but I was dealing with a lot. I had to think about someone other than myself for once, and I was scared. I did the best I was capable of at the time."

His smile is weak, and understanding washes over his face. I'm such a fucking asshole. All I've ever managed to do is hurt this perfect man who never did anything other than love me. This is why I'm not cut out for relationships.

"She's beautiful," he says after a long, pensive moment.

I smile and peek over at her sleeping form. "Yeah. She's kind of perfect."

Bren gets up and paces in front of me, throwing an icy glare my way every few steps. "I missed out on a whole year." Another step.

"I'm sorry."

"That's all you have to say, Sofia? I'm sorry?" He keeps pacing.

"Shhh. You'll wake her up."

He glances over at our sleeping child and winces a little, then sits back down.

"We were so careful, Sofia. We always used a condom. How could this have happened?"

I shrug. "You know how it goes. They aren't always effective. I'm guessing one broke at some point, and we didn't notice."

He nods, thinking. This is so much for him to take in. And he found out about it in the most awful way possible. God, I can be such a bitch. All I can do is apologize, but he's already made it clear he doesn't want to keep hearing it. Neither would I, to be honest, if I were in his shoes. Those words are weak when such a betrayal happens.

Bren's eyes glisten as he keeps looking at the top of Addy's head. I am sure he will burst into tears soon, but he takes a deep breath and reels them in.

"What now?" he asks.

I take a deep breath. "We'll have to come to some sort of agreement."

His head falls to the side as he studies me. "What does that mean?"

"We've been fine on our own this past year. I'm able to provide for us comfortably. I have a great support system with all my friends. We don't need anything. If you don't want to be a part of this, you don't have to—"

"I didn't say I don't want to be a part of it."

I smile. "I know. I'm just giving you your options. If you need to walk away, I understand. We don't need anything from you. But if you want to be part of her life, Bren, it's forever. I don't want you around if you don't mean it, so think about it very carefully—"

"I want to be in her life," he says firmly.

"Bren, I had an entire eight months to grapple with this. You need more than one angry day to make a decision like this. Think on it—"

"I don't need to think on it. She's my daughter—"

I wince a little at those words, and my attentive Bren doesn't miss it. His eyes narrow slightly.

"She *is* my daughter. Right?" That muscle in his jaw is popping again.

How could I tell him? I know in my heart Audrey is Bren's. My soul knows this kid is all him. How could she not be when she has her dad's very eyes? But there is that slight chance. That one percent doubt I've always carried and thought I'd be taking to my grave with me.

"Sofia? Is that little girl over there mine?" His voice rises, and Addy stirs a bit.

"I'm pretty sure she is. Yes. But not without a shadow of doubt."

Bren springs to his feet and can't stop himself from shouting. "Fuck, Sofia! What the hell?!"

Addy lets out a full cry then, and I scurry over to pick her up in my arms.

"Please stop shouting. You're scaring her."

"I can't!" he roars, and Addy responds in a higher pitch.

I wince. "It's okay, baby. It's okay. Daddy's just a bit upset."

"I might not be her . . ." He trails off, looking at the back of Addy's head as I support it in my hand.

"We can get you a DNA test, Bren. Calm down. But I don't need it. I know in my heart she's yours."

"You *were* always sleeping around," he says and laughs bitterly.

I rear back. "Bren!"

"Do you even have any idea who else's she could be? How many candidates for father are there, Sofia? Huh?"

"Bren, I—"

"Tell me, god damn it! How many paternity tests will you subject your daughter to?"

My eyes drift closed. I have to remind myself that he is so angry. He doesn't mean these hurtful words. I need to make allowances for him because I already hurt him too many damn times. I'll take the punches now if he needs me to.

"Only one other possibility. The timing . . . it's—"

Bren picks up a dining chair, intending to throw it, but watching me holding the baby, he only slams it back down in its place. Addy still winces at the sound and cries harder.

"Who?" he yells.

"Bren."

"Sofia, I swear to god if you don't tell me right now who else could be her father . . ." His eyes narrow when he trails off. Then he studies me, those chocolate brown eyes roaming my face as I chew the inside of my lower lip.

His eyes widen when realization washes over him, and he stumbles back a step before catching his balance on the back of a chair. "No," he croaks out.

"I'm so sorry, Bren."

He shakes his head, the long trails of tears rolling down his face making my own tears spill over. And isn't this a fucking perfect sight? Bren, our daughter, and me, all crying.

"You can't have a baby with Finn." His voice cracks. "You just can't." His voice cracks again. "Not with my best friend. Please, God. No. Anyone but him."

"Bren, I'm ninety-nine percent sure she's yours. But I had to be honest. I had to tell you that even I have some doubt."

"Get out!" he hisses, and Addy cries louder. I have to get her away from him. My protective instincts kick in, and I grab the sling from the coffee table, making quick work of wrapping her in it.

"Get the fuck out of my house!" he yells. I startle when rapid footfalls come down the hallway, and Fritz is at my side in no time. He holds on gently to my elbow.

"Come on," Fritz says over Addy's crying, escorting me away. "I'll get you home."

WHEN THE ELEVATOR DOORS SHUT, I WIPE MY TEARS AND ASK Fritz, "Did you hear all of that?"

He nods. "I'm sorry. I didn't mean to, but I didn't want to leave you alone with him."

"Did you really think he would hurt me?"

"No. Not physically, but Bren can be . . . explosive."

Addy is settling down in my arms, cooing softly, allowing me to relax and finish wiping my own tears away.

"I can't go home, Fritz," I say finally. "I have nowhere to go."

He looks down at me and arches a brow in question.

"My house is surrounded by reporters."

He sighs. "Right." When we get to the lobby floor, Fritz pulls me back into the elevator and presses a number only a few floors below Bren's penthouse.

"Where are we going?" I ask.

"My place."

I look up at him in question. "You live here?"

"I'm renting an apartment. Bren and I had plans to work on the next album, so I wanted to be close by."

———

FRITZ'S APARTMENT IS LESS LAVISH THAN BREN'S BUT IS STILL upscale and modern, though it lacks any warmth. The leather seating, glass, and concrete fixtures . . . all of it screams bachelor pad.

I settle onto the couch with Addy.

"What now?" Fritz asks.

I shrug. "I don't know. I've never seen him so mad, and we used to . . ."

"Fight a lot?" Fritz asks.

"Yeah."

"You both have tempers. I'm surprised at how calm you've been about all of this."

I crinkle my nose and make a funny face at Addy, earning me a little giggle. I'm glad I'm able to soothe her so quickly. "She's taught me patience, I suppose."

"May I hold her?" Fritz asks, completely surprising me.

"Uh, sure."

He stands and grabs Audrey under her armpits, keeping her away from his body, studying her like Bren had only moments ago. I suppress a giggle building in the back of my throat.

"That man is insane," Fritz says. "Those are Brenner Reindhart's eyes, or my name isn't Friedrich Hartmann."

"I know," I say.

"Then why'd you let him think she could be Finn's?"

"There's a chance. The timing, it's just not one hundred percent certain. You know?"

"You could have lied," Fritz offers.

"I'm not the lying type, Fritz."

"Yeah. I'm starting to see that," Fritz says with a small smile. "He's upset. Let him calm down. He'll come around." Then his nose scrunches up. "What is that smell?"

I stand to get close to them. "That is Miss Addy needing a new diaper. But, shit. In all the chaos, I didn't grab a diaper bag. I guess I'll have to brave the reporters."

"No. I'll have Everett get everything we need."

"Everett?"

"My security guard," Fritz explains.

That's rock bottom. I didn't even bother to get the other man's name who protected my daughter and me today. I'm not handling any of this right.

I give Fritz a list of supplies, and Everett goes shopping.

In the meantime, I do my best to clean Addy up with dampened toilet paper and rinse her in the kitchen sink.

"But you don't have a diaper yet," Fritz protests.

"I'm not leaving her in a dirty one while we wait for Everett, Fritz."

"What if she, uh"—he points at Addy's naked bum while I dry it—"you know, goes again?"

I laugh. "Well, we pray she doesn't. And if she does, oh well. We wash again."

"Right."

I dry Addy off, wrap her in a towel, and hand her to Fritz. "Can you hold her for a bit? I have to run to the restroom."

"No, wait," he protests but grabs on to Addy anyway. "What if she goes again?"

I shrug. "Then she goes."

When I come back out, Fritz is glaring at me. A wet trail begins on his shirt and almost reaches his jeans. I roar with laughter. I can't help it—and lord, I need the laugh right now. He looks so angry, glaring between the baby and me, but it only makes me laugh more. He tries handing her to me, but I shake my head.

"That's your *tío*, Fritz," I tell Addy.

"Uncle?" Fritz asks.

I blink at him. "You speak Spanish?"

"Not fluently," he says and looks down at Addy with a mocking glare, but his lips are already melting into a smile. "My niece just peed on me."

"Oh, relax. It washes out."

32

BREN

The phone on the coffee table blares again. I have over twenty missed calls, most of them from Roger wanting a statement for our publicity team to offer the press. Everyone wants to know if Sofia's daughter is mine.

Get in line. Fuck if I know.

My stomach twists into knots. What if I am her father? Then I'm the asshole who just kicked her and her mother out. I run my hand over my face, defeated. I came back for Sofia. To apologize. To win her back. To be with her again.

It wasn't supposed to be like this.

If she's right, and Addy is mine, I have a hell of a lot of more apologizing to do—the things I said . . .

"Yes?" Andreas says on the first ring.

"Bring the car around."

"On it. Where to?"

"I have to go back for Sofia—"

"Um . . ."

"What is it?"

"She's still here."

"What?" I shoot up to my feet. "What do you mean? I thought Fritz and Everett took her home?"

"No. Everett's with me. We've been here the entire time. No orders to take Sofia anywhere."

What the actual fuck? I toss the phone on the couch and storm to the elevator. Getting off on Fritz's floor, I stomp to his door and pound on the door. Fritz opens up.

"Is she here?" I hiss.

Fritz nods.

"Let me in," I demand.

"Your daughter peed on me," he deadpans.

This asshole thinks he's funny. "Fritz, let me in."

"No," Fritz says calmly.

"Fritz, I swear to god, it's not the time to—"

"You can see them when you're calmer."

Them. It isn't just Sofia anymore. It's them. I run a frustrated hand through my hair, pulling it back. "I'm calm."

Fritz studies me, then shuts the door on my face. I hear some muffled sounds, and he comes back.

"You can't shout around Addy," he says.

"I won't—"

"You did earlier," Fritz interrupts.

My teeth grind together. "I'm sorry. It won't happen again," I say.

Fritz's eyes narrow, but he makes no move to open the door any wider.

"Why is she in your apartment, Fritz?"

"She had nowhere to go—her place is swarmed with reporters. She doesn't want to go there right now."

Fuck. Of course she wouldn't want to be there right now. I should have thought of that, but I'm not thinking straight. "Right," I say. Then I call out over Fritz's head. "Sofia, I'm calm now. Please come back upstairs. Both of you."

Her delicate hand opens the door wider. She's been right

next to him the entire time. My stomach lurches, thinking that she sought refuge with Fritz instead of me. But what else was she going to do? I kicked her out, didn't I?

"I don't have a sitter, Bren. We can talk again when I can have someone pick Addy up."

I blink at her then look down at the baby in her arms. "You don't need a sitter. Please come up."

Sofia chews her bottom lip then looks between Fritz and me, and I hate that she thinks of him as an option for safety and comfort right now. "You won't yell again?" she asks.

I shake my head sadly. "I won't yell."

"I won't have shouting around Addy. Do you hear me? One more outburst from you and that's it. We are gone for good."

"I promise I won't shout. Now please. Come upstairs with me."

WE STRETCH A BLANKET IN FRONT OF THE TV, AND AUDREY entertains herself with some cartoon about a pig family of some sort.

I make good on my promise and keep calm while we talk for the rest of the evening.

"Sofia, the things I said earlier—"

"You were upset. I get it."

"Still, I owe you an apology for what I said, and especially for how I said it. Yes, I was hurting, but that doesn't give me the right to speak to you like that, and I'm so incredibly sorry."

"Thank you."

I take her hand in mine, feeling soothed by their presence now. I don't understand how I can be so angry one minute and yet feel like I'm exactly where I'm meant to be.

"Bren?"

"Yeah?"

"Do you need a paternity test?"

I try to smile at her, but it's forced. "I'm sorry, Sofia. It didn't come out right earlier, but yeah. If you would be willing, I need to know. I wish I didn't need to know, but even if that were the case, Finn has a right to know if she's his. He'd want to know."

She smiles sadly, and I know I hurt her with this one request. "I'm sorry," I say.

"Don't be. You have every right to be sure. And you're right about Finn too."

"What if she's Finn's?" I ask.

She shakes her head. "She's not."

"But just humor me. What if she is Finn's?"

"I doubt it, but if she were Finn's, I'd at least try to tell him."

I smile sadly at her. "If she's his, he would want to know. He's a good man. He'd show up."

"You think so?"

"I know so."

We both grow quiet as I contemplate that possibility and what it could mean for us. Maybe I'm a petty man, but I can't see myself with her while she shares a child with Finn. My stomach gets hot just at the thought of the lives they would share. Then there's the much bigger 'what if.' What if sharing a daughter were to bring them closer together and then they ended up trying to make a family together? That would kill me for sure. Watching my best friend with the love of my life.

"Hey." Sofia brings a hand up to my cheek. "Get out of your head, Bren. I'm sure she's yours."

"How can you be so sure?"

She shrugs. "Call it a mother's intuition." She bites the

inside of her lip before speaking again. "Do you want her to be yours?" she asks almost shyly.

"Yes," I say, not hesitating so much as a second, and Sofia beams up at me.

"Really?"

I close my eyes and draw Sofia into my side. "I want this. You. Us. Addy. A family. It's what I wanted then, and it's what I want now. But I need to know. You understand?"

"I do," she says. "Now let's play out that scenario. The paternity test comes back showing you are her dad. Then what?"

"Let's take this one step at a time."

"No, Bren. If she's yours, I'm afraid you'll bring up . . ."

"What?" I ask.

"Old questions."

"You mean, I'll propose again?"

She hesitates before answering. "Yeah. I'm afraid you'll propose again."

"You don't want me to?" I ask.

She shakes her head. "I told you then I'd never change my mind about marriage. And it's true. I haven't changed my mind."

"Can we have a life together, though? A family? Just us? No one else?"

"I've always wanted that with you, Bren. You just couldn't see it."

"Wanted? Past tense?"

"Still do," she amends.

ADDY AND SOFIA STAY OVER, AND ADDY SLEEPS BETWEEN US ON my California king-sized bed. I don't sleep a wink, worried I'll roll over and crush her, even though Sofia reassures me

I won't. So I spend the night awake, watching my girls sleep.

They both snore.

Addy's is softer, but not unlike her Mom's. God, I need this little girl to be mine. It feels like . . . like I love her already.

AFTER SPEAKING TO ROGER THE FOLLOWING MORNING, HE arranges for a paternity test. A nurse does a house call, takes our samples, and leaves with promises he will expedite the results.

My next order of business is to have Andreas shop for a crib. The genius returns with a box we have to build ourselves. When he says it isn't part of his job description to do handyman work, I offer a generous Christmas bonus if he helps. Sofia only mildly laughs at us as we try to put the crib together.

Sofia never leaves the room as she makes many calls for business and to friends to help get her things to the penthouse. I smile when she sends nervous glances my way when she speaks to her business partner. I'll never be happy about that partnership; I'm already thinking of ways to dissolve it. I think I could pair up with her manager, Joe, to buy back *La Oficina*. Then she asks her sitter, Lola, to go to her place and bring back clothes for her and supplies for Addy, who goes through more diaper changes than I could have imagined possible. When she asks for a car and security for Lola, I smile, proud she asks so easily. This can work.

Everything is falling into place, and all that's left is to wait a couple of days for test results that I'm starting to realize don't matter.

Fritz sits me down at one point and asks me if I'm blind.

That child is mine. He has a point. Addy does have a lot of Sofia in her, but also a lot of me.

Andreas leaves when the crib is set up, and we are both damned proud of ourselves.

"I think that earned you a brewski," Sofia says, handing me a cold one and a bacon sandwich expertly plated like the food at the bar, with stacks of chips.

"My angel," I say.

I'm amazed how she can multitask like this. She handles business, the baby, and keeps her damn cool. I have to remind myself she's been doing this for a year. Now I just hope I can be a source of help and relief for her. Not more stress.

"You haven't held her again," she says as I finish my sandwich.

"I haven't?" I ask.

Sofia shakes her head.

I think back to Addy in my arms and how she started fussing as soon as I grabbed her, even though she's so calm the rest of the time.

"I don't think she likes me," I say finally.

"She doesn't know you, that's all. I don't introduce strangers to her, so it's new. You'll need to give her some time to understand you're not a stranger."

"I know. I think we both need time to adjust."

"Here," Sofia says. "Stand up."

"What?"

"Stand up. When you have her, cradle her a little. She likes that."

Sofia hands me Addy before I can come up with a good excuse to get me out of it. I follow her advice and sway a little to cradle her a bit, but Addy's little head turns, trying to find her mom, and she reaches for Sofia, fussing. "See? She doesn't like me," I say and try giving her back, but Sofia steps away. "Sofia, take her. She's going to cry."

She shakes her head. "Nope. Sorry."

Addy keeps tracking Sofia with her eyes, wanting the hell away from me. "Sofia!" I hiss under my breath, mindful I'm not supposed to yell, but Sofia only laughs.

"Sorry. This is the only way."

"What do I do? What do I say?"

"Try singing to her."

My eyes snap up to Sofia again. "What?"

"She loves *Industrial November*. That will soothe her."

I blink at this woman. "You play her our stuff?"

She nods.

"Sofia, some of those songs aren't appropriate for a baby!" I whisper-snap.

Sofia busts out laughing. "Bren, it's okay. She doesn't understand what the lyrics mean."

Addy is on the verge of crying, I just know it, and I panic. "Sofia! She's going to cry. Please," I beg.

"'Girl from Kansas City' is her new favorite," she says with a grin and sits down, not at all intending to help me out.

Addy, for her part, keeps stretching out her arms toward Sofia. I change the tempo to a softer one, but I sing her the song Sofia suggested—a lullaby remix.

"FRONT ROW CENTER,
   Girl from Kansas City
   My tormentor

ADDY'S LITTLE FACE TURNS UP TO LOOK AT ME, HER HEAD COCKED to the side, but she stops fussing for one second. Her gaze freezes up on my face. Her little round face seems confused but also expectant now.

"Keep singing," Sofia says.

"Right. Um . . ."

"WITH HER FULL LIPS, THE SPELL SHE CAST ON ME,
With tequila nights

"SWIMMING IN THE VALLEY
*Sharing Mount Olympus
Dwelling place of gods*

ADDY WIGGLES IN MY GRIP LIKE SHE'S TRYING TO BOUNCE AND starts smiling as I sing.

"WITH HER FULL LIPS, THE SPELL SHE CAST ON ME, *I* WAS BEWITCHED.

"THE GIRL FROM KANSAS CITY
*My tormentor, front row center,
Girl from Kansas City*

BY THE END OF THE SECOND CHORUS, ADDY IS FULL-BLOWN giggling, and she brings her little chubby hands to my face. I kiss one of her palms.

"Hey, little girl," I say, and Addy beams up at me, then bounces on my arm again.

Sofia throws her head back with laughter, and I blink up at her.

"She wants you to keep singing," Sofia explains.

So I do. I perform the entire album like a lullaby—bleeping out the curse words—and little Addy bounces in my arms, what I now understand to be her form of dancing, and giggles the entire time.

She is tuckered out by the end, and I lay her down in her brand new crib for a nap.

"That was so wrong," I say to Sofia when we are alone.

"What?"

"Of all the songs you could have played her."

"I've played here all your stuff, Bren. And let's face it. With what you write about, if I had to sensor what I could play her, I'd be left with, like, two songs. Tops."

33

SOFIA

I f I didn't have to think about Addy and her safety, the
security detail would seem obnoxious. Everett now drives
us everywhere, not that we venture out often, and never
drops eyes from us. Once he is assigned to our security detail, I
do my best to get to know the man but fail miserably.

He is a man of few words. He is tall, muscular, and handsome—very military type. When I ask, he confirms he is a
former marine but declines to provide any further details.
Instead, he reassures me that he is more than capable of the job,
as if that is the reason for my questions.

I'll never get used to Bren's lifestyle. That's for sure.

Bren reassures me Everett is temporary until we can vet and
hire someone else, then he can go back to his original assign-
ment with Fritz. Despite the security company having someone
ready to start now, Bren is being paranoid and insists on doing
independent background checks, stalling the process even
further.

At this rate, Everett will be driving Addy to college, and poor
Fritz will be left to his own devices. Though from what I hear,

Fritz is the least troublesome in the band, so I doubt he needs a security guard to begin with.

Then the emails start flooding in.

After the first scathing message, I decide I won't tell Bren. But then there is a third. After half a day, I have collected twenty emails that would seem to be from the same person, if it weren't for the unique originating addresses.

Bren is chatting with Andreas when I finally work up the courage to show him.

"What is it?" he asks when he sees my concerned face. "Andreas? Give us a moment?"

"No. Andreas should stay," I say.

"Yes, ma'am," he says, and both men watch me set my laptop on the coffee table.

I upload my work email and turn the laptop so they can read the screen. "I've been getting these emails from some of your fans. At first, I thought I should just ignore them, but they're getting a little out of hand."

Bren's brows furrow as he scans through the emails, his jaw tightening further with each click. I take deep breaths, knowing what he is reading.

One fan writes that I should die because I don't deserve a man like Bren, and he is hers. Another calls me a homewrecker because, as far as the fan is concerned, Bren belongs with Emma Johanssen. The rest are variations of calling me awful names or wishing me harm. But the last straw is the email insinuating harm would come not only to me but also to my daughter, in much more graphic language, of course. That last email boiled my blood scathing-hot and forced me to tell Bren.

"I'm so sorry, Sofia," Bren says, looking up at me with apologetic eyes as he stays on the sofa while I stand with my arms crossed.

"Me too. I wasn't going to say anything, but then they mentioned Addy, and that sent me over the edge with anger."

"You should have told me. But you don't need to be scared," Bren says. "Nothing's going to happen to her—"

"I'm not scared something will happen to her. I'm scared someone will try to hurt her, and I'll go to prison for murder."

Andreas snickers until Bren silences him with one look.

"We'll expedite your new security," Bren says. "Andreas? Take care of it?"

"On it," Andreas says before leaving us alone.

Bren stands and pulls me into his arms. My shoulders relax instantly. "There's nothing to worry about."

"Has this happened to you before? With exes?" I ask and look up at his face.

Bren nods. "Yeah. This is very common. But please don't let them get what they want," he says.

"I won't," I say.

WE STILL DON'T HAVE THE PATERNITY TEST RESULTS THE following day, and I still haven't left Bren's penthouse. Everything starts to feel like I'm getting caged in, and Addy can sense it. She hasn't been out in fresh air in a long time, and she was used to our daily walks in the park. She is starting to fuss more than usual, and it is affecting both our sleep.

"When you and Fritz go to meet the producers at the recording studio tonight, do you mind if I have a friend over?"

"A friend?" Bren asks.

"Yeah. Lola misses Addy, and it'd be great to ask her to get a few more things from my place."

"Of course you can have friends over, Sofia. I want you to feel at home here."

"Thank you."

"Everett will stay here with you, and I'll have Andreas drop us off at the studio then pick up Lola, so she doesn't have to get around on her own." Bren pauses and rubs his bottom lip. "Actually, we may be having a lot of people over soon."

I raise an eyebrow in question.

"Roger called. Adrian and Karl are coming to KC."

"To record?"

"To stay. I mean, temporarily. But yeah, we're thinking of recording here. Roger got Adrian an apartment here, so Fritz and I can keep an eye on him."

"And Karl?" I ask about their guitar player.

Bren rolls his eyes. "He wants to party, so he's renting a secluded property where he can raise hell."

I laugh.

"I guess your band's been preparing you for fatherhood for a long time, haven't they?"

"Don't *you* start with that," Bren says. "I don't need you encouraging the guys to keep calling me *Dad*."

WHEN I CALL AND ASK LOLA TO COME VISIT, SHE IS ALL TOO excited. I ask her to run errands and pick up things for me so I can also have an excuse to throw a little money her way. I know she needs it.

So when the front desk rings up to say a friend is downstairs and asking to come up, I don't think twice about it.

When I get to the elevator doors to greet her, it is a different blond who steps out into the foyer.

The tall, Swedish bombshell squares her shoulders as she eyes me up and down. She wears a curve-hugging, cream-colored dress. Her perfectly styled waves cascade down the pale gold skin of her naked shoulders, and her beautiful green eyes never leave me.

What a great time for me to be wearing sweats, a messy bun, and have a crusted milk stain on my t-shirt because I haven't had a chance to change from Addy's spill earlier in the day. This is my life. I force my spine rigid and do my best to fake the confidence Emma exudes. "Can I help you?" I say after we size each other up.

"I'm Em—"

"Emma Johanssen. Yes, I know," I say and do my best to smile and offer her my hand. She looks at it for a moment before shaking it. "I'm Sofia. Nice to meet you."

"You as well." Emma looks uncomfortably around the space, no doubt for Bren.

"I'm afraid Bren is out, and he may be a while. You're welcome to wait for him here if you'd like."

Emma's face falls for a second before she looks behind her at the elevator doors as if deciding what to do, then faces me again. "Would that be all right?"

"Of course," I say.

Emma makes herself at home in the living room at the same time that the baby monitor goes off with Addy starting to cry. Then Emma's eyes fix on the monitor, and I don't miss her wide eyes. "I'll be right back," I say.

I run to the spare bedroom Bren has haphazardly turned into the baby room, then take Addy into Bren's room where I change into one of his workout shirts because I have no clean ones left. When I get back to the living room with Addy in my arms, Emma springs up to her feet.

"So you are *the* Sofia from the song?" she asks, her eyes boring holes at Addy's back.

I smile. "Guilty," I say. "At least, I think I am."

"And the baby . . . is Bren's?"

I shift my weight from one foot to the other. "I think you should talk with Bren. It feels a bit . . . odd, being the inter-mediary."

Emma nods. "To tell you the truth, I'm not sure why I'm here. My agent called me to warn me of an oncoming media circus headed my way, and I was on my way from New York to LA for work." Emma's eyes glisten, and the tip of her nose turns red, but she sniffs back her tears. "I guess I needed to know if it was true that Bren has had a baby with someone. And, well, I guess he did." She laughs then, trying to play off the hurt.

I stand there for a long moment, unsure of what to do.

"I really messed things up with Bren," Emma says. "And he's one of the good ones. It's clearly too late for us now."

"I'm sorry, I don't know what to say," I admit.

She laughs again, though she lets a tear out, wiping it swiftly away. "Are you together now? One big happy family?"

I look away from her. I know why she is asking. She wants him back. But the truth is, I have no idea what we are. Since he has learned about Addy, Bren and I have slept in the same bed, but it's been platonic. Though we have never discussed it, part of me thinks he is waiting for the paternity test before committing to a relationship with all this baggage. I don't push the matter because I understand his apprehension, but damn it! That has left us standing on uncertain ground, and I have no idea how to answer Emma. "I'm sorry," I say finally. "But you should really talk to Bren. He's a very private person, and he has the right to decide how much to tell you. I shouldn't get in the way of that."

She nods, almost approving of my answer. "May I look at her?" Emma asks.

I turn Addy around in my arms so she can face her, and Emma takes a few steps toward her. Addy giggles and wiggles in my arms. "I think she thinks you're my friend Lola," I tell Emma. "She has long blond hair too, though hers is curly. I wouldn't get too close if I were you. She likes pulling on Lola's hair."

Emma smiles sweetly at my daughter. "She has Bren's eyes," she says, and I smile at her. "I don't think I'll wait after all. Say hi to him for me, will you?"

"I'll tell him you stopped by."

Then Emma's eyes lock with mine. "He's one of the good ones—the best one. If you let him go a second time, I don't plan on giving him up again."

Once she is gone, I realize she said 'again.' Emma knew about me before the media got wind of me. Bren told her about me. She knew I broke his heart, and she is warning me not to do it again.

BREN

When we wrap up our meeting with the producers, Fritz and I head back to my penthouse, and his eyes grow wide at the sight of a beautiful young blond sitting on my couch.

"Lola, right?" I say as we walk up to her.

She does a doubletake, then shoots up to her feet to greet us. "Yeah. Nice to see you again, Bren."

"Where's Sofia?"

"Putting Addy down for the night."

"Right. Oh, this is—"

"Fritz. Yeah. I know," Lola says, then clears her throat. "Sorry, Friedrich."

Fritz takes her hand and eyes her carefully. "Fritz, please," he says.

"Want a beer, Fritz?" I ask him.

He nods but says nothing. I walk toward the kitchen as I yell behind me to ask Lola if she wants anything, but Sofia is back and nearly yelling at Fritz and me.

"She's not old enough to drink a beer," she snaps. "Fritz! One word: Jailbait."

I shake my head and snicker as I join them and hand Fritz his beer. To his credit, Fritz nails his gaze to his shoes after that.

Lola looks like she wants the earth to swallow her whole, and she is shooting Sofia daggers with her glare. It's a little funny.

"Sorry," Fritz says. "Won't happen again."

Then Lola jumps in, looking at Fritz. "It wouldn't have worked out anyway," she says. "I once saw an interview where you claimed the *New York Dolls* were better than *Iggy and the Stooges*. I fell out of love with you right then and there."

Fritz's jaw slackens with the surprise of her statement, sending both Lola and Sofia into a fit of laughter. "When exactly do you turn eighteen?" he asks with interest.

"And on that note," Sofia says, ushering Lola out and into the elevator, "Andreas will take you back home now."

Fritz leaves shortly after, and for the first time since Sofia quasi-moved in, it feels awkward. Without the buffer of Lola and Fritz, she has a hard time so much as looking at me. Something happened while we were out—of that much, I am sure.

"Everything okay?" I ask.

She nods and busies herself with picking up toys off the floor and tidying up the place.

"Sofia, look at me," I say as I follow her around the room until she stops to face me. "What happened?"

"You had a visitor," she says.

My brows furrow. I wasn't expecting anyone. "Who?"

"Emma." Sofia's gaze drops from me and lands on her hands, where she squeezes a small stuffed elephant.

"Emma?"

"Yeah. She was in New York when news about Addy broke, and she wanted to see if it was true."

"Sofia . . ."

"Do you still love her?" she asks as she forces her eyes on mine.

"No. I haven't loved her for a long time."

"She seemed to think she could get you back."

"She can't," I reassure her.

Sofia lets out a long breath and sits on the couch, so I take the spot next to her. "What's going on through that pretty little head of yours, huh?" I ask with as soothing a tone as I'm capable of.

"Bren, what are we?"

I blink at her. Where is this coming from? Things have been great since we both agreed to the paternity test. "What do you mean?" I ask.

"I thought we were . . . before you knew about Addy, I thought you wanted to reconnect. I don't feel that anymore. Granted, I know everything is about Addy now, but I need to know. Is a future together no longer part of what you want?"

"Sofia." I scratch my jaw. She's right. We are in limbo. Do I want her back? Fuck, yes. But am I afraid of saying that and then not be able to back out if Addy turns out to be Finn's? Probably. It might make me an asshole, I know that, but I can't change how I feel. "Listen," I say, "we've been through the wringer. Let's take things one step at a time. Once we get the test results and Roger can give a statement to the press, things will calm down. I'll feel better when you two have your own security sorted. Then we can start to build on this. Okay?"

"That's a rather vague and politically correct answer that covers all your bases, isn't it?"

"Sofia, I—"

"Hey, don't worry about it." Her smile is lopsided. "I understand that if you're not her dad, you will want nothing to do with us."

"That's not what I said."

"You didn't have to, Bren."

She gets up and walks down the hall to Addy's room. I've realized whenever she needs an emotional boost, Sofia likes to be around her daughter, as if merely by looking at her, she has all the answers.

I follow her into the mostly dark room save for one night light. Sofia stands over the crib, watching Addy's little chest rise and fall with each breath, her puny hands balled up at her sides. I wrap my arms around Sofia from behind until her head leans back on my chest, and I squeeze her tight.

We stand there for a long moment looking at our daughter, because yes, Addy already feels like mine, even if I can't admit it to Sofia—or to myself.

I can't say it out loud because I'm a coward and afraid. I'm afraid not so much because of Finn, but afraid to lose them—afraid to lose the family I'm clinging to. "It'll get better. I promise," I whisper into her ear. Sofia only nods. "Would you like to decorate this room? Maybe something Addy will like better?" I try to lighten the subject and redirect her emotions.

"No," Sofia says. "This is perfect."

"White walls?"

She nods and breaks free from my embrace. She walks over to a small table next to the changing table I had Andreas buy (prebuilt) and clicks a button on a projector.

A constellation of stars floods the dark room with changing light colors from red to green, then blue and purple, rotating every ten seconds. Every inch of her room is covered in constellations with colorful nebulas.

Sofia smiles wide at me—stars spanning the length of her face. "Easiest and cheapest decorating device ever," she says. "And Addy goes nuts for it."

"You've been really resourceful, haven't you?" I ask.

Sofia nods. "I have to be."

My heart squeezes when I think of everything I could have given them if only I had known of Addy's existence. I know Sofia is a smart businesswoman, but the fact that she had to sell half her bar told me she did that because she had to provide for someone else on top of her mother and grandmother. She's been tight with money when I could have offered them the world.

I'm such an ass.

BY LUNCHTIME THE NEXT DAY, SOFIA IS BACK TO NORMAL. SHE doesn't bring up Emma again after I reassure her that I will not be connecting with her ever again, which she seems to believe, so the strain lifts from both our shoulders.

Addy sits next to me in her highchair, squishing banana between her fingers and playing with the fruit before eating it from her hands. Babies are a mess.

Sofia and I order Pad Thai from a restaurant nearby after I convince her she should take a break from cooking for a day and relax. The afternoon starts off easy, and I could get used to having my family at my table every damn day of my life.

But the mood shifts when both mine and Sofia's phones ping with a text message from the lab informing us the results are in and have been emailed to both of us.

Sofia pushes her plate away, her eyes glued to the screen in her hands. "You got the message?" she asks.

I nod. "Sofia. Look at me, please." When she does, her eyes are glistening, and I want to lunge forward over the table and take her in my arms to beg her not to cry, but I can't. I swallow the lump in my throat hard, but my throat is dry. "I'm sorry, I have to know, I—"

"I know, Bren," she says. "I don't begrudge your need to know. I understand. And if I'm wrong, Finn has to know."

I nod again and scroll through my phone until I find the email from the lab. Next to me, Addy giggles and outstretches her hand, full of mashed banana, in a way that seems like an offering, and I laugh. When I don't take it, she shoves it in her mouth and blinks at me. God, I need this little girl to be mine. I love her. And I love her mom.

Looking up at Sofia, and with a shaky voice, I speak again. "Please forgive me for this, Sofia." I open the email.

I skim through the first page that includes Addy's and my full name and some laboratory numbers until I get to the section I need to read:

Conclusion: Based on our analysis, it is proven with >99.9999% certainty that Mr. Brenner Reindhart is the biological father of Audrey Michelle Ocampo Reindhart.

My sight gets blurry with the welling tears, and my gaze snaps up to Addy. Her little head cocks to the side as she looks at me, and I stand to pick her up in my arms. I hold her tight and don't even care when a tear rolls down my cheek.

My eyes draw closed as I let the news sink in. "You're my little girl," I whisper as I rock her in my arms from side to side. "And I'm going to protect you from the world," I promise.

"Can you watch her? I need a minute," Sofia says.

"Sure."

She hurries to the guest bathroom, and when she takes too long, Addy and I make our way to the door to make sure she's okay, but the sobbing makes it past the door before we even reach it.

I knock softly. "Sofia, please. Come out here."

"Just a second," she says.

When she comes out, the sight of her red-rimmed eyes and rosy nose breaks my heart. "Sofia—"

"I'm all right, Bren. That was a lot to take in. As sure as I was about this, I still sometimes wondered, and it's good to know."

"It is?" I ask, hopeful.

"Yeah. Oh my goodness! You have banana all over your shirt. Here, give her over. I'll clean her up, and you go change."

Sofia needs a bit of space to lick her wounds, and I do my best to give her what she needs. After I change, I go downstairs to tell Fritz the good news. The oaf just blinks at me like I'm not telling him something he didn't already know. "Yeah? Duh."

SOFIA

I've come to understand that Roger, the band's manager, and their public relations team work fast. Within three days of getting the paternity test results, Karl and Adrian settle in their new temporary homes and the press release follows. Then we all have to hide out like hermits.

The first week is chaos. Even from the penthouse, I can see the mass of reporters and paparazzi casing the entrance. It isn't until the second week, when every news outlet and blog delivered the same sensational story, that their numbers dwindle, and thank god, because Addy and I are going insane only staying inside. "We're like princesses in a tower," I joke to my daughter.

There is a change in Bren those few weeks too. The way he looks at me, with big wondrous eyes, or when I catch him daydreaming as he watches Addy play and giggle.

He's been hell-bent on getting her to walk, and while she can stand and giggles when we applaud and encourage her, she has yet to take a step. If either of us tries to guide her forward, she throws her weight back to the floor until her diaper-clad rump lands with a soft thump.

But Bren keeps trying.

I chew on my piece of bacon as I stare at him in his sweats, slung low on his hips, as he runs around picking up after our daughter or redirecting her from crawling away to another room. He is shirtless, his expansive chest and rippling abdominals displaying playful wisps of black hair. I lick my lips and keep stuffing bacon and eggs into my mouth. I've gained four pounds since coming over to Bren's, and I blame him.

We've been here over three weeks total, sleeping in the same bed, with no sex—not even after the paternity results came back.

And yet, somehow, we're more intimate than we've ever been. He holds me all night, every night, as he asks me questions about Addy and me before he came back into the picture. He wants to know everything about her birth, her personality, what our life was like, and we talk for hours every night, mostly him asking questions and me answering them.

Then we just sleep, unless Addy keeps us up, which is rare anymore.

And sure, before he came back, I didn't exactly have an active sex life—or one at all—but that night we were here in this apartment before he knew about his daughter, he'd opened up an insatiable beast that I'd forced into hibernation for nearly two years when he'd had his way with my body.

And the beast is famished now.

I need to get a babysitter but getting Bren to agree to let Audrey out of our sight would surely prove difficult, especially after I showed him those emails from his so-called fans.

"Are you okay?" Bren asks, looking up at me.

"What?" I ask through a mouth full of food.

"You're forgetting to chew, *Schatzi*," he says, and I blink at him. I can't remember the last time he called me by his weird little endearment for me.

Then I try chewing and realize the last three bites I took are building in my cheek. I chew vigorously and gulp it down.

"Everything okay?" Bren asks.

"Yep. Watch her?" I don't give him a chance to reply before I shoot up to run to the bathroom. I turn on the shower to cold and jump in, welcoming the shock to my skin and my system.

"WHERE'S ADDY?" I ASK WHEN BREN FINDS ME GETTING DRESSED in our room.

"Napping."

As I towel my hair, Bren approaches me until his naked chest is flush against my back, and he can wrap his arms around my waist. "What's wrong, *Schatz*?"

It's been so long. I decide to be honest, because staying quiet and making no moves is getting me nowhere. "I'm horny, Bren. And you need to put a damned shirt on when you're walking around the house being a great father and provider. My Neanderthal brain kicks in wanting you."

A chuckle rumbles low, caressing the side of my ear. "I'm sorry. I haven't done a good job with all my responsibilities, have I?"

I shake my head. "No, Bren. That's not it. You have. You've been nothing but wonderful to Addy, to me—"

"But I need to take care of you too," he says before lifting his hand to cup my breast. "I miss your body, Sofia."

"You do? You haven't said . . . or done anything."

"I'm too good at compartmentalizing. It's hard for me to multitask. I've been so preoccupied trying to be the best father, I completely forgot I have to be the best partner too."

I spin around so I can take in his beautiful face. "Partner?"

Bren nods. "Yes."

"You still want that?"

"I could kill myself if I haven't made that clear yet."

"Oh," is all I manage to say.

He hasn't changed his mind. He doesn't want just his daughter; he still wants us—both of us.

His hand travels down to the hem of my shirt, but before he can work it off me, Addy cries softly from the baby monitor I didn't realize he'd set on the dresser. He lets his head fall until our foreheads meet and chuckles. "We should get a sitter and have a proper date soon," he says.

"You want to date? Aren't we doing this a bit backward? A baby before dating?"

"When have we been conventional, Sofia? All that matters is that I love you. And I hope you love me."

"I do," I hasten to say. "I love you, *tonto.*"

Then he walks out of the room, and I follow to watch that perfectly chiseled man, shirtless, as he cradles his daughter in his arms, holding her bottle for her. I take my phone out and snap a picture of this perfect scene, the moment right after he told me he loves me.

He still loves me.

Halfway through feeding Addy, Bren's phone dings, and he answers the call. "Who was that?" I ask from my place doing dishes.

"Roger. He wants a band meeting tonight. Mind if I step out this evening?"

I laugh. "You don't have to ask permission, Bren. God knows I won't ask you for permission to do my thing when it comes to *La Oficina.*"

Maybe that was the wrong thing to say because Bren is scowling when I look behind me.

"Right," he says and places Addy back in her new playpen.

Bren goes off to his band meeting, and I take the opportunity to check on the bar. It's Wednesday night, and shouldn't be too busy. I'm delighted when it's Ileana who picks up the phone.

"Sofia! We haven't seen you in ages," she says warmly.

"I know. I'm sorry. I miss you," I say.

"Will we see you around soon?"

"I don't know. I'd hate to put *La Oficina* under any more public scrutiny. Tell me the truth, Ileana. David's been vague with his responses so far. How bad is it?"

"I won't lie to you. The press was bad that first week, but when they got the idea neither you nor Bren would be showing your faces, they died out. We get an occasional straggler here and there, but Joe handles it great."

My shoulders relax, knowing I haven't done any real damage. I still rely on the bar income for our living expenses. "Business reports have been great," I say.

"Yeah. It's picked up a little. That first week was chaotic. Everyone and their mother showed up, trying to get a glimpse of Brenner Reindhart. But their poor little hearts could only take so much disappointment, so that crowd died down for the most part, and now we are back to our regulars."

I smile with pride, grateful my little place managed to retain its heart. Though with Joe and Ileana, I knew my first baby would be in excellent hands while I took care of my second baby.

"Listen, Ileana, if you aren't working there tomorrow night, you think you could sit for Addy in the evening? I can take her to your place and pick her up. Won't be too late."

"Hot date?" Ileana asks, and I can just envision her wiggling her eyebrows, so I laugh. I miss her face. I miss working. I miss leaving these damn walls.

"From your lips to God's ears," I tease, and she laughs.

"Listen, it's picking up, and Joe's glaring at me, so I gotta go. But yeah, I'd love to have Addy, and so would Isael. You know I always wanted him to have a little sister, and Addy's probably as close as he'll ever get."

"I'll let you go then. And Ileana? Thank you," I say. She's

never declined a request to sit, though, probably because I don't abuse that ask.

Not long after I hang up with Ileana, Bren comes back from his meeting.

"You weren't as long as I thought you'd be," I say with a smile that fades when I take in Bren's angry features. "What's wrong?" I ask.

"Karl didn't show," he hisses. "Fritz and I are heading over to his place to drag him out by his little blond ponytail if we have to."

I can't begin to understand the kind of pressure Bren is under. If I didn't get along with an employee or someone slacked off, I could fire them and hire someone new. But Bren doesn't have that luxury. I decide I'll be the supportive partner he deserves.

"Can Addy and I come with?" I ask.

"You want to go with us to Karl's?"

I nod. "Addy's a fantastic buffer for bad tempers, and we really—and I do mean really—need to get out of these walls. We're starting to feel like caged animals.

Bren scratches the back of his head. "It's only six, so I doubt he's up to any real trouble so early in the evening. Sure. We'll have Andreas and Everett both come with us."

Whatever it takes, I think, but just smile at him as I run to take Addy in my arms before he has a chance to change his mind.

I GASP WHEN WE GET TO THE GATES OF THE MANSION ON THE outskirts of Kansas City. It's beyond a mansion; this must be what people say when referring to a property as an estate, like for royalty and shit. I get a sweet flashback to Napa.

I worry for all of one minute that Karl will squander his money in idiotic ways like this, then laugh inwardly. He can probably afford to live in this type of luxury for three lifetimes and still not be able to spend down his fortune.

Unfortunately, the inside isn't quite as lovely as the outside. Roger has given us the codes to get in, predicting correctly that Karl won't open up. Only one word can describe what we find inside:

Hell.

The trash, debris, empty bottles, and sticky stains from at least a week's worth of partying are scattered over every surface, floor, nook, and cranny of the main floor.

I almost want to weep at the sight of such a lovely place trashed like this. The black marble floors and every surface are covered in trash and food. An enormous floor-to-ceiling slab of quartz is the entryway's focal point, encasing a double-sided fireplace. The glass covering the fireplace is smeared, with . . . something. When I glance at the high ceiling, I wince at the sight of an intricate and modern chandelier with a red bra hanging from it. This should be a crime.

"What a *schwein*," Bren mutters under his breath.

"Guess he's not home," I say when Karl doesn't materialize at the intrusion.

"Oh, he's home," Fritz says. "He's sleeping." Fritz throws me a wicked grin and runs up one side of the twin staircases two steps at a time, I presume to find Karl and drag him back down-stairs by the ear.

I shake my head, and Bren catches sight of it.

"Sorry you have to see this," he says with his own shake of the head.

"I own a bar. I've seen rowdy," I say. "But this . . . is extreme. Though really, I'm most upset about the house. It's spectacular, and now it's so . . ." I trail off, looking for the right word.

"So what?" Bren asks with interest.

"Defiled," I say at the same time Fritz descends the steps with a groggy Karl slouching behind him.

Bren's eyes darken when he takes him in, and I act quickly. "Here," I say and hand him Addy before he can decline the baby handoff. *I'm getting really good at this*, I think to myself.

But Addy serves her purpose, and Bren, I can tell, forces himself not to curse or scream.

"What are you doing, Karl?"

"I was sleeping," he says, mocking Bren, whose nostrils flare to the point where I can almost see the steam coming out of them. It's quite a funny visual with him holding a baby, but I don't laugh.

"You need to clean up your act. Or do we have to find yet another guitarist?" Bren asks.

Before Karl can answer, Fritz speaks up with a more tactful approach. "You're talented, Karl. We don't want to lose you. We gave you the first year of touring to party and let loose because we know what it's like. We've been there. But when it came down to it, we all got down to business. And you're not, man. You're fucking up."

"Language in front of Addy," Bren hisses.

As if seeing her for the first time, Karl smiles wide. "This must be the first *Industrial November* baby," he says, stepping toward Bren, his arms outstretched. But Bren tucks Addy closer to his body with one arm and stretches out the other to stop Karl midstride.

"Have you even showered?" Bren asks, and Karl hangs his head.

Fritz places a hand on Karl's shoulder. "Go get cleaned up. We'll work on hiring a service to clean up the place, and we'll head back to my place. Roger and Adrian are waiting." Karl winces, and Fritz goes on. "And Roger ain't too happy. You'd better hurry."

"We're going to have to vet a service that'll sign an NDA," Bren says, and Fritz nods darkly.

I forget their lives are up for public consumption almost as much as their music.

"In the meantime," Bren says, "what about Lola?"

"What about her?" I ask.

"You think she can clean up around here?"

I take the place in. A job of this magnitude would take one person days. "She's just one person. Karl needs a crew," I say.

"It doesn't have to be perfect. Just have her sort the basics, get all the trash out. Get it going while we vet and process a service to sterilize the damned place."

"I don't know."

"You trust her, don't you?" Fritz asks.

"I wouldn't let her babysit my daughter if I didn't," I say sharply. "I'm hesitant because she's a great person, but only human. This job, it's too big."

"Just the basics to start. I'll make sure Karl pays out the ass for her trouble."

I sigh and take my phone from my back pocket. "Let me give her a call," I say and step outside.

When I wrap up my call, Bren, Fritz, and Karl walk out of the house, all their jaws set.

Fritz stops Karl in his tracks by the shoulder. "What about Pix, man?" he asks.

"Dog walker has her. I'm not a total idiot," Karl says with an eye roll. Fritz only shakes his head.

I'm horrified Karl has a dog in this house that looks more like an environmental hazard than anything else.

"What did Lola say?" Bren asks, ignoring Fritz and Karl.

I nod. "She'll do it, but Karl's paying premium."

"What are you talking about?" Karl asks, looking between us.

"You have a cleaning service coming in the morning," I say and smile darkly. "You're paying her a grand—cash—for eight hours of work, whatever she gets done in that time."

Karl has the decency to hang his head and slouches all the way to the car.

"I can't believe you didn't think to hire maids when you moved in," I say almost as an afterthought.

"I did," Karl whines. "They all quit."

I snicker and look up at Bren.

"I'm not looking forward to Addy as a teenager," I say and laugh when Bren's eyes snap down to inspect his daughter.

"Why'd you have to make my day worse?" he asks.

SOFIA

"I'm sorry I can't take you out on a proper date," Bren says when we get back to his penthouse after dropping Addy off at Ileana's for the evening.

We decide we needed some alone time, a proper date.

"This is life with a baby," I say.

"This is life with a band," he counters.

I press my hand to his chest. "Your band is your first baby."

He holds my hand over his chest and caresses the length of my jaw with his index finger. "You understand me, Sofia."

"Because we're the same," I breathe out. "*Industrial November* is your first child, your first commitment. Mine is *La Oficina.*"

His head dips down to kiss me gently, tenderly, slowly. He sucks my lower lip into his mouth, playing with it on the tip of his tongue. This is so different from the kisses I've known from Bren. This kiss is all emotion and tenderness.

When he pulls away, he's smiling.

"What?" I ask.

He eyes me up and down approvingly, and I return the favor. The dark denim and muscle-hugging, ribbed, long-sleeved shirt he has picked out leave him looking like sex on a stick.

Taking my hand in his, he leads me to the bedroom, where he proceeds to slide down the spaghetti straps of my A-line, emerald-green dress. As he does this, the pads of his fingers draw down the bare skin of my arms.

"Bren." I say his name without thinking, and his eyes lock on mine.

"I want you, Sofia," he says.

I swallow at the sound of that world-famous voice of his, husky with his arousal. "I want you too," I say.

It's been so long since I've had Bren; my instincts are to tear his clothes off and fuck—like we always do—with abandon like animals.

But there's something there, in Bren's eye, something flickering in his irises that I don't recognize. It's not the primal glare I'm at the receiving end of when he wants to fuck me—it's sweeter than that. His hands move slowly over my body as he wraps his arms around me to unzip my dress, and I gasp, every sensation charged tenfold. It's been so long.

When my dress pools at my feet, revealing my naked body because I decided to go bare under the dress, Bren steps back to take me in.

He smiles and groans, bringing his thumb to rub his lower lip. "Fuck, Sofia."

I step forward as slowly as he's moved since we walked into the room, letting him set the pace for tonight and doing my best to tame my hurried and desperate impulses.

I peel off his shirt and unbuckle his belt to help him out of his jeans. God, I've missed the sight of this naked body.

Bren leads me by the hand to the bed. Without pulling away from my lips, he lays me down on the bed with care. He only rises off me once, to step out of his jeans and underwear, then climbs back on top of me.

I feel the hardness of him pressed painfully over my mound, and my pelvis pumps upward, searching for him. Bren's eyes fly open to lock on mine. "Sofia," he whispers, his eyes searching.

"Bren."

"I love you," he says and kisses me again for the longest time. He's silencing me with his mouth, I can tell, afraid I won't say the words back, and tears spring to my eyes. *Oh, Bren, you fool*, I think as he continues to kiss me. *I love you too, you idiot*. Our tongues find each other, and the taste of Bren sends my toes curling against the bedsheets.

We both gasp for air when he finally pulls away from my mouth. I force myself to look him in the eye when I say, "I love you too." I need him to believe me.

Bren pulls away briefly to roll on a condom, then wraps his hands around my face, cupping it like something precious, while at the same time positioning his tip at my entrance.

"Say it again," he pleads.

I oblige. "I love you, Bren."

It's been so long, and I'm so turned on, the cream slicking out of me welcomes him as he toys with my entrance before sliding in slowly—inch by inch.

"I need you," he says gently in my ear, but his voice is so full of emotion; I get the feeling he means so much more with those words than I can possibly imagine.

I fuck. It's what I know how to do.

I'm good at fucking.

But this . . . this is making love, and I have no idea how to do . . . *this*. I'm terrified I won't be any good at it—that I won't be what he wants.

What he needs.

I didn't know love could be expressed beyond the words that always seemed so shallow to me. I thought maybe gestures—actions—for the one you love were the best way to show said love. I had no idea love could be exchanged through the sealing of naked skin against naked skin—that it could be exchanged like a current between two bodies. With every caress, with every gentle kiss, with every dusting of his lips over my shoulder, my collarbone, my breasts, I come alive under Bren's touch. It's more than a physical, sexual awakening. Through our physical connection, Bren reaches deep into my chest to claim my heart as his, and I never want to get it back.

BREN

I surge into the wet warmth of Sofia and watch her eyes go wide as I enter. Her walls clamp down around me, welcoming me in, and my cock twitches at the sensation. My body wants to go into overdrive, to fuck her like I've always fucked her, and for her to fuck me like she always has; quick, rough, and dirty. But I take it slow once I say those three words, and she returns them with sincerity. *I love you.*

The three words that disarm her for the first time since I've known her. Something is different in her tonight, though. With wide eyes, she locks her gaze on mine, like she is doing something she's never done before. She's a little unsure with her touch and a little shy with her words, which is so unlike her. For only one second, I think she might be self-conscious of the changes in her body after having a baby, but that's not Sofia.

So it must be something else.

When her nose turns red and a single tear rolls down the side of her face, she kisses me more sweetly than she ever has, and it hits me like lightning down my spine.

She's never made love before.

Until now.

I'm the first man she's made love to, and I can't fuck this up.

With my thumb, I wipe the tear away, and she turns her head to kiss my hand. I take my time with slow and deep thrusts, pausing and pulling out when I need to before I'm too far gone because fuck, I want this to last forever. Wordlessly, and with our gazes locked, we make love late into the night.

I never imagined I'd be the one to give her a first like this.

I'm the luckiest man alive.

———

SOFIA OCAMPO WILL NEVER SLEEP ANYWHERE THAT IS NOT MY BED again, if I have anything to say about it. I watch her sleep, and I hate that I have to wake her up soon because I could look at her all night. But we made love for hours, and we have to go pick up our daughter soon.

I'll remember this night until the end of my days because tonight was the night Sofia opened up to me. Truly opened up to me. I felt it the moment it happened, the flicker in her eyes as she told me she loves me back.

The love of my life loves me back.

I don't even care if she never wants to get married anymore. So long as I can keep her and Addy. So long as Sofia is my life partner and we can grow old together—that's the only important thing in my life now. I want everything that comes with the marriage, but I don't need the wedding, or the contract, not if it means I can't have her.

———

Her eyes flutter open, and she smiles at me. "We have to go soon, don't we?" she asks. I kiss her forehead and nod.

Sofia sits up and brings the sheet over her breasts, which is strange, then she grabs her phone from the nightstand. "Before we go, there's something I want to show you."

"Oh?"

She takes a deep breath. "I honestly really, really don't want to, but I think I should."

My brow furrows. She's acting strange.

"My Mom was here when Addy was born. She helped me a lot, and she was in the delivery room."

I know my face lights up because Sofia beams at me. She's going to tell me about Addy's entrance into this world. I stay quiet so she can go on.

"And so was my friend Mandy. And Mandy, without my permission," she pauses and rolls her eyes, "had a camera with her."

I shoot up into a sitting position with excitement. "She recorded it?"

The phone goes up to Sofia's chest, where she clutches it. "You are about to see something I wish you wouldn't, and once you do, you can't unsee it. So, Bren, how badly do you want to see the birth of your daughter?"

I caress her arm soothingly. "If I had known, I would have been there, Sofia. There's no doubt in my mind. I'd like to see it if you're okay with it."

She nods and hands me the phone.

I press play to find a different version of Sofia on the screen. Her face is a bit rounder, her hair longer and matted against her face with sweat. Her cheeks are red, and she's panting and screaming between breaths.

"Mandy!" she shrieks, and the camera pans away from Sofia, but the audio recording continues. "Are you filming this?!"

"No, of course not—"

Another shriek rips through Sofia, and I wince at the sound, but it must allow Mandy to bring the camera back to Sofia.

Sofia's mom is at her side, holding Sofia's hand as the doctor asks her to push once more, and Mandy manages to film as Addy's head starts to crown. My stomach grows hot. This is so . . . unnatural. I peer up at Sofia over the phone in awe of her and her strength.

"One more push," the doctor says, and Sofia screams for a longer stretch that time. "This is your fault!" Sofia roars.

Mandy speaks behind the camera. "My fault?"

She screams again, and when she stops, she continues. "Yes! If you hadn't dragged me to that stupid concert, this wouldn't be happening right now!"

"What are you talking about . . ." Mandy trails off. "Wait, don't tell me—"

"If you hadn't forced me to the concert, Bren would never have put a baby in me!"

The camera falls away from Sofia with a thud. Mandy must have dropped the phone. Another long scream follows, not captured on camera. Then Addy's first cry follows once Sofia quiets. The camera doesn't catch the visual, but Mandy has given me the gift of hearing my daughter's first cry.

My eyes sting when I look up at Sofia again, and I lean forward to kiss her temple. "Thank you," I say.

"For what?"

"For showing me that, and for the best gift you've ever given me. Thank you for giving me Addy," I say.

"There's more," Sofia says shyly.

"What?"

"I debated on whether I should tell you—I don't want to make you feel bad—but I think you'd want to know."

I push a strand of hair behind her ear, encouraging her with a smile.

"When you first found out, you said I should have done more to find you—"

"Sofia, I'm sorry." I let out a regretful sigh. "I was upset. I didn't mean—"

"No, it's okay. But you should know I did try."

"What do you mean?"

"I messaged your band's social media page when I couldn't reach you or Andreas by phone."

My face scrunches up. "I never saw anything. We have assistants who field those comments."

"I don't think any of the messages were ever read."

I nod, thinking. "We get thousands of comments a month. I'm sure many go unread."

Sofia nods, scrolls through the phone, and hands it back to me. "Scroll through these outgoing messages. I'll give you a minute while I shower."

With shaky hands, I take the phone and start reading.

First message: *This is Sofia trying to reach Bren. It's impor-tant. Please have him call me back.*

Second message: *Bren, I hope you see this. I'm out of ideas to contact you. I wanted to tell you in person, but I guess I can't. I'm pregnant.*

I draw my eyes closed with pain. She told me. She told me about Addy. Regret brings a sharp sting to my eyes, and I keep scrolling through the messages.

Third message: *I had my first OB-GYN appointment today. Both Spawn and I are healthy. Wanted you to know.*

Spawn? What the literal fuck? I'm going to have to ask Sofia about this.

Fourth message: *I heard Spawn's heartbeat today. It was beautiful, and it has me thinking about you a lot. I hope you are well.*

Fifth message: *I hate you, Brenner Reindhart! Being pregnant is the worst. I pee all the time, and my feet are the size of an elephant's. I can't wait for the day science catches up and we can force the men through the hell that is pregnancy!*

I chuckle. I can almost hear Sofia yelling at me all through the late stages of her pregnancy.

Sixth message: *I picked up my mom from the airport today. She'll be helping out after the delivery and will be joining me in the delivery room. Wish it were you, but I'm happy she's here. We are both doing fine, and Spawn is healthy.*

Seventh message: *It's a girl. She was born at seven pounds, three ounces. She's perfect, Bren. I wish you could meet her. I named her Audrey. And I gave her your last name. I hope you won't mind, but I want her to know who her father is one day.*

A long, regretful tear rolls down my cheek. I wipe it away so I can clear the blurriness from my eyes and keep reading.

Eighth message: *I was a little worried and took Addy to see the doctor. She isn't crying all that much, and I thought something might be wrong. But the doctor checked her out, and she is perfectly healthy. She said I was lucky to have such a calm baby, and it just means she's happy. I feel better now. Our daughter is perfect. Thought you should know.*

Ninth message: *The bigger she gets, the more she looks like us. She has your eyes and my lips. She's going to be a looker. I can tell.*

I keep reading message after message with updates from Sofia. I stop counting, but I estimate somewhere between one-hundred and one-hundred-and-fifty.

The last message came through a week before I showed up at her bar: *She stood up today! I thought it was a little odd she isn't walking even though she's almost one, but the doctor assured me it's still within normal range. Lola and I haven't been able to get her to take a step, but at least she's standing up! I'm so excited! But also sad. She's growing up so fast.*

Sofia's face falls when she sees me full-blown weeping as she comes out of the shower—the phone pressed to my chest.

"Bren." Her own eyes turn glassy.

"I'm so, so incredibly sorry, Sofia."

She sits up next to me on the bed and brings my head to her chest, cradling it in her arms. "It's okay, *tonto*. Don't cry. We're here now."

ILEANA IS A NICE WOMAN, AND I WANT HER TO CONTINUE TO SIT for Addy when Sofia and I need a night. I thank her when I pick Addy up. She's fast asleep and doesn't stir as I bring her back into the car.

I take my girls home, unable to break my ear-to-ear grin.

Addy gets a bottle once we are home and goes right back to sleep, so I tuck her in her crib.

"You're really good with her," Sofia says. I signal her to be quiet and lead her out of Addy's room and into the living room.

"Sofia, we need to talk. Really talk."

Her hand instinctively cups the side of her neck, and she nods. "Yeah. We've been avoiding it, haven't we?"

"No. I haven't, at least. I wanted things to calm down—to have time to process."

Leading her to the couch, I sit and pull her in to sit on my lap so her feet can rest up on the couch.

"Let's talk about Addy first," Sofia says, and I nod.

"I want to be involved," I say.

"Are you sure, Bren? Once in, you're in. That's it. You don't get any more outs."

"I don't want an out, Sofia. I want to be in my daughter's life."

I sound a bit angry but cool my temper when I see Sofia's grin. I must have said the right thing.

She lets out a long breath. "Good. That's what I hoped you'd say. Everything else we can figure out."

I pull her in and press a kiss to her forehead. "Can this really be so easy?" I ask.

"It won't be easy, Bren. We both have a lot on our plates. You have *Industrial November*. I have *La Oficina*. You'll need to travel, and I'll need to be here for my business."

"I know," I say and kiss the back of her head this time. "How, um—" I clear my throat. "How do you feel about the public attention? The fans? The security? The press?"

"The fans, I can handle. I understand the attraction," she says with a bite of her lip. "I'm not a jealous person, Bren. I know what's mine, and I know the second it's not." The way she says it, with a slight arch of her brow, I know it is intended as a bit of a warning, but I think it's also true. Sofia has excellent intuition. Then she keeps speaking. "It's the press that makes me weary. And the threats. I understand they're just that—threats—but something snaps inside when they include Addy."

"I know, baby. I swear you'll always be protected. Security around the clock, always."

"It'll take getting used to, but it's worth it for Addy to have her father in her life," she says.

"I'd like to take you to Berlin," I say. When she throws me a questioning look, I add, "My parents want to meet their granddaughter."

"Right. I'm sure we can make it happen."

We discuss nothing further tonight. We don't bring up that we said 'I love you' or that I know it was her first time making love. The most important thing is that I'm here to stay, and that seems enough for her to be content.

We go to sleep, and my heart soars, holding her in my

arms the entirety of the night, knowing our little girl is sound asleep only next door.

My life feels complete for the first time.

IT'S NOT EVEN LIGHT OUT WHEN ADDY WAKES US VIA THE BABY monitor. We both stir, but I tell Sofia I'll get her.

When I get to my daughter, she smells like she's gone rancid, and I understand immediately why she woke up so darned early. "That's how it's going to be, is it, *Schatzi?*" I ask her as I take her to the changing station. I start unclasping the buttons in her footie pajamas when Sofia's soft voice swims into Addy's room.

"Since when do you change diapers?" she asks from her place leaning against the door frame, her legs crossed at the ankles.

"I'm her dad, aren't I?" I say firmly like I'm not nervous at all about what's about to go down.

When I finally wrangle her little chubby legs free, I realize there's a second layer—another onesie. My nose scrunches up, and not just because of the smell. That's odd. But then I peel the outer layer, and on the white fabric underneath, scribbled with child-like letters, reads: "Will you marry Mommy?"

My eyes widen, and my head snaps up to Sofia, who's smirking, arms crossed in front of her. I raise an eyebrow at her.

"She gets the craziest ideas sometimes," Sofia teases.

"You're really proposing to me over a dirty diaper?"

She smirks. "It wasn't exactly planned like that, but it's rather poetic, don't you think? You've always known how I feel about marriage," she teases, and I drop my head back with laughter.

"Come here and tell me what to do," I say, annoyed.

The trick, I learn, is to wipe backward. Always backward. Never forward. This particular instruction was drilled into my brain over and over. I had no idea this was so important for a girl. I shiver when Sofia explains the reason why.

With a clean baby in my arms, dosing off again against my chest, I whisper, "Sweet dreams, *Schatzi*."

Sofia blinks up at me, and also whispering, asks, "She's '*schatzi*' too?"

I nod and she smiles at me. "Are you ever going to tell me what that means?" she asks.

I smirk at her. "Do you want to know?"

Her eyes narrow. "You want me to ask, don't you?"

"Not if you don't want to know what it means." I play it off as if disinterested.

Sofia rolls her eyes. "Fine, Bren. What does your pet name for me and Addy mean?"

I look between them both with the biggest smile. When I answer, I mean it from the bottom of my heart. "*Schatz* means my treasure. *Schatzi* is the diminutive. You are each my treasures, and I will protect you both with my life."

Sofia's hand flies to her chest, and her eyes well with tears, so I change the subject.

"What was that?" I ask. "With the onesie?"

"Do you want to marry me?" she asks, a smile spreading on her lips.

"You'd be willing to do that?" I ask.

Sofia nods. "I meant what I said last night, Bren. I love you. If that's what you need, yes. I'd be willing to do it."

I lean in and kiss her forehead. "I love you for saying that, but no. I won't marry you."

She smiles wider, and I return the grin. "I don't need the marriage as much as I thought I did. I love you because you're you—because you're free. I realize now that trying to change you would be my biggest crime in this life."

"But it's okay for me to change you?" she asks, a little sad now.

"I've changed, yes. My love for you and Addy has changed me. But you didn't force it on me. I'm just so damned happy to have you both in my life."

"And you're sure that's enough?"

I nod. "Move in with me. Be my partner. Let's start a life."

"That's what I want," she says.

"Good."

Addy stirs in my arms, and she looks up at me. "Da-da," she says, and tears well in my eyes. Sofia must have been teaching her that word when I was working. "Yes, Addy. I'm here to stay."

"Oh, Bren, one more thing," Sofia says.

"What's that?" I ask, looking up at her again.

"Just because we aren't getting married doesn't mean I don't intend to keep you for the rest of my life."

EPILOGUE

Something big and dramatic always happens on Audrey's birthday—a tradition that started on that first birthday when her dad walked into my bar and laid eyes on his daughter without knowing it.

Nothing changed after that. There's something about my daughter that magnetizes huge life events to her birthday—the little witch that I swear she's turning out to be. I expect her letter from Hogwarts any day now. Last year, when she turned seven, Bren released a solo album as a side project. It was meant to be a birthday gift for Addy, a little sweet and clean acoustic album, a little folksy, a little bit pop—something she could listen to without having to censor it. He didn't expect anything to come of it, but it did. It topped the charts for longer than all the other *Industrial November* albums combined, and he was nominated for his first solo artist Grammy.

He hasn't left the band, even as his solo career has skyrocketed. The band has slowed down a bit, but they continue to make music and tour some. I can almost see them old and wrinkled but rocking it like Mick Jagger on the stage.

The year before that, when Addy turned six, was just as big

for me. I got a call from David on the morning of her birthday. He took the *La Oficina* franchise national and has been building the brand for the last few years. Sure, *Industrial November*'s unintended promotion helped boost the brand's visibility, but I'll ride any wave I can get. I'm ecstatic I'll never have to worry about money in my life and can provide for my mom in her old age without having to rely on my partner.

Life is good.

This year is no different. Addy's little witchy ways brought about yet another big change, and I bite the nail on my forefinger as I watch Bren frosting a cake, nervous about telling him.

But now is not the time. We have a million things to do before everyone gets here for the party. Instead of getting to it, though, I sit at the kitchen table watching my partner, Brenner fucking Reindhart, in an apron, frosting a crimson red cake with black spikes because that's what his heavy-metal daughter requested. He lives for his daughter, and he really is the best dad.

Addy is better off for having him in her life and he for having her in his. They learn from each other, and the love between them is unreal. Girls and their daddies—I never understood until now.

We decided to have a big party this year because next year we'll be in Germany. We alternate where we live every year, a compromise that nearly drew blood to achieve. In the end, it's the best thing we could have done. Our little Addy is already trilingual, though she reads best in English. We'll get her up to speed on German and Spanish, though—little sponge brain.

"What are you smiling about?" Bren asks with a smirk of his own, oblivious to the streak of red frosting across his cheek, and I laugh.

I get up to join him by the island and swipe the frosting with one finger. "This," I say, showing him the red. "You have frosting all over."

Bren chuckles and raises an eyebrow. "Is that so? Care to lick it all off?"

His voice, thick with arousal, still sends shivers down my spine, even after all these years.

"Absolutely not," I say. "We need to hurry up. Everyone will be here soon—"

The ring at the door cuts me off. Guess my daughter's not the only one with witchy ways.

"I can't believe how late it is," Bren says, looking at the clock on the stove. "Time just slipped away."

I take the room in, and everything is just about ready. Black and red matte balloons are taped to every wall. The caterer has the buffet table ready, and the place is tidy.

"Addy!" I yell up the stairs. "Your guests are here. You need to hurry, baby!"

My voice echoes back from the tall ceiling of the foyer as I walk to the front door.

We live in Karl's house now. Well, it's not his house anymore. When Bren saw how much I liked it on that first day we visited Karl, he basically forced Karl to trade the mansion for the penthouse. It also served to calm Karl's partying ways down a bit, and we needed the space for our family.

We have a house, not quite this big but just as beautiful, in Germany, and when we visit my mom in Mexico, we stay at the home that I bought for her three years ago.

When I open the door, I find Carolina and her husband, Hector. Hector holds a present, and Carolina holds her enormous pregnant belly. My eyes widen at the sight of her. She looks like she's about to pop.

I gasp. "You look like . . ." I was about to say she looks like she's about to pop, but Hector's solemn shake of the head and a gesture of his index finger slicing across his neck in a *You will die, run fool!* warning stops my sentence midstride. I clear my throat. "Uh, thanks for coming." I chuckle nervously. "Please come in."

Carolina's eyes narrow. "You were about to say I look like a beached whale," she accuses.

"No, I wasn't!"

"It's almost like you don't remember what it's like to be pregnant!" she whines as I usher them in, but she's throwing me a teasing smile.

"Addy! Your tía Carolina and tío Hector are here."

"One minute!" Addy yells back down at us.

"I feel like I should have you sign a waiver," I tell Carolina as she takes a seat straight away at the dining table.

"What for?" Hector asks, helping his wife settle by taking her purse and hanging it on the back of her chair. He holds her hand for her to ease slowly into the seat. I smile, watching how tenderly he dotes on her.

"You know something always happens on Addy's birthday. Please don't burst at her party," I plead.

Hector chuckles but stops when Carolina glares at him. Then she smiles creepy-sweet at me. "But how cool would it be for our daughters to have the same birthday?" she asks.

Bren comes up to us, wrapping an arm over my shoulders. "Hi," he says to our friends. "What'll you have to drink?"

"Water's fine," Carolina says.

"Me too, please," Hector says, and when I throw him a questioning look, he shrugs. "Solidarity."

As big as the house is, the place could burst at the seams with people in no time. Sara shows up with her sons, Oscar and René, though their dad had to work and couldn't join us today. Mandy and Elio show up with their son Lulu, who is the same age as Addy. Karl surprises us all by coming to a child's party. Joe shows up with his wife and kids, and we are still waiting on Ileana to arrive with her family. Fritz is in Germany, but he sent a gift for his favorite niece.

Give me strength. This place is going to be a mess before the night's over.

"Addy, baby, everyone's here!"

"I'll go get her," Bren huffs. "I gotta change my shirt anyway."

Within ten minutes, Bren descends the staircase with his daughter in his arms. She's wearing a black tulle skirt, black velvet boots, and her favorite band's black t-shirt that reads 'Jaguaristica.'

She runs up to Mandy first and wraps her arms around her middle. "Tía Mandy!" she squeals. And like the well-mannered girl she is, she makes the rounds and gives all her guests a kiss on the cheek, conspicuously leaving Lulu for last. I bite back my smile, hoping Bren doesn't notice how nervous she gets when she gets to Lulu. Bren's been worried about her starting to like boys, though he's reassured knowing it's all still reasonably innocent at their age.

When it comes time for presents, Addy goes straight for the biggest one, which I'm pretty confident came in with Karl—the showboat.

Addy rips the card from the top of the box and reads it first. "OhmygawdOhmygawdOhmygawd," she squeals. "It's from Tía Lola!"

Bren groans next to me as Addy rips wrapping paper like a badger digging. When she opens the box, it's an electric guitar. Addy looks stunned at the sight of it, and you could hear a pin drop as everyone stares at her and her present. Then she shrieks and starts jumping in place, completely losing her cool.

Bren rolls his eyes. "It breaks my heart that you'd rather play the guitar like your aunty than sing like your dad," he admonishes.

Addy jumps like a bunny toward Bren and wraps her arms around him. "Sorry, Daddy," she says, but she's still smiling and jazzed about the gift.

"Give the kid a break," Karl says. "Guitarists are the coolest." He flashes everyone his million-dollar, toothy grin, earning him another eye roll from Bren.

Lola already called Addy this morning to wish her a happy birthday and apologize for missing the party, but she couldn't get out of her tour date. She also promised never to schedule a concert over her birthday ever again. Addy seemed satisfied with that, despite the initial disappointment. She worships the ground Lola walks on and has already informed Bren and me that she will be in *Jaguaristica* when she grows up. Because what band doesn't need a third guitarist?

I'M SURPRISED WHEN IT'S CAROLINA AND HECTOR WHO CLOSE down the party. I expected the heavily pregnant lady to be the first to leave, but that'll teach me. I'm exhausted and running on fumes when I slump back down on the couch next to her.

"You look worse than me," Carolina says.

"Thanks," I say dryly.

She must be more tired than she's letting on, though, because I catch her gawking at Bren, as I have many times before. Even after all this time, she's still a little starstruck. I can't blame her too much, though. *Industrial November* has been her favorite band ever since I can remember. "Will you stop ogling my man?" I snap, and she winces.

"Sorry," she says. She looks up at her husband with an apologetic look, and Hector only laughs. "It's the hormones," she whines, sending us all into laughter.

"I get it," I say, remembering when I was pregnant with Addy and desperately wanted to hump everyone in sight but couldn't. Luckily for Carolina, Hector is one of those uber-confident men who isn't threatened by a little wandering eye. He knows what they have, and they are pretty perfect together.

For his part, Bren has gotten used to the fact that Carolina will never be able to stop fangirling around him. He's wisely chosen to find it endearing since she's one of my best friends.

When they finally leave, I almost want to cry as I scan the mess. I get a sickening flashback to the first time I saw this house in Karl's hands. Bren pulls me into his arms and rubs my back. "It'll be taken care of," he says.

"I know. I don't think I'll be able to look the housekeeper in the eye, though," I say. Inwardly, I one thousand percent blame Isael and Lulu. They're a menace to society with that level of energy—and the horror of boys strikes down my spine for the first time.

"How about we give her a ridiculously large bonus?" Bren asks, still talking about the housekeeper.

I nod. "It's the least we can do."

I SINK INTO THE WARMTH OF THE TUB, READY TO RELAX AFTER THE long day, and don't expect Bren to come in when he does. He pulls up a chair behind the tub and massages my shoulders. I could kiss his feet. I groan. "That feels good," I say.

"Good."

He lets me enjoy the massage for a long while before speaking again and bringing me back to earth. "Addy looked happy." And though I can't see his face from behind me, I can hear the smile in his voice.

"She's a very happy kid, though you know, Lola screwed us over getting her that guitar."

Bren lets out a breath that lands on the back of my neck, and my nipples pebble in one second flat. Stupid hormones. That's all it takes—one hot breath from him on my skin.

I totally get what Carolina meant.

"I'll soundproof a room for Addy to practice in," he says, and it warms my heart that he is willing to encourage Addy even when she's following in Lola's footsteps instead of his. I couldn't have asked for a better father for my daughter.

It's time. I have to tell him.

I clear my throat. "Bren? Can you come here where I can see you? I want to tell you something."

He steps over to the side of the tub and kneels next to me. "Everything okay? You sound off."

I nod. "Bren, I—" I chew my lower lip and take a deep breath. "Um, how would you feel about another baby?"

His eyes widen as they roam my face, then drop to my belly. "Sofia?" he asks tentatively, his giant hand submerging under-water, where he presses it gently to my lower belly.

I nod at him even as his eyes start to glisten. "I'm pregnant."

The End

BONUS EPILOGUE

To find out if Addy gets a little sister or brother and to watch Bren become a dad for the second time, you can download an extended epilogue at: <u>ofeliamartinez.com/freebooks</u>.

In the meantime, have you already read Hector and Carolina's story in *Remission*? Keep reading for the first chapter of *Remission*.

ALSO BY OFELIA MARTINEZ

The Heartland Metro Hospital Series

Carolina & Hector's Story: *Remission*

Valentina & Rory's Story: *Contusion*

Izel & Logan's Story: *Incision* (Novella)

The Industrial November on Tour Series

Sofia & Bren's Story: *Hiding in the Smoke*

Lola & Karl's Story: *Running from the Blaze*

REMISSION

REMISSION EXCERPT:
CHAPTER ONE

SATAN IN THE AUDIENCE

The interview was going well, and I hadn't barfed or passed out once. As we neared its conclusion, the muscles in my legs relaxed, and I uncrossed my legs, taking a taller posture in my chair. The question-and-answer bit, my favorite part, was next. Reaching young girls and women wanting to become doctors was reason enough to put myself through the stress of getting on stage to lecture at universities.

"Dr. Carolina Ramirez, everyone. Can we all please give her a round of applause?"

The packed auditorium erupted, and my cheeks would have been tomato-red had I not prepared with extra layers of makeup. I was thirty-five years old, for crying out loud. I should've been over stage fright by this point in my career.

"Please, that's enough. Thank you," I said, waving down the audience.

"We would like to thank you so much for being with us today," said the interviewer. "Before we turn it over to the audience, I would like the students here today to know that when you signed on for this guest lecture and interview, you did so only on the condition that there would be extensive time for a Q&A."

"That's right. It's a standard request on all of my speaking contracts."

"Why is that important to you?" The young journalism student interviewing me smiled as she asked. She let the note cards rest on her lap, a sure sign the interview would soon be over. During the course of the interview, she had collected a constellation of sweat droplets on her upper lip and continuously wiped her hands on her black slacks. I had done hundreds of these interviews, and on this occasion, the interviewer seemed more nervous than me. I smiled reassuringly at her as if to say, *We may both be nervous, but we are in this together.*

"If I'm honest, if I could, I would skip the lecture and interview, and instead take each of you for coffee to talk one-on-one. Sadly, unless I clone myself, time does not allow that luxury."

"If anyone could manage *that*, surely it would be you," the interviewer said.

I laughed. "No. For now, I'm still going to focus on my oncology research and my patients. I will always follow my passion. Let's leave the cloning to someone else."

"We have a few people with microphones in the audience. Please raise your hand if you have a question for Dr. Ramirez."

I placed my hand in front of my forehead to block the blinding spotlight, so I could see the person asking the first question.

The young woman couldn't look up at me as she clutched my book in her shaky hands.

"Dr. Ramirez, I loved your book—" Her voice cracked a bit.

"Thank you. What is your name?"

"Araceli."

"Hi, Araceli," I said with an encouraging smile. "It's nice to meet you."

"You too, Dr. Ramirez," she said, giggling. She tucked a strand of hair behind her ear and fidgeted with the book. "Your book is mainly about research. Honestly, a lot of it went over my head, but I couldn't stop reading. You made it seem . . . accessible . . . but you also talked about how you struggled to advance your career in this field. Why was it important to include that in a book that would have otherwise been a dry and boring publication about research?"

"Thank you, Araceli," I started. "That is a huge compliment to me. I worked really hard to make my book readable to anyone, even those not already in the medical community, hoping it might spark an interest in medicine. We need more soldiers in the trenches. But to answer your question, I was writing to my younger self, which means I was writing to any young woman intrigued by medicine but too intimidated to pursue it. The many female doctors who came before me made it so much easier, but it still is really, *really* hard to become a doctor. It's harder if, like me, you are a woman. Even harder if you are a minority. Even harder if you grew up with little money or opportunity. The list goes on and on. I want women in my same circumstances to know that it *is* possible. It won't be easy, but I swear to you that you will find mentors to help guide you in your career as a doctor."

"Thank you, Dr. Ramirez."

"Oh, before we go to the next question, Araceli, I see you have my book with you. If you'd like me to sign it, please stay after the Q&A. I'd love to chat with you some more."

Araceli smiled as though she had won the lottery, and I wondered if one day the letters M.D. would follow her name.

The next girl's name was Stephanie. She was much more self-assured, though she asked a more basic question.

"Why did you get into medicine?" she asked.

I hid my judgment because I would never embarrass someone publicly like that, but I always dreaded that question, and to my annoyance, it was the one most frequently asked. It was a simple question, but I didn't like sharing that truth, so I always gave a partial answer, which was not the same as lying. Not really. "Anyone who gets into medicine wants to save lives. If that is something you are interested in, then medicine is for you." I smiled, dismissing her more quickly than I had Araceli.

The microphone went to the next person, who was, unfortunately, sitting directly below the position of the spotlight, leaving me completely blind and unable to make out a face. I adjusted in my chair and craned my neck, trying to see the person, but it was no use.

"Hello," the voice said. This time it was a man.

"Hello." I smiled. "What is your question?"

"Your first grant," he said, and my blood went cold.

That voice. I knew that voice as well as I knew human anatomy.

"You got your first significant grant at a very young age. Most doctors are fellows or attendings before receiving that kind of research funding, but you were only a resident," he said.

My heart launched itself against my ribs, and, I swear, my poor lungs were caught in the crossfire because I couldn't breathe. The words were getting in, but I wasn't computing—not yet. I squinted, trying to make out the face that I knew in my bones belonged to the voice, but the lights were too bright. I had to give up.

I steeled my spine. *Fake it till you make it,* I reprimanded myself. *Feel confident. Be confident.* "I'm sorry," I said. "I'm not hearing a question in there."

"Please forgive me," he said. His accent had gotten softer over the years, but that voice was undeniably his. "My question is—where did you get the inspiration for your first research grant?"

The bastard. He was goading me. Here. In front of all these

people. Fine. I could play his game. I could give as good as I took.

"A researcher was working in the sub-specialty of cancer research I was interested in at the time. I read all of his research, and I found a way I could improve upon his work."

"Isn't that plagiarism of someone else's research?" he asked.

"That is actually a misconception," I fired back. "All medical advances are built on the foundations laid by research before them. A mentor once told me that research was a dance. One doctor takes a step forward, and the next doctor picks up the lead, spinning the research into a twirl, pushing it further." I grinned and challenged him with a raised eyebrow before realizing he was probably too far away to make out my facial expressions.

"Sounds like a wise mentor," he said.

"He had his moments," I said, and just like that, our banter was back. "Medical research doesn't necessarily mean living in a laboratory like a mad scientist inventing new medicine, though it could certainly involve that. A lot of research, mine included, is about adjusting existing medications and protocols into new modalities. There are drugs that are used now for one thing but were originally intended for something else. I haven't invented any of the medications or radiology methods in my research. Other scientists did that long before me. But what I *have* done is change dosing and experiment with different combinations of medications. A lot of my research also involves psychological components—how much can a patient take mentally before it becomes too much?" I sat back, pleased with my answer. He wouldn't publicly ruffle my feathers—he had already taken enough.

I hadn't heard that voice in over seven years, not since he left town after nearly destroying my career. Despite my hatred of him, the familiar back and forth we had always shared returned, and I resented the excitement that simple fact brought into my body.

"Thank you, Dr. Ramirez. If I may, a second question, or rather a request—"

"Sure."

"I also have a copy of your book here with me. Would it be okay if I also stayed behind to get a signature?"

"Of course."

The last thing I wanted to do was speak with him, let alone sign his book. And what business did he have buying my book anyway? I took a deep breath; this was the worst possible time for my hatred of Hector Medina to rear its head.

I answered about twenty more questions. The entire time, I couldn't see him but knew his glare was glued to my skin. I managed, somehow, miraculously, to concentrate on the questions, but I know I wasn't one-hundred-percent on my A-game. Luckily, my B-game was also rather spectacular. When the interview wrapped up, I took a break backstage to gulp an entire water bottle in hopes of cooling off and calming down.

After the auditorium emptied, I came back on stage to meet with Araceli, as promised. The spotlight was turned off, and I was aware of the second figure in the room only by my peripheral vision, but I refused to look at him.

I sat on the stage, my legs dangling off the edge as I took Araceli's book. I chatted her up for about ten minutes to get to know her a little better so my dedication could be personalized. She left with a dazed look, as though she might swoon, and I grinned like a fool after her.

I didn't see him move so much as I sensed him approaching, drawn to him like the pull of a magnet that had always been there between us, binding us together. That hadn't changed, and alarms started blaring in my brain.

"That was very kind of you, Dr. Ramirez," he said.

Crossing my arms, I finally turned to him as he walked over

to me, his steps a loud echo in the empty auditorium. I liked this position of power, sitting on top of the stage like a queen waiting for her peasants to come up to her from below. I smiled and clung to that image to give me the strength I would need to deal with the person I hated the most in this universe.

"Dr. Medina," I said. "How . . . *nice* to see you."

"Please call me Hector, Carolina," he said, his voice trying to soothe me like a child. The nerve.

"That's 'Dr. Ramirez' to you, *Dr. Medina.* Let's keep this professional."

He finally stood in front of me, and I reveled in this view from the higher vantage point. He looked up to meet my face from several feet below. Letting out a breath, he handed me the book. I arched an eyebrow.

"I wasn't kidding," he said. "I would very much like a dedication."

"You are kidding." I scoffed.

"No, Carolina. I'm serious. I'm very proud of you."

Proud? That gave me pause. Why would the man who nearly ruined my career be *proud* of me?

Disbelieving, I snatched the book from his hand. I opened the cover to the third page, which had the most blank space for a dedication. I smiled devilishly. I couldn't resist:

To the Devil himself—
   You couldn't pull me down to hell with you.
   Hate always,
   Dr. Ramirez

Jumping off the edge of the stage, I landed squarely in front of him and handed him the book. Standing on his level, I hated the height difference. I was tall, but he still had a good three inches on me. He encroached on my space too much with his height. I damned him for looking more handsome than ever. In the seven years since I'd seen him, his impossibly good looks had actually improved. His dark-brown, tanned skin glowed even more. What had once been salt and pepper hair was now nearly white at the temples, and his face was a bit rounder. He'd gained weight. The good kind. He was broader at the shoulders than he'd been back then, and I hated myself for noticing he'd clearly been working out. The man was like freaking wine.

He opened the book to read the inscription and laughed.

"That's funny, huh?" I said.

What in the world was happening? I didn't understand any of this. Why was he here? Why was he happy, smiling of all things, and *proud* of me? Nothing made sense, but I would be damned before I'd ask him.

"I will treasure this forever," he said, clutching the book to his chest. "I see you remain judgmental and critical of me."

"I see you remain tactless and careless," I shot back.

He laughed, and I noticed the sparkle in his eye. A sparkle I knew well, but it was so much brighter now.

I slung my purse over my shoulder, ready to get going and forget this crazy day ever happened, but Hector grabbed my wrist as I turned to leave.

"No, Carolina, wait." I looked at his hand on my wrist at the same time he did, and we both froze. We only connected for two, maybe three seconds, before he withdrew his hand, but those seconds electrified us. Nine years since the first time I'd touched him. Seven since the last time I'd spoken with him. I couldn't believe my body still reacted to him the same way after all this time.

"I'm sorry," he said.

"It's okay," I said, palming my wrist with my other hand to calm the fire on my skin.

"Can I please take you out for a drink, or coffee perhaps?"

I was speechless, so I could only shake my head.

"Please, Carolina. I have so much I have to say to you."

He said my name in nearly every sentence like he was pleading. I took too long to answer, and he pulled off his glasses to clean them. I knew that tell well. He was thinking. He wanted to find an argument that would persuade me to have drinks with him.

"Even if I wanted to," I said, "which I don't, I can't. I have a flight to catch."

"How about in Kansas City?" he asked, hopeful.

My entire body stilled. "In Kansas City?"

"Yes. Tomorrow. That little café on Westport Road you liked so much. Wait, is that still open?"

"It-it is, but you're going to be in Kansas City?"

"Yes. Does five sound okay to you? Tomorrow?" He smiled, and in that moment, he looked like a little kid.

"Why?" I asked, closing my eyes, seeking patience from within. "Why are you going to be in Kansas City? Please don't tell me you're coming back."

"Is the idea so terrible?"

"I-I, um, I have to go."

"Okay, but please. Meet me tomorrow. Five p.m."

I finally nodded. I would at least have to find out why my nightmare was back in my hometown. Then I ran out of the building as fast as I could because there was no air left in the vast auditorium.

Remission is available now on all major book retailers.

ACKNOWLEDGMENTS

I would like to thank my girlfriends, Anny and Liz. I've looked up to your confidence since the day we met. You are the strongest women I know and inspire me daily.

Also, much gratitude to my beta readers without whose feedback this book wouldn't exist: Amanda, Michelle A., Michelle M., and Tamara. Big thanks also due to the editors at Midnight Owl Editors. Your team is amazing, and I couldn't do this without you.

Lastly, to my partner and best friend, Robert. Though you never understood the dream, you fueled it with your encouragement and love. Thank you for putting up with me having no days off and never shutting up about my books. I love you.

ABOUT THE AUTHOR

Ofelia Martinez writes romance with Latinas on top. Originally from the Texas border, Ofelia now resides in Missouri with her partner and their dog, Pixel.

This is Ofelia's third book.

She loves good books, tequila, and chocolate. She proudly shares a birthday with Usagi Tsukino. When not writing, you can find Ofelia making visual art.

Visit OfeliaMartinez.com to learn more.

facebook.com/OMartinezAuthor
twitter.com/OMartinezAuthor
instagram.com/omartinezauthor

CPSIA information can be obtained
at www.ICGtesting.com
Printed in the USA
LVHW090501181121
703620LV00001B/47